Challenge
for Two

A Dave and
Katie Adventure

Kit and Drew Coons

Enjoy! Kit Drew

Challenge
for Two

A Dave and Katie Adventure

Kit and Drew Coons

Challenge for Two

© 2018 Kit and Drew Coons

ISBN: 978-0692895580

Library of Congress Control Number: 2017908494

Edited by Jayna Richardson
Illustrations by Julie Sullivan (MerakiLifeDesigns.com)
Design: Julie Sullivan (MerakiLifeDesigns.com)

First Edition

Printed in the United States

21 20 19 18 17   1 2 3 4 5

To all couples who take the challenge
to work together as a team.

Two are better than one,
because they have a good return for their labor.
Ecclesiastes 4:9 (NIV)

Principal Characters

Dave Parker • accountant
Katie Parker • science teacher, homemaker
Old Yeller • cat that comes with the mansion
Susie Holmquist • waitress and owner of The Blue Ox,
husband Charlie
Betty Larson • Cook at The Blue Ox
Mrs. Mary Johnson • older lady with cats, husband Sam
Tom and Maureen Swanson • owners of mansion
Tuffy • Maureen's dog
Annie Jordan • African American housekeeper
at Old River in the 1940s
Ramona Watkins • KAAK TV news reporter
Henry Henderson • Mill striker

Historical Society

Frank and Helen Pederson • President
Ed and Nancy Williams
John and Ellie Foster • Pastor of Lutheran Church

McReady Clan

Thaddeus P McReady • clan patriarch 1860-1933
McReady cousins • Jud - 40s, Bogus - 30s, Lars - 30s
Fred McReady • Mrs. Lancaster's brother
Clyde McReady • nightclub owner, Fred's son

Washita Police and DA

Billy McReady • Patrolman
Chief Oleson • Chief of Police
Darlene Clark • Patrolman/Detective
Gary Hobson • Detective
Pete Thomas • Patrolman
DA Richard Christensen • married to Lisa

Marriage Discussion Group

Billy McReady • young police officer
Caroline McReady • librarian, married to Billy
Tommy Bryant and Jane Jenkins • unmarried couple
Rick and Beth Larson • Betty's son and daughter-in-law
Lyle and Leslie Rogers • snowplow service, daughter Elsie

The Town of
Washita

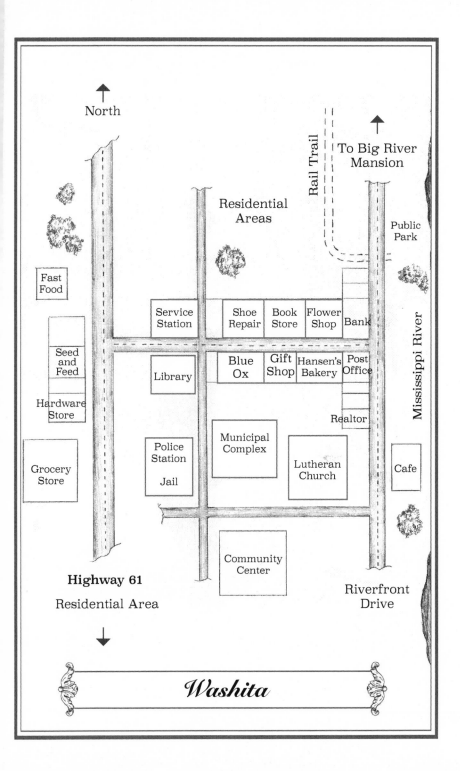

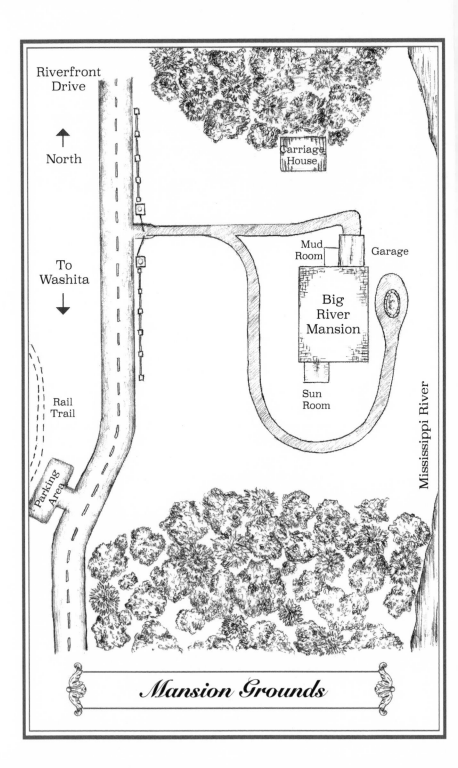

Riverfront
Drive

↑
North

To
Washita
↓

Rail
Trail

Parking
Area

Carriage
House

Mud
Room

Garage

Big
River
Mansion

Sun
Room

Mississippi River

Mansion Grounds

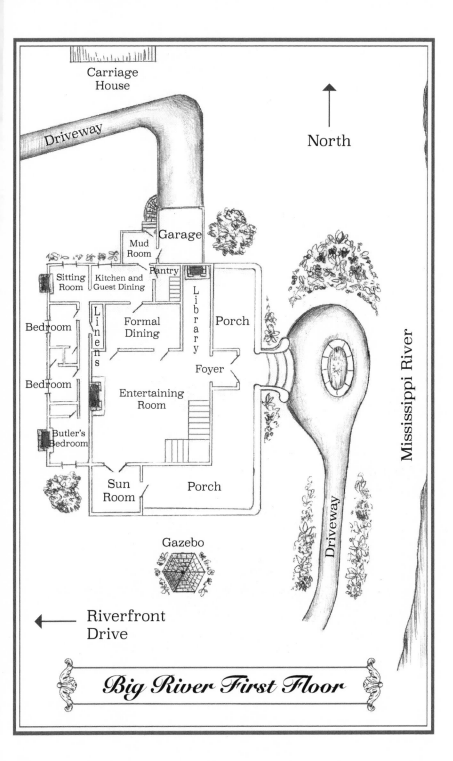

Carriage House

Driveway

North

Garage

Mud Room

Pantry

Sitting Room

Kitchen and Guest Dining

Library

Porch

Bedroom

Linens

Formal Dining

Foyer

Bedroom

Entertaining Room

Butler's Bedroom

Mississippi River

Sun Room

Porch

Driveway

Gazebo

Riverfront Drive

Big River First Floor

Acknowledgments

———•———

We would like to thank our partners for their invaluable help on this, our first novel. Jayna Richardson and Anne Tjaden provided professional editing and proofreading. Julie Sullivan provided artwork and formats for publishing. Rita Bryant, Marnie Rasche, Robin Dill, and Leslie Mercer read the manuscript and made valuable corrections and suggestions. All of them, plus Angie Fraser and Mary Larmoyeux, gave us generous encouragement. This project could not have been completed without their help. Our thanks also to Kylie Potuznik, our Marketing Specialist.

BIG RIVER
BUILT 1897

PLACED ON THE
NATIONAL REGISTRY IN 2007

Chapter One

"The Swansons expect us at the mansion at ten," Katie Parker reminded Dave as he first stirred. Always slow waking up, Dave dragged himself out of the hotel room bed to the shower without comment. Katie heard the shower running. She knew her husband of thirty-four years stood sleepily in the spray of hot water. She had sometimes wondered if he had fallen back asleep during his long morning showers. He emerged after twenty minutes, about average for a Dave wake-up shower. She had hot tea ready in the room.

Katie had already googled directions from the hotel to the mansion and packed up their overnight belongings.

"From I-90, we follow Highway 61 north past Winona to Washita. Riverfront Drive parallels the river going north from the town." She felt glad to see the journey nearly over. Her husband's drive-orgy to get from south Alabama to Minnesota in only two days had exhausted her.

Dave sipped the tea and nibbled on a stale bagel. "Thanks."

By 7:00 a.m., they started in Dave's ten-year-old mid-sized pickup truck. As they passed hardwood-covered hills and ravines, Dave commented, "I didn't know that Minnesota had mountains."

"It doesn't," Katie responded. "The Mississippi River cut a valley into a relatively level plain. The hills and bluffs appear to be mountains because we're down in a broad valley."

"Where's the snow?" Dave demanded. "I thought there would be snow, and I expected to see spruces and fir trees. These woods look a lot like Tennessee." Katie only shrugged. Dave had been complaining the entire trip. No need to get into another exchange.

The four-lane bypassing Winona featured fast food restaurants, gas stations, and chain retail stores. The Parkers continued north on Highway 61 to the Main Street of Washita which took them through the center of town toward the Mississippi River. There they found an old-fashioned shopping district on a wide street. All the storefronts displayed Christmas decorations on this Saturday after Thanksgiving.

"This is charming," Katie remarked as they passed shops and businesses. She would love to have stopped at Hansen's Bakery, but they didn't have enough time.

Near the river, they intersected Riverfront Drive and turned north. Soon they located a huge three-story house of beige limestone block about a mile north of downtown. A wrought-iron fence separated the mansion grounds from the road. Entrance columns with an open iron gate guarded the asphalt driveway. A cast bronze sign announced "Big River—National Historic Register—1897." Through the mansion's grounds, they glimpsed a body of unfrozen water. "I believe that's the Mississippi. From here it flows south all the way into the Gulf," Dave said. Privately he wished that he were headed toward the Gulf.

◂◦▸

At precisely 10:00 a.m., they drove up the long driveway leading to a circle between the mansion and the river. Katie looked at a printed email. "They said to take the left fork in the driveway and come to the door by the garage."

The couple walked to the door by a garage that didn't look like part of the original construction. Dave theorized, "I'll bet they added this on after cars replaced horse-and-buggies." A decrepit building nearby which could have been the carriage house added credibility to that theory. Three steps led up to a solid-looking white door. Katie pushed a ceramic button. Both Dave and Katie unconsciously leaned inward listening for a doorbell. From within the house came a deep *bong, bong, bong*. Immediately, a small dog started yapping.

In a minute, the dog sounded closer. The door opened to reveal an attractive and surprisingly young woman. A Shih

Tzu dog with a ribbon in its hair peeked at them from behind her legs. "We are the Parkers . . . " Katie began.

"Come in. Come in," the fortyish and stylishly dressed woman insisted. Inside, she offered a thin hand. "I'm Maureen Swanson." She quickly turned without waiting for a response. "We're in a bit of a hurry, so I'll make this fast. As we agreed on the phone, we'll give you $200 a week to watch over our home while we're in the Caribbean for the winter. Plus, we'll pay for the utilities."

Dave hadn't been part of the phone conversations between Maureen and Katie. "What are we supposed to do again?"

"Just watch over the place. Phone the police in case of an attempted break-in. Call the plumber if there's a leak. That sort of stuff. Oh, and they pronounce the town name 'Wa-shi-taw,' " she exaggerated each syllable.

"Sounds Native American."

"I suppose," Maureen answered. "This is your first experience house sitting, isn't it?"

"Yes," answered Katie, "But we own a home . . . "

"That's in Mobile, I think." Maureen interrupted. "You'll find a Minnesota winter a *lot* different." Her tone indicated regret that she had hired the Parkers. "Well, you'll manage somehow."

"Our truck has four-wheel drive and has been winterized," Dave offered to appear prepared.

Maureen sighed and continued, "You're in what we call a 'mudroom.' " That small antechamber contained a clothes washer and dryer then led to another substantial-looking door.

4

After passing through the inner door, Maureen made a sweeping gesture with one arm. "This is the kitchen and the guest quarters where you'll stay. Everything you need should be in here. The kitchen includes a dining table, and you can see the sitting room over there." Maureen indicated a cozy corner room with an open fireplace and a window facing the woods. "The hall past the sitting area leads to three bedrooms. In the old days, the butler stayed in the largest on the far corner. The maids, cook, and other help lived in the other two. The linen closet is on the left." Katie also spotted a walk-in pantry opening from the kitchen.

"Do you still have resident help?" Katie asked attempting to slow Maureen down.

"Only Emma. She's our housekeeper and cook. We gave her the winter off. She went to Florida to stay with her sister. We have a lawn service and other temporary help during the summer, when we entertain a lot of clients here. But there's no one in the winter. You'll be here alone."

Katie extended her closed hand palm down toward the dog. "Hello, little friend."

"Grrrr . . . ," came in reply. Katie quickly withdrew her hand.

Maureen made no sign that she had noticed. "Let's look at the main house." A door from the kitchen led into a large formal dining room with dark walnut paneling. A beautiful mahogany dining table had chairs for sixteen places. Without comment, Maureen led them through the dining room into a luxurious living room.

There a pile of luggage waited by the mansion's front door. The front door led to a foyer with a tiled floor from

5

which the outer doors opened onto a wraparound porch. In the foyer, Maureen opened a cabinet to reveal a security pad. "You know how to use this? Just enter 'T-u-f-f-y' to arm or disarm the system. All of the first-floor doors and windows are monitored and connected to an alarm."

Dave nodded to indicate understanding. "Who is Tuffy?"

"This is Tuffy," Maureen responded, indicating the small dog that sat looking suspiciously at Katie. "We're taking him with us." Dave and Katie glanced with relief at a dog carrier among the pieces of luggage. "Our contact numbers and a few instructions are on this list." She handed Katie a typewritten sheet. "Here are keys to the outer front doors and the mudroom door. Let's give the rest of the house a quick walk-through." Dave and Katie followed obediently.

All-dark natural wood finished the first-floor walls. Even the ceilings had wooden panels and molding in a grid pattern. The mostly Victorian furnishings filled nearly every space. Drop cloths covered the upholstered furniture. Katie tried to slow Maureen's whirlwind tour down by asking, "Who is that?" She pointed to a beautiful oil painting of a teenage girl holding a horse by its bridle hanging over the main fireplace.

"I have no idea. The painting came with the mansion." Maureen showed the Parkers double glass doors opening from the entertaining room into a large sunroom. Another outside door connected the sunroom to the wraparound front porch. Next Maureen led them up a broad oak staircase with turned banisters to the second and third floors. Stopping on the second floor, Maureen said, "This is where my husband Tom works when he's not at his Minneapolis office." She indicated a large bedroom that had been converted into an office. Through the door, the Parkers could see a man about their age sitting in the glow of several computer screens and talking on a phone. "He manages a hedge fund."

"Can he take the winter off?" Dave asked, doubting that Tom ever took any time off.

"His clients are scattered through the Caribbean islands until spring. Of course, with computers and cell phones, he can stay in touch with the office every day," Maureen explained. To Tom she shouted, "The shuttle will be here any minute." Tom partially turned and raised an arm in response.

A second-floor sunroom sat atop the ground floor sunroom. Bedrooms and sitting areas with floral wallpaper completed the remainder of the second and third floors. A service stairway connected to the kitchen pantry served each floor independently of the main staircase. Maureen explained that the 12,400-square foot house had been remodeled in 1922, 1984, and 2009. "We bought Big River in 2011 and did some updating and decorating of our own."

After leading Dave and Katie back down the formal staircase to the ground floor, Maureen hesitated in front of an unopened door under the stairs. "This is the basement. We don't go down there very often." Carefully she started to crack the door. Immediately, a tawny yellow streak of fur burst through and disappeared into the house. "Umm . . . that was Old Yeller. Tom's daughter, Tricia, from his first marriage, picked the cat up at a shelter. Then she moved to New York to try out as an actress. Her apartment building doesn't allow pets. She begged her dad to keep him for her. He can't say 'no' to her," Maureen said with apparent disapproval of her stepdaughter.

Dave and Katie looked at each other. A cat? "You can keep him in the basement," Maureen continued. "Do you like cats?" she asked in afterthought and looked at her watch.

"We don't know. We've never had one. We're more large-dog people," Katie answered. "Why the name Old Yeller?"

"Tricia thought the name was funny. I don't think that she ever actually saw that old movie with the yellow dog. He's nothing special, just an ordinary cat. If he happens to get lost or something, don't worry."

The front doorbell rang. Through the window, Dave and Katie saw a van waiting in the circular driveway. "Tom, the airport shuttle is here!" Maureen called up the stairs. Dave helped the shuttle driver load the Swansons' luggage while Maureen forced a resistant Tuffy into the carrier. In a few minutes, Tom arrived flustered and still talking on his cell phone. He extended a hand to Dave in passing and without breaking his phone conversation, seated himself in the van.

"We keep the thermostat at sixty degrees in the winter. But there are space heaters in the guest quarters," Maureen added. Before Dave could answer, Maureen joined Tom in the van. "Have fun exploring. See you in April," she said as the driver closed the sliding door.

Chapter Two

———•———

The airport shuttle carrying the Swansons pulled away leaving Dave and Katie standing in the driveway. They looked at each other. "I expected more of a transition than that," Katie commented.

Dave turned back toward the mansion. "They didn't know that we've not been house sitters before?"

"That never came up," Katie answered and followed Dave. "I'm sure they were just excited about their trip and in a hurry." Katie pointed toward the door by the garage. "Why don't you pull the truck around to the back door?"

Dave unloaded plastic containers and suitcases they had stowed under the truck's shell. Katie met Dave at the mudroom and guided him to a hall leading to three transom-topped bedroom doors. "Let's make this first bedroom our temporary storage area," she suggested. Two single iron beds, two chairs, two lamps, and two bureaus furnished the monk-like room and its twin next door. Both double bedrooms had a small window, a few coat pegs, and a tiny white tiled bathroom containing a bathtub and a porcelain sink. The

Alabamians stored their possessions in the first bedroom and started looking around.

The largest bedroom at the end of the narrow hallway faced woods in the opposite direction of the sitting room windows. A large old-fashioned wardrobe sat next to a king-sized bed. A sturdy oak desk and couch completed the room. The bathroom had both a bathtub—the type with feet—and a shower, which, as a retrofit, looked a little out of place.

The common sitting area appeared surprisingly cozy and inviting. Three large windows provided a view of the woods and old carriage house. That structure had been built from the same limestone blocks as the main house. "It's so picturesque nestled into the edge of the woods," Katie commented. Economical overstuffed furniture, obviously not of the best brand, appeared comfortable.

An old-fashioned forty-eight-inch TV provided entertainment. "I'll bet they replaced that with the high-resolution flat screen we saw upstairs," Dave suggested. The room also included a table for games, some high-backed chairs, and a desk phone sitting on an end table.

The sitting area, plus the three bedrooms, the kitchen/dining combination, and the pantry would comprise their living area. Dave held both arms wide indicating those rooms. "They call this the 'guest quarters'?"

"These are actually the servants' quarters. 'Guest quarters' just sounds better," Katie explained. "I'm sure that guests of the family stayed upstairs."

"That makes sense."

Katie started exploring the kitchen while Dave wandered off. The lighting, plumbing fixtures, and appliances, although not remotely new, were functional and spotlessly clean.

Thanks to Emma, Katie theorized. She started making out a list of items they would need. As she worked, Katie thought, *Dave really needs this diversion. The stress of the last few years is just now catching up with him. He's starting to grieve the loss of our old life. Maybe this trip can help us move forward. I wonder where he went.*

⁕

Dave had found a door from the mudroom into the garage. A Mercedes and a Jaguar sat inside. Storage items filled a third vehicle spot. *Could put the truck here, if I needed to,* he thought. Next, Dave wandered outside. Woods separated the mansion from neighboring houses. But a front lawn between the mansion and river had been well maintained. A white gazebo and perennial flower gardens decorated the grounds.

The lawn sloped twenty feet down to the river where dark, clear water swirled. The flowing river looked young and vigorous compared to the muddy and sluggish Mississippi in the Deep South. Looking at the river, Dave already felt homesick. *I would rather still be down South. But Katie needs this. She's been through so much the last few years. Maybe an adventure will help her forget.*

The old carriage house drew Dave's attention. A side door had been padlocked shut. The dark interior prevented him from discerning much by looking through the dirty windows. *That could be fun to explore later,* he speculated. *I'd like to know more about the history of this place.*

Returning inside, Dave saw some of the items Katie had unpacked. Several pictures of their son Jeremy had been positioned in prominent places. Katie had moved their clothes into the wardrobe in the butler's bedroom. She placed a favorite comforter from home on the big bed.

"Dave!" he heard Katie call. "We need to go into town."

"What for?"

Katie came into the kitchen and waved her grocery list at him. "Do you want to eat while you're here?"

"That would be nice." Dave looked around. "Have you seen the cat?"

"You mean Old Yeller?" Katie smiled. "There are a thousand places it could hide. First, we need to get into town."

"I'm leaving the door to the basement open so that he can get food and water. I'll bring the truck to the front."

Katie joined Dave at the truck. Wearing her favorite sleeveless light-blue puffer jacket, she shivered from the cold wind.

"Did you lock the doors?" Dave asked.

She turned the truck's heater on high. "Yes."

"How about the alarm?"

"T-u-f-f-y," she spelled out using her schoolteacher voice.

The previously open gate had closed behind the Swansons. The gate sensed the truck approaching from the inside and automatically opened. "On to find a grocery store," Katie reminded.

"How about a late lunch first?" Dave suggested.

"Sure, why not?"

—◦◦◦—

"Aren't you worried about leaving your doctors in Mobile, Tousle Top?" Dave used an affectionate reference to her short salt and pepper hair as they drove into town.

"Hello. We're near the Mayo Clinic. I'll be okay," Katie reassured him.

Returning to Washita on Riverfront drive only took a few minutes. Dave suggested a couple of fast food places. Katie closed her eyes and shook her head, "No." On Main Street, she pointed out a quaint storefront restaurant called "The Blue Ox." On the street, a painted wooden statue of Paul Bunyan decorated with a red Santa hat guarded the door. "That place looks interesting."

Dave pulled into a diagonal parking space. Even with Christmas shoppers, the town wasn't crowded. Multicolored strings of lights spanned the street. A fresh evergreen wreath decorated each light pole. Christmas carols played from hidden speakers.

Inside the restaurant, the smells of fresh coffee and French fries welcomed the couple. Two rows of old-fashioned booths lined a linoleum-floored aisle. Tin ceiling tiles remained from the 1896 store. One of the walls displayed pictures of local sports teams thanking their sponsor. The other wall displayed cooking implements from years gone by. The Parkers hung their jackets on a coat tree near the door. A robust middle-aged waitress wearing an apron over a T-shirt with a picture of a Blue Ox greeted them with a husky voice. "Welcome to The Blue Ox. Pick any booth."

At 3:00 p.m., the establishment wasn't busy. The Parkers were the only customers. "What'll you have to drink? Coffee, tea, pop?" the waitress continued. They selected a booth near a picture of a high school hockey team holding a championship trophy. On closer examination, they observed one lone girl posed among the boys. Laminated menus,

13

condiments, silverware wrapped in paper napkins, and a set of salt and pepper shakers that looked like blue oxen waited on each table.

"I'll take hot water with lemon," Katie replied.

"Could I have unsweetened iced tea with lemon?" Dave asked.

"You betcha." The waitress disappeared as they pulled menus from behind a napkin dispenser.

Almost immediately the waitress had returned with their drinks. Pulling an order pad from a pocket in her apron she asked, "See anything you like? We serve breakfast all day if you're interested. Our skillets can't be beat. They're a local favorite."

"What are skillets?" Katie asked.

"Skillets are like an omelet still in the pan. You can get them with anything you want. Most places cook their omelets directly on the flat top grill. We cook ours in a skillet placed on the flat top. Then you eat the omelet right out of that skillet. Plus, they come with the best hash browns in town."

Katie responded, "I'll try one of your skillet breakfasts with onions, cheese, and tomatoes plus the biggest order of hash browns you serve." Dave ordered the "Daily Special," a three-quarter pound burger.

"Be right up." The waitress disappeared again.

"Right up" proved to be accurate. In just a few minutes, the waitress returned with their food. Katie's omelet and hash browns still sizzled in a cast iron skillet. Dave looked at her plate. "That looks great." A huge pile of hot French fries accompanied Dave's burger. The appetizing odor made Dave and Katie extra hungry.

As they ate, the waitress wandered back. "Anything else I can get you?"

"No, this is perfect," Dave replied as he added a little artificial sweetener to his tea. "But where do y'all keep the snow?"

"We haven't gotten any yet. Some years are like that. Then when bad weather comes, you'll think a whole winter of cold had been stored up. My name is Susie Holmquist, by the way. You're not from around here, are you?"

"How did you know?" Katie answered for Dave, whose mouth was full.

"Well, locals don't ask about snow. They're just glad not to see any, except for the ski slopes up the road, that is. Your husband ordered 'unsweetened' tea. That's the only kind we make here. Both of you have nice suntans. Then there's also the way you talk. Are you from Louisiana?"

After swallowing, Dave resumed the discussion. "No, we live near Mobile. I was born and raised in South Alabama. My wife, Katie, is originally from Minnesota, though. My name is Dave Parker."

"Oh, another mid-western girl. I've been living here all my life. Whereabouts in Minnesota are you from?"

Katie laid down her fork. "I'm originally from Duluth where my father worked for Weyerhaeuser. My entire family moved to north Florida when I was just eight. I don't remember much or even know anybody up here now."

"So, are you just visiting?" Susie's voice indicated a perpetually friendly individual.

"No, we're house sitting for the winter out on Riverfront Drive. The place is called 'Big River.' "

"You're staying at the Big River mansion?" Without waiting for an answer, Susie yelled back toward the kitchen, "Betty come out here! This couple is staying at Big River." Turning to Dave and Katie, she explained, "Betty cooked your lunch. We call her 'British Betty' because she's from England."

A stout older woman first looked around the corner, and then walked toward them while wiping her hands with a dish towel. "You're at the Big River mansion?" she repeated Susie's question with a distinct cockney accent.

"Yes, we just started today. We'll be here until April. You're not originally from here either."

"Me mum brought me as a wee girl over to Canada from London in the 1960s. Then she met this American chap from down south and got herself married."

"Did he come from Alabama?" Dave finished a bite of burger and jumped back into the conversation.

"No, he came from Iowa."

Dave and Katie couldn't help but smile at the thought of Iowa being "down south."

"That's how I came to America." Betty moved closer to the table and asked, "You know anything about the Big River Mansion?"

Katie spoke with frustration, "Not much. The Swansons were hurrying to leave when we arrived. They almost acted like they didn't want to answer any questions."

Susie and Betty looked at each other. "Maybe they were afraid you might back out," Susie suggested. "Every year, somebody different stays there."

Chapter Three

Betty's voice became authoritative. "That's because the mansion has got a haint. People have gone missing. Some say bodies are buried on the grounds. Their restless souls can't leave the mansion. I knew this girl who worked as a maid there. The stories she could tell."

"Now don't you go scaring them, Betty. You know there aren't any ghosts."

"Well me mum always said . . . "

Susie burst in, "These folks don't want to hear about your mother." As Betty headed back to the kitchen, Susie admitted, "There are some dark stories about the mansion. But maybe most people just feel it's safer to blame ghosts than criminal activity. Folks around here know to not ask many questions. A few break-ins have been reported in your area. But none at Big River that I know of."

Dave and Katie sat wide-eyed, their remaining food forgotten. "Did the houses broken into have security systems? How do they get by them?" Dave wondered aloud.

"Some did have security systems. The police haven't figured out yet how the thieves avoided them. Hey! Don't let your food get cold." Susie placed their bill face down on the table and headed back to the kitchen.

The sun setting at 4:00 p.m. as they left the restaurant surprised Dave and Katie. Being so far north in late fall made Minnesota days shorter than they expected. "Did you leave a nice tip?" Katie asked as they headed down the street. She had been a waitress in college and always wanted to be generous.

"Twenty percent, actually a little over," Dave answered.

Katie held onto Dave's arm as they explored downtown. The mostly two-story buildings had been built in the 1890s. The air temperature, just below freezing, felt frigid to the southern couple. Katie wrapped her scarf around her neck. The cold, music, and decorations made Main Street feel like a town from a storybook. Besides The Blue Ox, gift shops, a travel agency, an antique shop, and a charming locally owned bookstore lined one side of the street. On the other side, they noticed a shoe repair shop, an old-fashioned pharmacy, a real estate agent, and most important, Hansen's Bakery. A three-story bank building with "1893" carved into the stone door lintel dominated the corner of Main Street and Riverfront Drive.

A turn-of-the-century post office sat across the street from the bank. Inside the post office, brass mailboxes lined wood-paneled walls. Each box had a glass viewing port, a combination dial, and a number. Dave gave their name to a kindly looking older man at the service window and asked for general delivery. Their forwarded mail included financial statements, bills, and a couple of early Christmas cards. "Would you like to rent a box?" the postal worker offered. "Only ten dollars a month." Dave gave him fifty dollars to fully cover their expected stay in Washita.

Next, they tried the bakery. Unfortunately, that treat shop had closed for the day. So they walked back towards the truck. On the street, a young woman approached leading a Labrador Retriever puppy on a leash. Katie gushed, "What an adorable puppy." The young woman stopped to let her admire him. When Katie leaned over to pet the little dog, the end of her scarf fell from her neck and dangled down. No puppy could resist that. He snatched the scarf in his little teeth and pulled. Quickly Dave reached out and grabbed the scarf to prevent the puppy from strangling his wife. He gently removed the scarf from the puppy's mouth. Katie didn't mind and continued smiling at the puppy.

"I'm so sorry," the young woman began. But Dave and Katie laughed merrily. Holding her scarf in one hand, Katie knelt and petted the little Labrador, who relished every bit of the attention.

"Thanks," Katie said to the young woman as she stood up. "We had a Labrador Retriever until she died earlier this year. Her name was Ruthie. We miss her so."

"Aren't they wonderful dogs?" the young woman asked as she walked away with her puppy.

"People here seem quite friendly," Dave observed.

"Southerners aren't the only ones who practice hospitality," his Minnesota-born wife mildly reprimanded him. "Now I need a grocery store." They took the truck back out to where Main Street intersected the highway. There they found a nice but unremarkable local grocery store. The shelves featured less organic produce than in Mobile. A seafood counter displayed pickled herring rather than catfish fillets. Otherwise the grocery store seemed normal. Katie filled a shopping cart half full and asked Dave, "Do you need anything?"

"Yes, but the grocery store doesn't carry it."

"What do you need?"

"I'm not sure myself."

The couple felt a brisk wind from the northwest leaving the grocery store. The southerners hurried to load the groceries and get into the truck cab. With the truck's engine running, they sat shivering until the heat from the vents warmed them. Twinkling lights in closed shop windows made Main Street look even more charming as they drove through town.

—◆—

"Why doesn't the gate open?" Katie wondered aloud as the truck approached the driveway to Big River.

Dave stopped the truck. "The Swansons had probably opened it for the airport shuttle when we came. I didn't think to look for an electric opener. Do you have the instruction sheet? Maybe the gate combination is listed there."

Katie looked in her purse and then at Dave. "I didn't realize we needed to bring our instructions."

"You didn't bring the instructions?"

"Did you?"

"Maureen gave the sheet to you." Dave's irritation grew.

"I don't even want to be here."

"That's apparent. Being here alone would be more fun. Go home to Alabama, if you want to."

Dave sat still for a minute. "I don't think my going home would help us. So, let's stop bickering."

"I'm not bickering. And don't blame me."

"Uh-huh." Dave started rummaging in the extended cab. In a minute, he came out with a flashlight that could have doubled as a searchlight. "Sometimes there's an open button. Otherwise, we'll need to climb the fence and walk up to the house to look at the instructions. Or maybe the electronic eye will think I'm a car trying to leave and open the gate. If that happens, you drive the truck through." Katie stayed in her warm seat while he approached the control box that had both numbers and letters. He couldn't find a button. Commonly used combinations didn't work either.

As Dave examined the fence for the best place to climb over, he heard, "Try Tuffy." With that entry, the gate opened.

He returned to the truck shivering from the cold wind and acknowledged, "Nice guess."

Katie nodded. "A lot of people use the same password for everything." The driveway seemed dark as they approached the even darker mansion. "We should leave some lights on when we leave next time."

Dave kept the truck headlights directed toward the house while Katie opened the front door. He watched as a porch light came on, then some interior lights, and finally the light by the guest door. Dave parked the truck and started bringing in the groceries through the mudroom.

21

Katie began storing them in the refrigerator and pantry. Dave started one of the portable electric heaters.

After putting away the last items, Katie found Dave clicking through TV channels in the sitting area. His mood lightened on finding a football game. Soon he fell asleep to the soothing lullaby of blitzes and touchdowns. Katie then switched the channel to a romantic made-for-TV Christmas movie. The reassuring climax soon lulled Katie to sleep as well. Eventually Dave and Katie woke up and stumbled into the butler's bedroom. The old house creaked in the howling wind.

Late into the night, Dave felt a nudge from his wife. "Dave, I hear something."

"You hear the wind blowing against this old mansion," he replied, only partly awake.

"No, this is different. Something is moving through the house."

"You're not believing Betty's ghost stories, are you?" he teased.

Katie nudged him harder. "Get up and see what it is."

Dave tucked the comforter under his chin. "I'm warm and comfortable here."

"You're the man. You're supposed to . . . " An unmistakable moaning cut short Katie's words.

Chapter Four

—•—

As the couple lay still in fear, the moaning grew louder. The source came closer. Something applied pressure on the foot of the bed. Two eyes gleamed green in the reflection of the porch light. Dave fumbled trying to find the lamp switch. Suddenly, light from the lamp flooded the bed. The eyes disappeared, leaving a large yellow cat blinking in the light.

Filled with relief, Dave sat up to stroke the apprehensive feline. Feeling Dave's gentle hand, Old Yeller immediately rolled over, wiggling with delight. Loud purring came from somewhere within the cat's body.

Katie peered over the comforter that she had pulled up over her face. "How did it get in?"

"I left the door to the dining room open a crack so that we could hear anything in the house. That's our job after all." Dave leaned back and reached for the lamp switch.

"You're going to leave it here?"

"Better than letting him creep around the house. Right now, I'd rather know where this cat is."

Old Yeller curled up at their feet and contentedly fell asleep. The humans took a while longer.

Dave woke up slowly after the sun rose. Neither Katie nor the cat had remained in the bedroom. Dave could hear a tea kettle whistling. Stumbling bleary eyed from the bedroom, he walked into a Christmas wonderland. Familiar decorations dominated nearly every available space. "Where did you get these?"

"You said that I could bring whatever I wanted." Katie deliberately placed several boxes of small colored lights on the counter top. "We'll also need a tree." Privately Dave agreed that their traditional decorations did add comfort and cheer to the guest quarters.

His wife had brewed her English breakfast tea in a beautiful porcelain teapot she had found in a china cabinet. Then she put some milk into her cup and added the tea to the milk in the old English fashion. Her grandmother who had grown up in England insisted that the tea tasted better because the boiling liquid slightly scalded the milk.

Dave simply poured hot water onto a generic tea bag, which had already been placed in his favorite Christmas mug. He poured a little lemon juice into his tea and noticed a saucer with untouched milk on the floor. "Where's the cat?"

Katie sipped her tea. "The cat was here earlier. I offered it milk."

Dave stepped around the lightly humming space heater and went through the servants' door into the formal dining room. The air seemed chilly compared to the warm kitchen. At the top of the basement stairs, he punched a button light switch. A bowl of cat food, dish of water, and a litter box sat near the bottom of the steps. The litter box appeared to have been used. "Here Old Yeller. Here boy." His voice sounded hollow in the large basement.

"It isn't a dog." Katie had come behind him wearing a cozy bathrobe. "Kitty, kitty, kitty . . . " she tried. Still no cat appeared. She wrinkled her nose at the musty basement smell. "Let's look for him in the house."

Overnight, the wind had died down. Quiet dominated the big house. Dave and Katie each felt silly recalling the previous night's drama. The big staircase to the second floor included a landing where the stairs turned. There they found Old Yeller curled up in the morning sun on an east-facing window seat. The cat cautiously looked up at them. Dave rubbed his soft

25

yellow fur. "He seems happy." Old Yellow relaxed and rolled on his back in pleasure. "Let's leave him here."

Back in the kitchen, Dave re-warmed his tea in the microwave. Then sitting at the table with some cereal, the couple discussed their day. "Let's go for a walk," Katie proposed. "We both need some exercise after the long drive from Mobile, and there's a trail nearby like our Eastern Shore Trail." Katie's doctor had instructed her to get exercise after her surgery. They had started slowly at first. Eventually, as Katie recovered, a brisk walk or bicycle ride had become an enjoyable habit for both. Her husband accepted her idea readily.

Outside temperatures in the mid-twenties seemed formidable to the Southerners. Each of them dressed in layers—lots of layers. They headed down the long driveway to Riverfront Drive. Katie's Google map had shown a walking trail across the road that had been built on an old railroad bed. After following the road for about 100 yards towards town, they found a small parking lot and access to the trail. It roughly paralleled Riverfront Drive in both directions. Katie quickly dubbed this the "rail trail." Southward the trail led into downtown Washita. The northerly direction headed out into the Minnesota countryside. Dave and Katie turned north away from town.

The trail followed a fifty-foot right-of-way from the old railroad. Birch trees with white trunks along with wild rose bushes grew on both sides. Wild grapevines with dried fruit from the previous summer tangled the undergrowth. Embankments had been built to level the original train tracks where they crossed frozen ponds and marshes. Brown mounds of vegetation protruding through ice showed muskrat lodges. A few ice fishermen spread out trying their skills on a frozen lake. Elegant newer homes lined the larger lakes.

Dave noticed a few wild ducks occupying spaces of open water. "I thought ducks fly south in the fall."

Katie shrugged. "I guess these didn't get the memo."

Minnesotans had even created some spaces where blue spruces made the trail's effect park-like. The gently winding path remained mostly empty. But occasionally, Dave and Katie passed others who nodded or spoke politely. Dogs accompanied many of the walkers. A few runners, more focused and intense, passed. Suddenly, a white cat-sized animal darted in front of them. Near the edge of some bushes, the animal paused to reveal itself to be a white rabbit. Dave pointed. "Look! Somebody's pet bunny has escaped."

"No, that's a snowshoe hare," Katie corrected. "Look how big its feet are."

"Rabbits are white in Minnesota?" Dave asked as he stood very still.

The former science teacher in Katie started to emerge. "Only in the winter. They turn brown in summer."

Dave pondered the improbable. "You're saying that these northern rabbits are chameleons?"

"You could say that." Katie turned around. "I'm cold. We'd better turn back. How far do you think we've walked?"

"About three miles." Dave rubbed his hands together to warm them.

"How do you know?"

"We're walking at about four miles an hour. Forty-five minutes have passed," Dave smiled. "That, and these markers along the side." For the first time Katie noticed little brass disks with numbers anchored to the path. In mile tenths, they told the distance from the trail's origin. "That would be four *Katie* miles."

"Why are my miles different?"

"Your legs are shorter."

She smiled and quickened the pace home. "You're a stinker."

Walking back to Big River seemed warm despite officially freezing temperatures. Soon Dave and Katie stripped off layers of winter clothing and carried them. Back at the mansion, Katie suggested, "Let's drive around a bit now. I found the gate opener by the security alarm."

Dave readily agreed and met Katie at the truck. "Let's look at the neighborhood." Impressive-looking houses lined Riverfront Drive on both sides. The larger houses, like Big River, overlooked the open water of the Mississippi River from a high bank. Most of the houses appeared to be about a century old with a mixture of Victorian and Federal styles. A few of the oldest houses looked rather run down.

At first Katie kept up steady chatter as Dave drove. She talked about people they knew, a TV program she had watched, an article she had read. To Dave, Katie's chatter sounded like listening to a happy mockingbird sing. He could remember days not very long before when pain had silenced her joyful noise.

Katie knew that the leisurely driving would make Dave relaxed and reflective. She scooted across the truck's bench seat to be closer to him. "Remember our first date?" she prompted. "You took me to a concert. I had to hint several times before you asked me."

"Yeah, I still can't believe you wanted to go out with me." They had met in a student group at Auburn University.

Katie had been amazingly pretty and popular, the life of any gathering. By contrast, Dave had been quiet and rather serious minded.

Katie smiled and deliberately bumped his shoulder. "I wanted a man of integrity and a man who would respect me. You looked quite handsome as well. You're even more handsome now," she added, loving her husband's patrician appearance.

They rode in silence a few minutes until Katie asked, "Aren't you glad we came to Minnesota?"

"I don't know. Maybe I miss the gulf coast area that's been home all my life. But I wasn't very happy even before we came." Dave drove farther before speaking again. "I think that I miss having a purpose for my skills and reaching new goals. Or maybe what I miss is having a future."

Katie waited, then added, "Everything seemed to pile on us at once: the stress you had at the firm, Jeremy growing up and leaving home, my cancer, the circumstances leading to your retirement, the house downsizing, even Ruthie dying. I feel like our old life was a boat that went over a waterfall with us inside. Now we're bobbing up in the pool below, glad to be alive, but without a boat."

Dave glanced her way. "Life was easier when we knew what to expect. Now everything feels uncertain. The only good thing is that we're treading water in the pool together. Aren't we?"

"Yes . . . we . . . are, Dinosaur." That was her favorite nickname for Dave, a compliment and mild tease about his chivalrous and old-fashioned values. Then with a little misgiving she asked, "Do you think we'll ever find a new boat?"

"I hope so. That's part of our purpose coming to Minnesota."

29

Needing gas, Dave pulled into a gas station along Highway 61. Katie remained in the warm cab while Dave operated the self-service pump. As his tank filled, he noticed a trio of large, unshaven, and roughly dressed men. Dave recognized the boisterousness of men who had been drinking and looking for trouble. The three started shouting innuendoes toward a red-headed young woman holding a baby in a pickup. A slightly built, clean-shaven man about thirty years old stood between the trio and the pickup. Dave guessed him to be the woman's husband. Several casual onlookers gawked at the unfolding scene.

As Dave watched with concern, the men stepped to within a foot of the young man. Each of the three troublemakers stood nearly a head taller and probably fifty pounds heavier than the husband. Dave could hear vile insults referring to the man's wife. The young man's fists closed as he prepared to strike. Quickly Dave pushed in between them. With his most exaggerated southern drawl Dave began, "Eggscuse me pullese. Does any of you all know the way to the interstate highway? I been drivin' 'round for hours."

One of the three men curtly answered, "Go south on 61. Now beat it, old man."

Up close Dave could smell the alcohol on the trio's breath. "Ooo . . . kay, south. I got it. Uhhh, which way *is* south?" Dave stood among them and turned in a circle looking in all directions. He noticed the young man glowering in anger with clenched fists standing his ground.

The thuggish speaker gestured toward the highway. "That way, you fool. For the last time, get lost."

"I woulda thought Rochester would have better signs. Back in Al-la-ba-ma we have better signs. This is Rochester, ain't it?"

As one of the big men reached to push Dave aside, everybody heard a shrill voice. "Rufus, if ah tol' you once, ah tol' you a thousan' time, you ask directions afore you get lost, not after." All the men turned to see a late-fifties woman with short gray hair approaching Dave. She turned to the trio of men to explain, "I been married to this idiot for pretty near forty years. He just gets dumber and dumber." Turning back to Dave, she continued, "And you promised me supper. I ain't had nothin' since breakfast." To all the men's surprise, she then swung a haymaker and hit Dave in the upper arm. As he cowered back, she continued to punch and kick at him while berating him for various inadequacies.

The three bullies had forgotten the young man and his wife as they enjoyed the sight of a woman beating on the irritating old guy. They started throwing in their own taunts toward Dave and laughing. The oldest of the three men used an expletive and shouted, "Come on guys. Let's blow this stinking dump." The three strutted toward an oversized pickup parked in the shadows. Their truck, jacked up with humongous mud tires, made Dave's mid-sized truck look like a pigmy. Dave and Katie watched as doors slammed and the monster truck roared away burning rubber to the highway. Cars braked and swerved as the huge truck pulled into traffic heedless of oncoming vehicles. Dave could not make out their license plate number.

Under the gas station lights, the young man approached Dave. "I wouldn't have left you, mister, if those guys had gotten rough. Anybody can get lost. Follow this road," he pointed to the highway, "to the interstate. Go west there. Signs will take you to Rochester."

Dave could feel his heart beating. "I know you would have tried to help me, son."

The young man immediately discerned the change in Dave's carriage and voice. "What's going on?" he questioned. "Aren't you really lost? Were you two acting?"

"Yeah, we played that out. Those pig-heads were trying to goad you into swinging at them first. Then they would have beat the crap out of you and called the fight 'self-defense.' " Dave's voice sounded serious.

The young man began to realize the danger he had been in. "I guess you're right about that. Thanks."

"You're welcome, son. Is that your family?" Dave waved toward the man's pickup and received an affirmative nod. Katie had moved over there to reassure his wife. Dave continued speaking to the young man. "I'm a father myself. Fathers like us don't have the freedom to let imbeciles like those guys provoke us into putting ourselves at risk. Watching out for ourselves so that we can take care of our families is being responsible." The young man nodded again and stuck out his hand, which Dave shook firmly. Without another word the two fathers returned to their respective pickups. The casual onlookers continued to stare.

Katie joined Dave in the truck cab. They drove toward home in silent tension until Dave demanded, "What were you thinking? Why didn't you stay in the truck? You could have been hurt!" His foot pressed the gas pedal hard.

Katie reacted to Dave's anger with her own. "Me? You were the one about to get his brains knocked out. That is, if you have any brains. Now slow down!"

Dave eased up on the accelerator a little. "I had the situation under control."

"The heck you did. Those drunken morons would have spread you and that guy all over the parking lot. If anybody's going to beat on my husband, it's going to be me."

Chapter Five

———•———

Dave's personal integrity had to privately concede the truth of Katie's words. But the adrenalin of his anger still partially controlled him. "Maybe I could have outrun them." He rubbed his arm, which still smarted from Katie's initial haymaker and protested in a calmer voice, "Did you have to hit me so hard?"

Katie also calmed down a little. "If I ever want to really hit you, you'll know that was a love tap." She paused and then added, "I had to make it look real to save your butt."

The couple rode in silence until Dave asked, "How did you know that I might need help?"

"I could hear most of the words from the cab. And remember that I saw you do that dumb-lost-guy distraction routine once before. Do you recall those drunken fraternity boys who nearly fought the rednecks after the Auburn-Alabama game?"

Dave took a minute before responding, "Yeah, I do remember that. I don't remember being as scared then as just now, though. But I hardly knew what I was doing either time." Dave looked over at Katie, who still trembled from her own fear and anger. "What did you say to the girl?"

"I told her that her husband had been brave. She said that she knew those guys a long time ago. They don't appreciate that she's moved on. She thinks maybe they have a jealous grudge against her husband."

At the gate to Big River, Dave heard Katie feigning a deep voice to mimic his words. "Does any of you all know the way to the interstate highway? I been drivin' 'round for hours."

Dave couldn't prevent himself from laughing. In a high-pitched squeak, he returned Katie's words, "And you promised me supper. I ain't had nothin' since breakfast."

Dave and Katie laughed and teased each other. Inside the mansion, Old Yeller greeted them with curiosity at their joviality. "Let's celebrate not being in the hospital," Katie proposed. She pulled a half-gallon of double chocolate ice cream from the freezer and picked up two spoons.

As they sat across the table from each other dipping into the carton, Dave concluded, "You know, we worked pretty well together. But next time call the police *before* you get out of the truck to save my butt."

Katie nodded in agreement. "You did the right thing tonight, Dave."

━━◆━━

"Aaaah!" A startled scream woke Dave from a deep sleep. Katie wasn't beside him. He rushed into the kitchen. Katie stood with both hands over her mouth and stared in revulsion at the floor. A dead mouse lay on the rug. "Look at this," she managed.

"Where did that come from?"

"The cat was sitting by it." Katie turned away.

Dave looked around. "Where is the cat now?"

"It ran away when I screamed."

No wonder, Dave thought. He glimpsed Old Yeller peering cautiously from the pantry. Dave nudged the mouse with his foot. This rodent was certainly dead. Old Yeller strolled in with his tail erect and sniffed the tiny remains. Suddenly the cat grabbed the mouse body and tossed it playfully into the air.

Katie backed away and shouted, "Get rid of it!"

"The mouse or the cat?" Dave smiled.

"Both of them."

Dave shooed Old Yeller out of the guest quarters. The cat, satisfied with his night's work, hurried up the stairs to the sunlit window seat. Dave collected the mouse carcass in a paper towel to dispose of in the woods. Katie threw the rug into the mudroom to deal with later.

Enjoying a leisurely breakfast, Dave and Katie discussed their day. They both wanted to see more of the town. They agreed to combine that exploration with another walk. Katie handed Dave two cloth shopping bags to carry. "We need to be prepared," she said.

After crossing Riverfront Drive and accessing the walking trail, they turned south in the opposite direction from the day before. The trail passed the outskirts of town, then a city park, and finally came to a marina beside the river. The marina had closed for the season. The trail crossed over

Riverfront Drive where a sign indicating "Main Street" pointed to the right. There they found Hansen's Bakery open and crowded with customers. A sugary smell of freshly baked pastries wafted out the door.

Donuts, cinnamon rolls, croissants, and artisan breads filled the bakery's display cases. Next to one of the cases a sign, "Bismark of the Day," announced a different filling for each day of the week. That day's filling was raspberry, Katie's favorite. "What is a bismark?" Dave wanted to know.

"A bismark is like a hole-less round jelly-filled donut with icing on top," his wife explained. The case also contained several kinds of cookies and a whole section of assorted dessert bars.

As Katie considered her purchases, Dave observed several small tables for snack-in customers. "Would you like a cup of tea?"

"Thanks. That would be nice, but let's keep exploring the town right now. I'll get some treats to go." Katie requested three bismarks, two cinnamon rolls, a lemon bar, and an almond bar. Then she saw frosted sugar Christmas cookies and added a few to her order.

The couple continued walking down the street with Katie stopping at several gift stores. "Looking at the bright and shiny things again?" Dave teased. Katie gave a little smile, but did not allow his words to deter her.

When they passed near the library, Dave left Katie to continue her shopping. Inside the virtually empty library, he asked a pretty yet bored-looking girl behind the checkout desk for books on local history. Although she wore a diamond ring and wedding band, to Dave she looked like a teenager.

"Sure," she answered, seeming to be glad to have any distraction. She led him to an aisle where, without speaking, she rubbed the back of a fingernail across a group of books. The clicking sound seemed loud in the quiet library.

"Thanks. Can I take several at once?" he asked, pulling one off the shelf.

"Whatever." The girl turned to go. "Just let me know if you need anything else."

Dave picked out *Settlement of Southeast Minnesota, Famous Minnesotans*, and best of all, *Mansions of the Upper Mississippi.* He settled into a chair in the reading section. Starting with *Settlement of Southeast Minnesota*, he studied about the early fur traders, loggers, and ultimately farmers coming in from Wisconsin. He read about the influx of immigrants from the Baltic Sea countries in the 1800s. These resulted in many Scandinavian surnames and influenced the modern culture. *They probably felt right at home with the lakes and the cold here*, he conjectured.

The words, "Sir, we close at noon today," broke Dave's concentration. The bored girl, only less bored in anticipation of leaving, appeared eager to go home. The clock said 12:04.

Dave picked up the books. "Can I check these out?"

"Do you have a library card?" she asked while walking toward the checkout desk.

"Not yet. We just moved here."

"Name? Address? Phone Number? Email?" The girl efficiently punched in Dave's relevant information. "Here's a temporary card. A permanent card will be mailed to you. Now let me check out the books." She finished in another minute. Then she reached for her jacket.

Dave headed for the door carrying the books in one of the cloth bags. "Thanks for staying late for me."

The girl smiled and shook her head. "Whatever." She locked the door behind him.

—•—

Walking back to the mansion, the couple passed another lake with ice fishermen. Dave became intensely curious. "Where are you going?" Katie asked suspiciously as he put his bag of books down and headed toward the lake.

"I just want to see the ice fishing. People are out there. The ice must be safe. Come on," he urged.

"I'll just wait here with the books, thank you."

Dave stepped out onto the ice. Immediately, the frozen surface broke, leaving him standing knee deep in icy water. Embarrassed, he looked back toward the fishermen. They walked around high and dry. Looking to where Katie stood, he demanded, "What happened?"

She answered objectively, albeit without much sympathy, "You broke through the ice. You're lucky the water there is shallow."

"I know that," Dave stomped out of the water and spoke with irritation. "I mean *why* did this happen?"

"The ice looks thinner at the edge where the ground warms it. There probably hasn't been enough cold weather yet to solidly freeze the ground." Katie pointed toward a large board someone had placed as a bridge between the bank and firmer ice. "That's how the fishermen kept their feet dry."

"Why didn't you tell me that before?" Dave spoke louder than he intended. His words carried across the ice, drawing glances from a couple of the fishermen.

"I didn't know before. My parents took me onto the ice when I was a little girl. They knew the safe spots to go." She couldn't help smiling a little to herself.

Dave, however, was not amused. "Thanks for nothing. You could have warned me about the ice."

Katie ruffled his mostly grey hair. "Oooh! Do you think your thin southern blood can't take a little cold?"

He still grumbled back, "That would be easier without wet feet."

Fortunately, the mansion wasn't far away. A hurried walk kept Dave's feet almost warm. They entered the mansion through the back door. While Katie went to disarm the security system, Dave stripped off his wet clothing in the mudroom.

"Now you know why they call that a mudroom," Katie teased. His implied blame hadn't spoiled her chipper mood. Buying some of the treats she remembered from childhood and going shopping had buoyed her spirits. "Do you know what I think?" Katie wanted to know.

"Certainly not. You think so many things so quickly that I can never imagine what you're thinking."

Katie put her arms around Dave's waist and looked into his eyes. She gave her husband a big kiss. "I think that we've made a good living, raised a wonderful son, and helped to make our community a better place. And recently, we've endured a lot. So, we should give ourselves a break and enjoy every day."

Dave enjoyed the kiss and softened in response. "That makes sense." Dave put his arms around Katie and hugged her to his chest. "Guess I was wrong, sweetheart. This time I could have predicted what you were thinking."

"Each day could be our last best day, you know. Let's try to make the most of every one."

"You're right. I'm not used to being a fish out of water. I've been irritable lately. I just don't understand what's bothering me."

"I've been touchy too. Let's try to remember that we're treading water together."

Dave gave his wife a last squeeze. "Let's do."

After Katie put away her bakery treats, she called to Dave, "How about French onion soup for supper?"

"Sounds good." Dave reclined in the sitting room easy chair with his feet warming in front of a space heater while locating a football game on TV.

Katie stuck her head into the room. "Okay, then you know what to do."

In the kitchen, Dave found five large onions and a knife on a cutting board. After doing his part for the soup, he returned to the game. Not long after, he became engrossed in the history books from the library. *Maybe this will help me understand this strange place,* he mused.

Chapter Six

With the soup simmering, Katie settled into the comfortable couch nearby with a cup of tea. "Who's winning?" Dave's silence didn't answer her. "Who's playing?" Silence again. "You're not even watching the game. Give me the remote!"

Without seeming to notice her demand, Dave began sharing his discoveries. "Thaddeus P. McReady built this mansion in 1897. He was born in New York state in 1857 and started work as a lumberjack in western Pennsylvania at age fifteen. In the early 1880s, he started his own logging operation in Minnesota, which was still mostly wilderness. Within a couple of years, he had built a sawmill on the river just south of where Washita is now. They used the Mississippi River to transport floating logs to market. That is called the 'Golden Era' of the Minnesota timber industry. Later McReady also built a rail line to his sawmill." Dave looked up. "I'll bet that became the trail we walked on today."

Katie listened, then reached for her laptop. Dave heard tapping. Katie cleared her throat. "Apparently, Thaddeus McReady was a ruthless competitor who commonly used shady practices. Some historians believe that he bribed federal government officials to remove Native Americans who opposed clear cutting on the land deeded to them by treaty. Certainly, he benefited and became one of the richest men in the Midwest."

"Where are you getting that stuff?" Dave looked up, amazed.

Katie turned the laptop so that Dave could glimpse the website. "McReady married a local farm girl, Sara Carlson, in his late 20s. She gave him three sons, but died in childbirth with the fourth child. The baby didn't survive either. In 1896, McReady married again, this time to a socialite from New York. He built this house for her. The mansion was placed on the National Register of Historic Homes in 2007."

Despite his pique at being out-researched, the history intrigued Dave, until the clamor of a game-winning touchdown grabbed his attention. Then he inquired, "Do you think the soup is ready?" The soup was ready. Each of them served themselves a big bowl and added a piece of bread topped with cheese. Next, they browned the top surface under the oven broiler. The odor of melting cheese filled the guest quarters. Before another football game could start, Katie pulled out several classic Christmas movies and her holiday viewing list.

Dave reacted with surprise. "You brought the Christmas movies and the list?"

Katie smiled. "Of course, I did. We can't celebrate Christmas without our annual countdown-to-Christmas movies."

"What else do you have in those containers?"

Katie only shrugged.

During the first movie, Old Yeller wandered into the guest quarters. He jumped up on the couch next to Katie, who ignored him. After a few minutes, she felt a little weight on her leg. Old Yeller had put his chin on her thigh. Absentmindedly, she rubbed him behind the ears. His fur felt soft and warm to touch. A quiet purring sound started. In a few minutes, the cat's head and forepaws pushed into her lap. She noticed the cat's encroachment. "What does this animal want?"

Dave looked over in amusement. "He likes you."

"Well I don't like him." She gently pushed Old Yeller off. Undeterred, Old Yeller waited a few minutes and started edging into Katie's lap again. "Maybe if I ignore him, he'll go away," Katie said under her breath. After a long time, the feline did seem to lose interest and wandered away.

After watching two Christmas movies and enjoying several Christmas cookies, Dave and Katie went to bed. They hoped for and enjoyed an uneventful night of sleep. Old Yeller slept in contentment on a soft chair.

—◆—

"Let's get our Christmas tree today," Katie greeted Dave as he struggled to wake up. After tea, the couple dressed for a day away from the mansion. From Main Street, they turned onto busy Highway 61 and drove slowly back toward the interstate. Many familiar chain stores lined the approach to Winona. "Other than the chill in the air, we could be back in Alabama," Katie observed.

Dave pulled into the huge parking lot surrounding a national discount store. In the pharmacy section, Dave found and purchased an electric heating pad.

"We have space heaters. What's that for?" asked Katie.

"You'll see. I'm going to try something."

Katie, used to Dave's experiments, didn't object. Outside they picked out a six-foot Douglas fir Christmas tree.

Back in the truck Katie realized she felt hungry. "Are you ready for lunch?"

Dave waved his arm toward the plethora of choices along the highway. "Pick any place."

"Could we go back to downtown Washita? I'd like to try The Blue Ox again."

They found a parking place on Main Street. Katie hurried to the bakery. She returned to the truck with a slice of apple pie for Dave, a cupcake, and two bismarks.

The Blue Ox felt warm and cheerful inside. Customers talking across the tables and sometimes with customers in adjoining booths filled the restaurant. Their previous waitress, Susie, greeted them again. "Glad to see you back. You can see we're more filled-up today." Without asking, she had brought hot water with lemon and iced tea to their booth. She took out her ordering pad. "What'll you have today?"

Dave pointed at the menu. "The skillet breakfast looked so good the other day, I'd like to try one."

"You betcha. What would you like Katie?"

Katie hid surprise that Susie would remember her name.

"I'll try the BLT on whole wheat bread with a bowl of tomato soup."

Susie had already headed for the kitchen. "Hash browns or French fries, Dave? Sorry to be in a hurry."

"Uhhh . . . hash browns," he called after her.

While waiting, Dave and Katie looked at wall photos of men and a few women posing with stringers of fish. In a short time, British Betty brought their plates out. "You doing fine, luv? Have you seen any haints out at the mansion?" Without waiting for an answer, Betty returned to the kitchen.

Dave and Katie ate slowly, enjoying the atmosphere and great food. "These hash browns are as good as cheese grits," Dave admitted, scraping his plate.

A big group left the restaurant together. Susie, obviously less busy after the group's departure, stopped by. "Need anything else?"

"We're fine," Dave answered.

Susie had heard Betty's earlier question. "Don't you mind Betty and her ghosts."

"Actually," Dave began with a serious facial expression, "we did have a visitation." Susie's mouth opened in surprise. "Tell her about it, Katie."

A good storyteller, Katie built suspense of the unknown until she revealed the cat frightening them in the night. Susie's congenial laugh could be heard all over the restaurant. Heads turned their way before customers returned to their food and conversation. Katie continued by telling Susie about the dead mouse the previous morning. "Why would the cat do that?" she wondered out loud.

"He was just bringing you a present. That's all." Again, Susie's laugh brought looks. "Mrs. Johnson here knows about cats." An elderly lady nearby heard her name and turned.

"How many cats do you have now, Mrs. Johnson? Six? Eight? You help these folks out." She pointed at Dave and Katie.

Mrs. Johnson looked frail, but moved eagerly to the Parkers' booth as Susie checked on other customers. "I only have five cats right now," she explained. "They all came as strays." She slid into the booth next to Katie. "You have a new cat?"

"We're keeping a cat for the owners of the Big River Mansion where we're house sitting," Dave clarified.

"Oh, the Big River Mansion. You'll need to be careful out there." Mrs. Johnson sat silent for a few seconds as if remembering. "What type of cat is it?" she asked.

"Just an ordinary tomcat," Dave replied as he described Old Yeller and told about the mouse. Mrs. Johnson confirmed what Susie said about the mouse being intended as a present. "A mouse is the best gift a cat has to offer." She suggested that the cat also wanted to show off his hunting skills. "Where did he catch it?"

Katie looked embarrassed. "Could have been in the pantry. I had seen mouse droppings when we moved in." She hesitated. "Would the cat have eaten the mouse?"

"Maybe, if you hadn't taken it away. He probably thinks you ate his present. But you wouldn't want a cat to eat a mouse. They can get parasites that way. Are you glad the mouse is gone?"

Katie shuddered at the thought of eating a mouse and nodded her head.

"Well, then the cat did you a favor," Mrs. Johnson concluded.

Katie added, "I gave the cat milk to drink, but he didn't touch it. Why not?"

Mrs. Johnson shook her head negatively. "A lot of cats

know milk isn't good for them. They can't digest dairy products very well. So never give a cat milk. That can make them throw up." She started to leave.

"One more question please, Mrs. Johnson. Why does the cat seem to be attracted to me? I don't even like cats."

"Honey, regardless of what folks say, most cats want everybody to like them. They just don't want to let on that they do. A friendly cat that senses somebody's uneasiness will try to win their affection. Give Old Yeller a chance. He could be a good friend." Mrs. Johnson hurried away to join her group as they departed.

Susie came back with their bill. "I'm a dog person, myself. But I keep a couple of cats around to catch mice. They're not so bad."

Dave handed her a credit card. "Has Mrs. Johnson lived around here a long time?"

"All her life and she's in her nineties. I heard that her husband was involved in the labor disputes back in forty-nine. Before he disappeared, that is."

"He disappeared?" Dave repeated.

"Well he never came home, is all I know."

"What happened in forty-nine?" Katie and Dave leaned forward in curiosity.

"Something about the old paper mill. I wasn't born yet. My parents would never talk about it."

———◆———

Returning to the truck after lunch, Dave shivered. "It's getting cold up here."

"Just you wait," replied the Minnesota native and buttoned her coat.

At the mansion, Old Yeller had abandoned the window

47

seat, which was shaded in the afternoon. They found him crouched in the pantry, waiting for another mouse with the endless patience of his species. The couple started a careful walk-through of the entire mansion. They considered this part of their responsibility as house sitters. "Come along, Mouse Mouth," Dave invited Old Yeller. The cat, taking no offense at his new nickname, joined them. Everything seemed safe and in order. Returning to the guest quarters, they settled in front of the TV to watch the evening news.

Old Yeller joined Katie on the couch. He started gradually working his way into her lap again. Dave left for the kitchen, leaving the instructions, "Pet him. Rub his fur. I'm going to try something."

Old Yeller enjoyed Katie's attention and wiggled on his back. Soon he fell asleep. Dave returned with a cut-off box. In the box's bottom, he had put the electric heating pad set on low. He placed the box on the floor beside the TV and plugged in the pad. "Now pick the cat up and gently put him in the box." The feline stirred a little as she did so. "Now stroke him a few times." Katie did. Old Yeller happily fell back asleep.

Katie sat back down on the couch. "How did you know to do that?"

"A little reassurance, a warm spot . . . he's a cat. This way we can keep an eye on him." With Old Yeller asleep in his box, they enjoyed decorating their Christmas tree. Katie thought of Christmases past as she lovingly placed each ornament. Dave also thought of the past. *What happened to Mrs. Johnson's husband, and why won't people talk about it?*

Chapter Seven

———•·•———

"This is what we have been expecting folks," the local weatherman predicted. "Snow flurries should start this afternoon, followed by three to four inches of accumulation overnight. Be careful driving out there!" Clouds began to overcast the sky. Old Yeller confirmed the prediction by remaining in his heated box.

Dave looked out the window. "Let's not go out in the truck today. We can have fun here."

Katie knew the real reason for his suggestion. Four-wheel-drive truck or not, her South Alabama husband remained apprehensive about driving on snow. She respected his caution. "I've got an idea. Let's walk into town."

Dave nodded in agreement. "I read somewhere that the Washita Historical Society has an office in the Community Center. I'd like to meet someone who works or volunteers there." Using Katie's cell phone, he dialed a number listed in an old telephone book.

An older male voice answered, "Hello."

"I'm looking for the Washita Historical Society," Dave said.

"You've found us. What can we do for you?" The voice sounded helpful.

Dave explained his interest in the history of the area, particularly the Big River mansion. The man on the other end offered, "I'd be willing to tell you what I know. We even have some exhibits and photo records down at the office in the Community Center."

"This isn't the Historical Society's office?"

"No, this is my home. I'm Frank Pederson, the president for nearly twenty years. I could meet you at the office this morning, though. Could you be there in about an hour?"

"Sure," Dave answered.

Without sunlight and with a modest breeze, that day felt like the coldest the southerners had experienced. Dave looked like an arctic explorer with his down coat and ski mask. Katie had a stocking cap on with a muffler wrapped around her face. Both had thick gloves and heavy hiking boots. Venturing out into the elements with winter weather brewing excited the Alabamians. Few people used the walking trail that morning. A fanatical runner passed them wearing earmuffs and gloves but otherwise was lightly clad. One man walked a Siberian Husky that obviously relished the cold. Reaching town, Dave and Katie felt completely out of place in their heavy winter apparel. None of the Minnesotans appeared to care about the impending weather. Everyone wore regular jackets.

The Parkers found the Community Center located on a side street near the center of town. Apparently, the building had been an elementary school in the 1950s. After the town built a new school, various community groups utilized the space. Dave and Katie found the front door unlocked and entered a dusty-smelling hallway. The Historical Society used an old classroom close to the entrance as an office. The room had a couple of partitions with old desks littered with papers and a conference table circled by folding chairs. The room felt nearly as cold as outside.

Dave and Katie found three senior citizens standing around a portable electric heater. A tall spry man of about seventy-five years with white hair stood and approached them. "You must be the ones who called. I'm the society president, Frank." Gesturing toward the heater Frank explained, "We don't use much heat in the winter when nobody's here." Two other seniors appearing trim and active for their ages shook Dave and Katie's hands. Frank continued, "These are the Williamses, Ed and Nancy. I thought they could help," Frank explained. "My wife Helen is visiting our daughter today. And your name is . . . ?" Frank leaned forward to hear clearly.

Dave introduced himself and Katie and explained their purpose in Washita. "I've always been a history buff. Big River has a fascinating story." He shared what he and Katie had already discovered about the logging industry, McReady family, the mansion, and even the ghost stories.

Frank led them to the conference table, cleared his throat, and spoke first. "I don't know about ghosts. But Washita pretty much built up around the timber business. In fact, Thaddeus McReady, who built the sawmill, named the settlement Washita after an 1868 George Custer victory over the Cheyenne Indians in western Oklahoma. Later historians

51

described 'the victory' as a 'massacre of women and children.' I guess the Indians had the last say with Custer at the Little Big Horn," he said with a wry smile.

"Anyway, the big timber in Minnesota and Wisconsin ran out around the first of the twentieth century. A Douglas fir takes one hundred years to grow to twenty-seven inches and three hundred years to grow to forty inches. After all the old growth trees had been cut, the lumber business was pretty much finished. The McReadys converted to a pulp and paper mill to use smaller trees. Back then, Thaddeus McReady pretty much ran the town. He even owned the bank and the rail line leading into town. His sons followed him into the business. They were a rough lot and thought that the town belonged to them."

Ed broke in with strong feeling. "Some of the McReadys still think the town belongs to them."

Frank continued, "Old Thaddeus lived until the early 1930s. The oldest son had taken over running the mill. The middle son managed the logging and shipping. And the youngest son took responsibility for the bank and other local businesses. Later, grandsons got jobs too. The family seemed to prosper even during the Depression when everybody else was hurting. Their combined family business was called 'McReady Enterprises' and continued into the 1980s. Nearly everybody in Washita had some member of their family working for the McReadys."

"What happened to McReady Enterprises?" Dave asked.

Ed answered, "They lost a couple of big liability lawsuits mostly from accidents due to unsafe working conditions in the 1970s. Then the EPA required the paper mill to stop polluting the Mississippi River. Over the years, a lot of the sons and grandsons were divorced. Every ex-wife had left with part of the family fortune. Finally, one of the great-grandsons had a manslaughter charge upstate. He had been drinking and driving while on company business and broadsided a school bus. Killed a couple of kids and injured more. Because of previous moving violations, he had no license or insurance."

"Yeah, all that was bad for them," Frank chimed in again. "But in addition to the financial settlements, a big Minneapolis law firm bled them dry with fees for all their legal troubles. Ultimately McReady Enterprises declared bankruptcy. The courts liquidated all of the assets in 1983 to partially pay the debts."

Curiosity stirred in Katie. "Who owned the Big River Mansion before the bankruptcy?"

"The family had always held the mansion as part of McReady Enterprises. That's why the authorities sold the mansion along with all the contents to the highest bidder, a doctor, in 1983. Until then, various sons or grandsons had lived in the mansion with their families until they built their own houses," Ed answered. "McReady sons and grandsons built many of the big houses on the waterfront. When a McReady daughter married a husband, the family business built them a smaller house on the other side of the road."

"We've got pictures," Frank offered. An adjoining classroom contained some display cabinets, pioneer implements, and blown-up photos of early days. The men stood up and led Dave into the display area. The Historical Society had collected plenty of old black and white photographs. Yellowed pictures showed the patriarch Thaddeus McReady, his sons, various wives, the sawmill, and the town. Even Big River had been documented starting with the construction stage.

Katie and Nancy Williams remained by the warm heater and began visiting about their families. Nancy and Ed had four kids, twelve grandchildren, and now three great-grandchildren. Katie showed a photo of Jeremy enjoying the beach in Australia and explained, "Jeremy inherited an adventurous nature from me. That spirit of adventure motivated him to work for an international corporation based in Atlanta. They recently gave him a two-year assignment in Australia. Both our parents are dead. He's our only close family."

"Maybe he'll come home with an Aussie wife," Nancy speculated. Katie only shrugged. She hadn't thought about that possibility.

They shifted to talking about the town and its people. Nancy had plenty to share about everyone. Obviously, Nancy liked Susie from The Blue Ox. "She was head cheerleader in high school. Perkiest girl you ever saw. She and her husband, Charlie, never had children. He used to be the high school principal, but had to give up his career after being diagnosed with colon cancer." Nancy paused a moment to think. "Charlie has struggled with cancer for maybe six years now."

Katie asked about Mrs. Johnson, the woman who had educated her about cats. Nancy knew her well. "She was a single mother. I had her son, Danny, in my class when I taught fifth grade before I married Ed. Danny was a smart boy. Mrs. Johnson's husband had been a real hero in the war. He won the silver star for knocking out a German pillbox on the beaches at Normandy." Nancy couldn't remember his name or what had happened to him.

Katie stepped nearer to the heater in the chilly air. "What about the McReadys?"

"They've always been pretty tight among themselves. Oh, there have been pictures of brides in the newspaper and a few of the boys played sports. But they're secretive about family business. One scandal they couldn't cover up, though." Nancy spoke more intimately. "After his first wife died, Old Thaddeus used his fortune to try gaining respectability for the family. He married one of the Astors in New York, more than twenty years younger than him. Big River was built to be her wedding present. After a couple of years, she went back to New York and divorced him. My parents said that she called Minnesota a backwater state and called the McReadys barbarians. After that, there were always women around Big River, but Old Thaddeus never married again."

Dave returned from the display area along with Frank and Ed. He and Katie thanked Frank and the others who all escorted them out. As they left, the Parkers heard a thumping sound from the old school gym. "That's just some of the local kids on their lunch break," Frank explained. Dave glanced inside the gym. There a group of middle-aged men warmed up to play basketball.

The mention of the men's lunch break made Katie hungry. "How about some lunch?"

"The Blue Ox?" Dave offered.

"Sure, why not?"

Susie greeted them loudly at the door. "Do you think you have enough coats on?"

The Parkers couldn't help but laugh at themselves while hanging their many wraps.

"How's your cat?" Susie asked.

55

Dave told about their success with Old Yeller. "Where is Mrs. Johnson? We have more cat questions." Secretly, Dave also wanted to ask Mrs. Johnson about the labor disputes and her missing husband.

"She comes in most Thursdays with her bridge group. You could phone her. Mrs. Johnson's first name is Mary. She lives over on 3rd Street. She'd love to talk to you."

Over lunch, Katie and Dave shared what they had learned. The food, as always, tasted delicious. After lunch, they dropped by the kitchen to greet Betty. On leaving The Blue Ox, big white snowflakes drifting down from a darkening sky delighted the southerners. The colored Christmas lights crossing Main Street had been lit. The town's Christmas wreaths collected a white frosting. Already snow almost covered the ground. Even the passing locals admired their first snowfall of the season.

Walking down the rail trail toward home felt like living inside a Christmas card. Mobile had experienced a couple of snow flurries during their thirty-four years there, but nothing in comparison to this snowfall. They marveled at the quietness of the falling flakes. Dave and Katie felt cocooned in silence, even with so much motion all around them. Katie, ever the science teacher, explained that the accumulated snow on the ground and evergreens absorbed any sounds humans or wildlife might have made.

At the car park access to the path, an inch of snow had already collected. They left the rail trail to finish the journey on Riverfront Drive. Near the driveway to Big River, they found a surprise.

Chapter Eight

A minivan had slipped off the road into a ditch at a slight curve. The vehicle wasn't damaged, but the back tires had lost traction and simply spun in the snow. Dave tapped on the driver's side window. The window lowered to reveal a mother with a cell phone in her hand. A preteen girl sat in the passenger seat with widened eyes. From the back seat came sounds of a toddler and a baby, both crying. Bags of groceries filled the back behind the children.

"Are y'all okay?" Katie asked.

"Sure, we're fine. I can run the engine to keep us warm." The mother sounded exasperated. "The tow service isn't answering. There are always a lot of fender benders with the first snow. My husband had a meeting in Minneapolis today. I'm on my own."

"Can we help?" Dave and Katie asked in one voice.

The mother looked at the couple on foot. "I don't see how. I just need to get these kids and the groceries home. We had to wait until Laura finished her ballet lesson, but I thought that we could get home before the snow built up. I was probably going too fast."

Dave got that determined look Katie had seen before. "We'll be right back." He started walking doggedly toward Big River.

Katie hurried after him. "What are you going to do?"

A short answer came back. "Get them out."

"How? You don't plan to use the truck, do you?" No answer. "You know that you aren't experienced driving on snow."

Dave left Katie by the gate. "When you see me coming, punch in the code. If I start to slide, I don't want to wreck the gate." In a couple of minutes, Katie could see the pickup coming slowly down the driveway. She opened the gate. Dave lightly touched the brakes to stop and pick her up. Then he drove the short distance back to the stranded minivan. Remaining on the road, he pulled ahead of the mother and removed a heavy rope from his extended cab. Seeing the truck, the mother had lowered her window again. "Could you turn off the engine, please, and keep the transmission in park?" Dave asked her.

After she turned off the engine, Dave crawled partway under her minivan and tied the rope to the front axle. Then he tied the other end to his truck's trailer hitch. "Start up and when I begin to pull, put it into drive, and give your engine a little gas."

The mother restarted her minivan and followed his instructions. Her kids became quiet and watched with curiosity. With Dave's truck pulling in four-wheel-drive and the minivan's wheels spinning, the vehicle returned to the road in a second.

"Turn the engine off while I untie you, please." Once he had untied the rope on both ends, Dave re-approached the driver's window. "We'll follow you to your driveway just to make certain you get home safe."

"Thank you so much," gushed the mother. "I feel like I've never driven on snow before."

"I feel the same way," Dave responded, smiling.

Following them, Katie questioned. "Why did you have her turn off her engine?"

"So she wouldn't accidentally run over me."

"Wouldn't tying to her bumper have been easier?"

"That might have worked. Or we might have pulled the bumper off."

After about two miles, the minivan turned into a driveway. The young woman's arm waved "Thanks" from the window. Dave and Katie waved back and turned around to go home. Katie looked at her husband and lovingly thought, *My southern gentleman.*

In a few minutes, they had returned to the mansion. Old Yeller left his heated box to stretch. He headed toward the basement, presumably to the litter box. As night fell, Dave turned on a floodlight outside the sitting room windows. Katie brought the comforter from the bed. Together they

59

romantically cuddled on the couch and watched the falling snow. Gradually the flakes got smaller as the air at higher altitudes got colder. But the snowfall intensified. Old Yeller returned to his heated box. They felt a wonderful sense of comfort and peace. Dave gently turned Katie's head to kiss her.

Mid kiss the phone rang. Dave and Katie looked at each other. The ringing came from the house phone. Who could be calling them? Dave picked up the old-fashioned rotary phone. On the other end a rough male voice rasped, "You've been askin' around about the McReadys. You'll mind your own business, if you know what's good for you."

"Who is this . . . ?" Dave demanded.

Click.

Dave told Katie about the call. They both felt better after giving the house another thorough walk-through. Old Yeller, unperturbed as usual, joined them through the entire mansion. Returning to the couch, Dave resumed the kiss. This time, no interruptions bothered them.

━◆━

Dave and Katie awoke to a pristine white world. Quickly, they put on coats, hats, gloves, and boots to go out into the cold. To their surprise, the last falling snow crystals reflected the morning sun. The very air appeared to be sparkling. Fine dry snow piled on the branches of the evergreen trees. Katie used a ruler to measure the depth on the ground. "Almost five inches."

The thought of a warm breakfast lured them back inside.

As they took off their outdoor clothes in the mudroom, the house phone rang again. Dave picked it up with some apprehension. To his relief, this voice sounded much friendlier than their previous call.

"Good morning, I'm Lyle Rogers."

Dave finished unbuttoning his coat. "Oh yes. We saw your name on our instructions from the Swansons. You're the summer groundskeeper."

"That's right. During the winter, I offer snowplow services. The town plows the main roads. But private property owners plow their own driveways or hire someone. I do most of the driveways out your way. I'm just calling to make sure you want Big River's done. The snow will build up if you don't keep it plowed regularly," Lyle warned.

Dave first asked the price, which turned out to be a reasonable monthly fee. "Yes, please do that for us."

"Okay, thanks. I should get to you later this morning."

Dave took an address for mailing a check. Then before Lyle hung up Dave asked, "Mr. Rogers, there's an old carriage house here on the property. What's in there?"

"Call me Lyle. Aaaah . . . There's not anything important in there. I keep a few tools inside. There's old furniture, a lot of boxes with papers, mostly junk the new owners moved out of the big house. A key to the padlock is in the light fixture by the side door, if you'd like to look around. Big River's driveway gate code is still Tuffy, right?"

"Right. Thank you very much, Lyle."

After breakfast, Dave and Katie decided on some exercise and a walk to enjoy the beauty of the newly fallen snow. Various animal tracks in the snow crisscrossed the trail. Returning to Big River's gate, they saw a young man in a familiar-looking pickup had just finished plowing the driveway. The pickup had been fitted with tire chains and the bed loaded with old bricks to improve traction. A snow blade had been attached to the front. Lyle waved in a friendly fashion as he passed moving toward the next driveway. Suddenly Lyle's truck-turned-snowplow jerked to a stop. The driver's side window came down. "That was you!" he shouted. "I hardly recognized you with all of your coats on."

Dave and Katie stood bewildered. Who could know them? A slightly built man opened the truck door and strode purposefully toward them with a bare hand extended. Closer, the couple recognized him as the husband from the confrontation at the gas station. Lyle shook both of their hands briskly. "Are you staying in the mansion?"

"Yes, we're house sitting until April. I'm Dave Parker. This is my wife Katie."

Lyle smiled broadly with a hint of mirth. "That was some act you two put on. You fooled me at first. But not Leslie. She's my wife. She majored in theater at the university and knew exactly what you were doing. How's the shoulder, Rufus?" he teased and reached out to touch Dave's arm.

Dave laughed with Lyle and hung his arm limply as if he had been injured. Katie added to the fun by rolling her eyes as if to question the sanity of men in general.

"Are you two professional actors?" Lyle asked.

Katie laughed, "No. Dave is an accountant. I worked as a high school science teacher. That act just came out of us to avoid an emergency."

To her, Lyle said, "I know Leslie would enjoy seeing you again."

Katie perked up. "Please have Leslie call me."

Lyle promised he would and turned back to his truck-snowplow. Leaving, he extended one additional friendly tease. "Thanks again, 'you all.' "

Dave and Katie waved as the young man climbed into his truck and resumed plowing snow.

⬛

Quickly kicking their boots off in the mudroom, the couple hurried to the space heater. Dave flexed his fingers in the warm air. "I'll bet that mittens are warmer on your fingers than gloves."

"That's what my mother gave me as a little girl. I never knew why."

After warming up, they settled into a relaxing day. Katie puttered around in the kitchen and then reclined on the couch with a blanket and a mystery novel. Dave continued reading the history of the region and occasionally shared tidbits with Katie.

Late in the afternoon, they made their customary walk-through of the mansion followed by Old Yeller. Katie noticed Dave squinting. Her own eyes felt itchy. Back in the guest quarters she looked carefully at her husband and then at herself in the bathroom mirror. The whites of their eyes had turned slightly pink. "I believe our eyes are sunburned.

Why didn't we wear sunglasses on our walk?"

"I never thought of that," replied Dave as he joined Katie at the mirror. "We weren't very smart, were we? We always wear sunglasses for a day boating. Snow reflects sunlight just as well as water."

Katie googled a first-aid encyclopedia on her laptop. "We have a mild cause of 'snow blindness.' We are lucky that we came back in when we did."

"What's the treatment?"

"Stay out of the sun. Keep your eyes covered. See a doctor, if the redness gets worse."

"Well, let's put on some music then."

The next morning, the Parkers' eyes did feel better, and the pink had diminished. "The Swansons said we could explore the property. I think that I'll look around the carriage house today. The sun won't affect my eyes in there. Want to come?" Dave offered.

Chapter Nine

———•———

Exploring dirty old places didn't appeal to Katie. "I have Christmas cards to finish." On the table, a stack of cards with envelopes waited. Not wishing to explore alone, Dave invited Old Yeller to go along. The cat wasn't interested in going out into the snow either.

Dave collected his big flashlight and dressed for the unheated carriage house. He found the padlock key hidden in the light fixture as Lyle had promised. Dave pushed in the door and stepped inside. Nearly twenty feet above him, the ceiling covered an area about sixty feet long and thirty feet deep. After the bright sun and snow outside, Dave couldn't see anything. The place smelled dusty with a hint of old leather, gasoline, and perhaps a little decayed horse manure.

Gradually his eyes adjusted to the dim light showing piles of . . . apparently, everything. The landscaping tools Lyle had mentioned leaned against the wall near the door. These weren't the only tools. Someone had stacked old tools from the timber business and sawmill in disorganized piles. Tools for the upkeep of horse-drawn carriages mixed in with old automotive tools. These added a slight odor of grease to the leather. Using the flashlight, Dave looked more closely at the open interior. Old furniture presumably from bygone eras filled the building's center. Cooking utensils, plumbing supplies, and even used clothes hanging on racks filled nearly every space. Stacks of old calendars and pictures covered former workbenches. Dave marveled, *At least a hundred years of history is in here.* He became immersed in the thrill of historical discovery as he picked up item after item, examining them.

Eventually, the flashlight revealed a dark doorway past the furniture. Maneuvering around the piles of "history," Dave reached the doorway and shined the light inside. Dust-covered wooden boxes on shelves lined the walls. Moving closer, he could see that each box had been dated. Careful not to disturb the dust, he removed the lid from the box marked "1929." Inside he found ledgers documenting financial records of McReady Enterprises. Different ledgers documented the mill, timber operation, and bank. Obviously, the records had been left behind when the house had gone through foreclosure. Dave set down the flashlight in a convenient spot, selected the ledger titled "Bank," and found October 1929. He started slowly turning the pages, trying to decipher the entries. Through their own bank, the family leveraged stocks heavily in speculation before the market crash. He remembered Frank's words about the McReadys doing well even during the Depression. As an accountant, Dave's curiosity intensified as he studied the records. *How did they manage?* he wondered.

Suddenly, from the quiet darkness an unexpected voice intruded, "What have you found?" Dave visibly jumped. "Sorry, I didn't mean to startle you." Katie stood at the door with Old Yeller under her arm. His tail twitched.

"I'm okay." Dave felt his heart slowing back to normal. "What are you doing out here?"

"You were gone for more than two hours. I wondered what you had found. And the cat seemed restless. I carried him over the snow." She put Old Yeller down. The feline started to explore.

"Look at all this stuff. I could stay busy all winter."

Katie took the flashlight and panned it around. *"Yes, you could,"* she answered with emphasis. Then looking at the open box she asked, "What have you got there?"

"These boxes are full of old financial records from the McReady family businesses."

"Aren't you cold?" Katie asked. For the first time, Dave realized that he shivered. She continued, "Come on back to the house for a while to warm up. What happened to that cat?"

Dave saw Old Yeller busily investigating whatever cats investigate. He looked back at the boxes. "I think I'll bring a couple of these over to look at."

Katie turned to go. "Okay, but please don't bring them inside until they've been cleaned off. And don't forget the cat."

Dave made several trips to carry the Depression-era

records to the house. Outside the mudroom door, Katie had placed a broom. On his last trip to the carriage house, Dave noticed a sizable stack of split firewood in a corner, likely from decades earlier. *That could be useful*, he thought, and called Old Yeller. The feline by then also suffered from the cold. After replacing the padlock on the door, Dave put the key back into the light fixture and carried the cat over the snow into the house. Back inside, the cat lay in front of the space heater while Dave warmed himself in the warm rising air. Katie served hot chocolate to Dave and heated a little cat food for Old Yeller.

That evening Dave resumed looking through the old handwritten ledgers. Figuring out records nearly a century old wasn't easy even for an accountant. Plus, accounting standards had changed, not to mention the introduction of computers. Katie watched her husband with resignation. She knew that the combination of history and financial records would be irresistible to Dave.

—◆—

"Wake up, sleepyhead. Do you want to miss Christmas?"

Dave woke to find Katie sitting on the bed. He covered his head with a pillow. "Christmas? When is that?"

Katie shifted her position to sit directly on Dave. "Strange coincidence that Christmas falls on the same day as last year, the 25th."

What Dave thought strange was his difficulty breathing. "We still have two weeks until Christmas." He gently tried to push the weight on him aside.

"No, only eight days left. I intend to enjoy every red and green moment."

More awake now, Dave wiggled his arms free and made a grab for Katie. She squealed and jumped free, scampering back to the kitchen. "Your tea is ready," she called.

In the kitchen, Dave found his tea waiting on the kitchen counter. "I'm guessing that you have a plan for the day?"

"Take me to the shopping mall of all shopping malls . . . the Mall of America." She handed him driving instructions.

"That's in Minneapolis, two hours' drive or more. Let's wait until the snow has melted on the roads."

"That would be in May." She knew that her husband still felt uneasy about driving in the snow. "You drove well during the first snow and even helped someone," she added. "Since then they've cleared the roads."

Without arguing, Dave acquiesced and started getting dressed. "Leave in half an hour?"

"You *betcha*." Katie exaggerated a Minnesota accent.

Thirty minutes later the couple headed down the driveway. To their chagrin, they found a load of garbage someone had dumped in front of the gate. "What happened here?" Katie wondered aloud.

"This must be deliberate," Dave suggested. "Maybe our caller the other night left this as a warning." He turned the truck around and started back to the house.

Katie's voice showed her disappointment. "You're giving up on the mall?"

"No, we just need some trash bags to pick this up first." Already a breeze had scattered some of the garbage.

Returning with trash bags, Dave and Katie started picking everything up.

"Why would somebody do this?" Katie asked.

"I'll ask them next time they call."

"You really think this is related to that phone call?"

"Probably."

Soon the filled bags went into the pickup bed to be disposed of later. The couple resumed their journey to Minneapolis, playing their favorite Christmas music. The drive through snow-covered Minnesota fit the music perfectly.

Katie initiated a friendly banter. "This is probably no surprise, but you married a woman with a flaw."

"Shall I start guessing what?"

"Go ahead. I'm curious to see how that might work out for you." Her husband wisely remained silent. "My flaw is that, while I'm enjoying being in Minnesota, I'm homesick too. How about you?"

Dave reluctantly admitted, "Yeah, I think about home a lot. But I'm warming up to Minnesota." Katie didn't miss the pun, laughed, and scooted next to her husband.

As they rode, Dave and Katie enjoyed reminiscing. Earlier that year the Parkers had sold their large suburban home in Mobile. They downsized to a much smaller and newer house in a semi-retirement community near Mobile Bay and the Gulf Coast.

An asphalt walking path shaded by live oaks and cypress trees covered with Spanish moss started near their house and tied into South Alabama's trail network. The path wound through the park-like residential community past a golf course and tennis club. Wherever the path passed near water, signs warned, "Do not feed the alligators." Only two miles from their new house, a marina lined both sides of a dredged creek. From there, recreational boats could pass downstream to Mobile Bay. The larger boats had access out onto the Gulf of Mexico.

Even when not fishing, Dave loved seeing the boats come into the marina and observing what types of fish had been caught. A flock of brown pelicans waited on the docks, always ready to grab anything dropped into the water. Katie loved the fresh seafood grills and restaurants near the marina.

"We'll be home again for spring," Katie reassured her husband.

"That's true. But being in Minnesota is a change we probably needed. Maybe I haven't provided you with enough adventures during our years together."

Privately, Katie *was* glad for an adventure.

"Are you sorry you left the firm?" Katie asked, not certain she wanted an answer.

"No, I'd be miserable there now. Also, you and I probably have more money than we can ever spend from the partnership buyout."

"You might be surprised how much I *could* spend." Katie enjoyed Dave's out-loud laugh to her quip.

He then continued with a serious response. "You and I have mostly lived in crisis mode for the last few years. Before that we worked toward goals, mostly separately. Now we need to figure out a new life together."

"We'll figure it out," Katie reassured. But privately she wondered how.

Chapter Ten

---•---

The "Mega Mall" appropriately named was mega with over 500 retail stores and restaurants, quite unlike Mobile's modest shopping malls. Opening in 1992, the Mall of America showed a little age, but the lavish Christmas decorations still delighted visitors' hearts. The hustle and bustle of shoppers brought back nice memories of Christmas gift buying at South Alabama's smaller malls. Dave and Katie enjoyed making slow circuits on each of the three floors. Dave frequently got disoriented in the mall. "I never get lost in the woods," he complained.

Katie pointed out the way. "I never get lost in a mall."

They enjoyed lunch at the biggest food court either of them had ever seen. After their meal, they walked through the amusement park in the center of the mall. Dave offered to take Katie on the roller coaster. She declined with, "Life with you is thrill enough." By agreement, they parted for an hour to do some Christmas shopping. Katie returned with several shopping bags, Dave just one.

As with many excursions, the return trip home seemed longer than the trip going. Dave and Katie talked about the garbage. Katie repeated Susie's words about vandalism and break-ins. "Maybe we shouldn't have left the house today."

"There's no way we can be there all the time. But I am glad that we had Lyle plow the driveway."

"Why would plowing the driveway help protect the mansion?" she asked.

"Otherwise our tire tracks could reveal that we're not home."

Still, Dave and Katie decided to spend the next several days close to Big River. A few dustings of snow fell, just enough to keep the countryside pretty. Every day, wearing sunglasses, they took a long walk on the rail trail. Although the weather remained cold, neither of them felt the need for as many clothes as they had in the beginning.

—◆—

One evening Lyle's wife, Leslie, phoned Katie. The women had a long talk getting to know each other. Leslie asked mother-to-mother advice about caring for her four-month-old daughter, Elsie. Katie invited Leslie and the baby to the mansion. Leslie promised to come after the hectic rush of the holidays.

Dave continued trying to make sense of the financial records from defunct McReady Enterprises. Katie busied herself baking in the kitchen. Each evening, she brought out the next Christmas movie on her countdown list. One night coming from the shower, she found Dave standing in front of a cheery fire burning in the fireplace.

"Where did you get the firewood?"

"There's a big pile in the carriage house."

"Shouldn't we ask the Swansons?" Her concern didn't prevent her from joining Dave in front of the fire's glow.

"I'd bet they don't even know that they have any wood."

Katie saw Old Yeller stretched out contentedly in front of the blaze with a cat's unwavering instinct for warmth. "I thought animals were afraid of fire."

"Apparently not this one."

━◆━

The next afternoon they walked the rail trail into Washita. At The Blue Ox, Susie placed a colorful glossy flyer on the table and inquired, "Are you coming to the Christmas concert?"

Katie picked up and examined the flyer. "Who's giving a concert?"

"Nearly all of the local churches combine each year to organize a Christmas program for the town. None of their sanctuaries are big enough. That's why they conduct the program in the auditorium at the community center. Still, getting everybody in takes three performances on successive nights," explained Susie.

Katie looked up and asked, "Do we buy tickets?"

"No, the concert is free. Just show up. The music starts at 7:00 p.m. I'd be there early, though, if you want a decent seat."

Two days later, Dave and Katie started on the rail trail toward town at 6:00 p.m. They hadn't walked on the trail at night before. The waning moon wouldn't rise for hours, making the trail dark. Dave turned off his flashlight. Within a couple of minutes their eyes adjusted. Starlight reflecting off the snow gave plenty of illumination to walk without artificial light.

By 6:30, they waited with others to enter the already crowded auditorium. A living nativity scene complete with animals decorated the community center lawn. Dave and Katie wondered about the historical accuracy of a llama being at the Nazareth stable, but made no comment. Inside the door, a skinny teenaged boy handed them a program. They found two empty seats closer to the back than the front. After a few minutes, violins and other instruments began warming up. *An orchestra in this small town?* Dave wondered. But there in front of the stage, musicians donned in formal wear prepared for the performance.

At precisely 7:00, a slender man of about forty wearing a clerical collar stepped through the stage curtains. "On behalf of the churches of Washita, I welcome you to our annual community Christmas concert." He gave a short prayer thanking God for the birth of Jesus. The orchestra started and the curtains opened as the pastor left the stage. A choir of about sixty men and women stood on risers. They began with "O, Come All Ye Faithful" followed by "Joy to the World."

The program continued mixing in various hymns with "White Christmas" and other Christmas favorites. Several soloists took turns on center stage, Susie from The Blue Ox among them. She looked different in a stylish evening dress. All the soloists had voices that amazed Dave and Katie. A couple of ensembles came in from the wings. The concert ended when all the soloists, ensembles, and choir performed Handel's "Messiah." Along with everybody else, Dave and Katie stood to honor the beauty of the music and the message.

Dave and Katie walked home silenced by the joy of the program until Dave observed, "Is that smoke ahead?" A greenish haze had appeared in the northern sky. As they walked, tints of glowing yellow and pink gradually emerged. "Could that be the northern lights, the aurora borealis?" In the starlight, he could see Katie's head moving up and down in affirmation.

Still in silent awe at the phenomenon, the southerners continued walking. Suddenly very near to them, came a loud, "Aarck!" followed by the sound of something crashing through the brush beside the trail. They both jumped back. Katie clutched Dave's arm. He pulled up the big flashlight. The beam seemed bright to their starlight-adjusted eyes. Three deer, all does, stood looking at them. Dave extinguished the light. "We must have startled them."

"I didn't know that deer made noise," Katie whispered.

"Only when frightened. Their cry is a warning to the other deer." The couple continued their walk in peaceful semi-darkness.

—◄●►—

The house phone rang early the next morning. Katie answered hesitantly, "Hello."

77

"This is Susie Holmquist from The Blue Ox. Is this Katie?"

"Hi Susie. Yes, this is Katie. You sang beautifully last night."

"Oh, thanks. I'm glad you came." Susie paused as if to take a breath. "Could I ask a favor please? I have a niece who just got married last spring. She has a few questions about marriage. Her husband is eight years older than her, a lot when you're nineteen. Would you be willing to give her some advice?"

"Wouldn't somebody she knows be better? Maybe you? I'm not a trained counselor."

"That's just the thing. The girl is embarrassed and would rather talk to somebody who doesn't know either her or her husband. Everybody knows everybody's business in this community. Her husband is a policeman. He doesn't want talk getting around. You may not be a counselor, but you and Dave love each other. I can tell."

"Okay, sure. I'll try. How will I get in touch with her?"

"She'll call you. Her name is Caroline McReady. Thanks." Susie hung up.

Katie's ears had perked up at the name McReady. She wondered if the girl was related to the McReadys mentioned by their late-night caller.

Dave stumbled out from the bedroom, drank a little tea, and headed for the shower.

The phone rang again. Surprised, Katie answered, "Hello."

"Mrs. Parker, my name is Caroline McReady. My Aunt Susie just called. She said that you might have some advice for me." The girl's voice sounded young and more than a little anxious.

"I'll do the best I can, Caroline. Would you like to meet?"

"Would *today* be too soon? I have an hour off work for lunch."

Katie sensed urgency in Caroline's voice. "Do you have a place to meet?"

"Any place you say," the girl offered.

"How about Hansen's Bakery downtown? We can have tea."

"I work near there. I'll see you at noon."

Katie said goodbye and hung up.

Dave came in drying his hair from the shower. "Did I hear you talking to someone?"

Katie explained the calls. "I don't know what I can do to help a struggling couple. But I hated to say no to Susie."

"Sweetheart, do you remember those marriage discussion groups we joined when Jeremy was young?"

"Yes," Katie answered reluctantly.

"We learned a lot that helped our marriage. I'm sure you remember some of those principles. You always had some of the best insights and even led some discussions."

That encouragement didn't convince Katie. "But that was different. This couple could have real trouble."

Dave smiled reassuringly at his wife. "Like our trouble wasn't real? Remember some of the fights we had? Just listen to the girl and then share some of your own experiences."

"What about us can I tell her?"

"You can tell any mistake I made or problem we solved as examples. Just do whatever you can to help." Katie seemed to be gaining confidence. "Would you like me to go with you?" Dave offered.

Katie gave her husband a big hug. "Thanks, but that might make the girl nervous. Well, I'll need to be in town by 11:45. Can you find something else to do?"

"Actually yes. I've wanted to talk to Mrs. Johnson. I could do that." Dave picked up the local phone book and then dialed Mrs. Johnson's number. "Mrs. Johnson, this is Dave Parker. You gave my wife and me advice about a cat at The Blue Ox."

Mrs. Johnson didn't act surprised to get the call. "How is your cat? Wasn't his name Old Yeller? Unusual name for a cat."

Dave assured Mrs. Johnson that Old Yeller was doing well and told her about him enjoying the heated box. Then he explained his interest and research on the area's history. "Would you let me interview you?"

"You mean right now? On the phone?"

"No; if you would allow, I could come to your house and ask some questions. Or we could meet at The Blue Ox about noon. Would today be convenient?"

"Today would be fine, young man. But come on to my house. I'll have tea ready."

"Thank you. I'll be there at noon," Dave concluded.

Katie had been listening while sipping her tea. "Sounds like we're both busy today."

Chapter Eleven

After Dave dropped her off, Katie hurried to the bakery where she selected the most isolated table. She ordered a pot of tea. A few minutes after twelve, she saw an attractive young woman, hardly more than a teenager, enter the bakery. By the girl's anxious expression, Katie guessed her to be Caroline McReady. Katie stood and waved her to the table. "You must be Caroline. I'm Katie Parker."

The girl appeared unsure how to proceed. "Thanks for meeting with me, Mrs. Parker," she said as she sat down.

"Please call me Katie. Would you like tea?"

"Whatever." The girl reconsidered, "No, I'd rather have coffee, please."

Katie waved to the waitress and ordered coffee for Caroline and several cookies. Knowing that time would be limited, she turned to the girl and asked, "How long have you been married?"

Caroline tried to conceal her nervousness by speaking slowly. "Eight months." She paused. "I was so in love with Billy that I just couldn't live without him. Now I don't know."

"What seems to be the problem?" Katie asked gently.

"We argue about everything. Billy wants to do everything his own way. His friends are more important to him than I am. I'm not sure he loves me anymore." A tear formed in Caroline's eye.

Katie's instincts told her to keep the girl talking and let her release some emotions. "Why do you think he might not love you?" That did it. Like a dam breaking, all the hurts and misunderstandings accumulated over eight months burst out. Katie listened and sipped tea for thirty minutes as Caroline's coffee got cold while she poured her heart out. Finally, Caroline slowed down, stopped talking, and sat silently with tears on her cheeks.

"I told Susie that my husband Dave and I are not trained counselors," Katie began. Caroline nodded. "That's still true. But what I didn't tell Susie is that we have led marriage enrichment classes for our friends and church in Alabama." Katie saw Caroline's eyes widen. "So, I'm going to give you the best advice I can before you have to go back to work." Caroline sat as still as a rock.

"First, Billy has what we call 'Young Husband Syndrome.' Nearly all newly married husbands are difficult in some ways. Very few men come into marriage with the understanding they need to make a marriage work." Katie went on to describe some of the characteristics of young husbands.

Caroline interrupted, "It's like you know Billy. Was your husband a 'young husband' too?" She looked hopeful.

"Oh yes. Dave was worse than Billy in some ways." Katie, the storyteller, went on to describe a few uninformed things Dave had done early in their marriage. "Punctuality is important to my husband. He always complained about me making him late. He used to wait with his arms crossed by the front door. One Sunday morning I would have been ready to go to church right on time, but I noticed that Dave had left the doors and windows wide open, all the lights on, and our puppy chewing on the couch. After I fixed those things, I went to the front door to find Dave had left me behind. I was so mad that I called a taxi to take me to church. I marched in during our pastor's sermon and sat down by Dave. When he found out how much I had paid for the taxi, we had a big fight. Afterwards, we hardly spoke to each other for a week."

Caroline started giggling a little. Encouraged, Katie continued, "On another occasion, I came home from a hard day teaching high school students to find Dave at home with three potential clients. He had promised them a home-cooked meal. The house was a mess and I didn't have anything thawed for dinner. While the men drank beer, and watched a game on TV, Dave learned how to *help me* in the kitchen." Katie could see her stories had given Caroline hope. She continued, "But he learned. *We* both learned a lot about what a good marriage takes." Then Katie asked, "Caroline, do you know what is the most important thing to make a good marriage?"

"Love?" Caroline guessed.

"Love is important. But commitment is the most important thing. But not just a commitment to stay married. A lot of couples that would not consider divorce are miserable in their relationships. What you need is a commitment to having a *good* marriage. That takes a lifetime of work from each of you. But a good marriage is worth the effort."

Caroline looked at the clock. "I'm already late. Would you meet with me again?"

"Let me make another suggestion. A good marriage takes two people learning together. If I tell you how to work toward a good relationship, and Billy doesn't cooperate, you'll just be more frustrated. We could make better progress if you and Billy met with Dave and me. Dave can tell Billy things better than you or I can. Do you think Billy would?"

"He might. I'll ask him." The girl looked at the check the waitress had left. "I'll pay the bill."

"No, you get on back to work. I'll take care of the bakery." Katie picked up the check. Caroline rose, hugged Katie, and rushed out the door.

⟺

Meanwhile Dave sat in Mrs. Johnson's parlor in a small-frame cottage that needed some repairs. She had not only hot tea ready, but also a tray of cookies and muffins. She was happy to have a visitor. "Mrs. Johnson, you grew up here in Washita. What was the town like then?"

Mrs. Johnson poured tea for each of them and began reminiscing about the town and even more about the people. She told him who was related to whom and how they had lived their lives. Frequently she added in anecdotes about people long dead. Cats wandered in and out while she spoke. Dave let her talk in general while he sipped tea and then directed her a bit. "I heard that your husband fought in the war."

"Yes, the army sent Sam to France. He followed General George Patton all the way into Germany. I worried and prayed every single day until he came home. My mother took care of our son while I worked in the grocery store. Sam won a lot of medals. Would you like to see them?" Dave didn't need to pretend interest in the medals. Mrs. Johnson left the room momentarily and returned with a cardboard shoe box. A large collection of medals and campaign ribbons plus a few old European coins rested inside. "Honorable Discharge" papers accompanied sergeant's chevrons and unit patches.

Dave reverently held the Silver Star for bravery in one hand and three Purple Hearts for wounds suffered in the other hand. He had difficulty speaking as he carefully placed them back into the box. "What happened after the war?"

"Everybody was so happy to see the men come home. We knew that Sam would be discharged in Chicago. But we didn't know for certain when he'd arrive here in Washita. Danny and I lived with my mother during the war. We had everything ready for a big reception at her house. Well, this house actually," she indicated her current home. "My mother left it to me. Sam surprised me by coming directly from the train station to the grocery store where I worked. When I saw him, all I could do was bawl and bawl. People came to see what had happened. Mr. Howard, the store owner, gave me the rest of the day off."

"Did life return to normal quickly?" Dave gently prodded as he nibbled another cookie.

Mrs. Johnson delayed a moment and sighed. "Sam wouldn't talk about the war at all. He acted different than before the war somehow, more determined maybe. He had worked at the paper mill before the war. The women employed at the mill during the war mostly went home. The men took their places."

Finally, Dave had arrived at the most important purpose of his visit. "What happened to Sam?"

"Things were good for a while. He worked hard at the mill. The work was dangerous. Accidents killed a couple of men and hurt several others. Wages weren't much different than during the Depression. Prices to buy everything went up after the war. We could hardly pay for food. The owners had the advantage because so many men returning from the war needed jobs. Then Sam and some of the men got together and asked the company for raises and better safety standards. Having fought the war for America, they weren't willing to be treated so badly at home. The McReadys who owned the mill refused to listen. A strike was the only way to get their attention. The workers picketed the gates to discourage replacements brought in from back east. Then the McReadys hired what they called 'security agents.' Those men were just paid goons. Some fights resulted down at the mill gates. Like the war, Sam would never talk about the fights."

Mrs. Johnson took a sip of tea. Then as if summoning her own determination, her words came slowly. "One day Sam came home from the picket line exhausted. I had spent the day at home taking care of our son, Danny. But I had heard that the biggest fight yet had happened that morning. I worried and prayed about Sam all day. He had a big knot on his head and some bruises. When I asked him about the fight, Sam only said, 'Nothing important. Don't worry about it.' That was just like him.

"I tried to get him to eat something and then lie down. I had made a soup from some fish I had caught plus a few early green peas and onions from our vegetable garden. Sam showed me a note he had received from the McReadys. The note said that the mill owners wanted to make a deal. They asked Sam to meet them alone out at their mansion, Big River. I protested, 'Why you? And why alone?'

"I can remember every word Sam said. 'I'm the workers' leader. We all know the owners have a lot of pride. Maybe they don't want folks to know they're giving in. Or maybe they're going to offer me a bribe. I won't take it. But just to get a chance to talk to them is worth the effort. We need to end this strike for everyone.'

"I kept on arguing with him, 'Do you have to go right now?' Sam got that determined look he had and answered, 'This could be the best opportunity we get. In the army, we learned that the enemy is most ready to surrender after losing a fight.' He did eat a little of the fish soup. I had removed every tiny bone with my fingers. I wished that I could have given him a piece of bread to go with that soup, but bread cost money we just didn't have.

"He started the long walk to meet with the brothers who owned the mill right after eating. The last words he said to me as he walked away were, 'I love you, Mary.' "

Mrs. Johnson sat quietly for a minute. "We never saw him again. I went to the Big River mansion the next morning looking for him. But they wouldn't let me in. They denied sending any note and said that Sam had not been there." Tears formed in the old woman's eyes.

Dave stood, gently touched Mrs. Johnson's shoulder, and looked at photos displayed around the room. He picked up one of a large well-built soldier in a WWII army uniform. "Is this Sam?" he asked quietly.

"That's him." She then pointed to a photo of a man with a wife and several children. "This is our son, Danny. I never remarried. Lots of women needed husbands after the war. Also nobody was ever like my Sam. Danny married a local girl, Paula, and they have four kids. They live in St. Paul now. He teaches chemistry at the University of Minnesota." Mrs. Johnson cheered up talking about Danny.

Dave noticed lots of pictures of grandkids and even a few great-grandkids. "Did the police ever find out anything about Sam?"

"Not a trace, not that they tried hard. I had no evidence to prove what I knew. Sam had taken the note with him. Several other men involved in the strike also disappeared afterwards. The strike fell apart without leadership. All the workers needed to feed their hungry families. I never let Danny even think about working at the mill. I made him study hard. He finished Washita High School as valedictorian and got a scholarship to the university. He had his father's determination." She rightfully felt proud of her son.

Dave looked at the clock. "Thank you very much, Mrs. Johnson. I need to meet my wife in town."

"Next time you come, please bring her along. She's such a cute little thing. If Sam had lived, we might have had a daughter like her." Mrs. Johnson wrapped up some of the cookies to send with Dave. "Take care of your cat." He thought to protest that Old Yeller wasn't their cat. Then he thought better.

Chapter Twelve

———•———

At The Blue Ox Susie brought their drinks. "I hear that you met with Caroline. She told me that you two have taught marriage classes." She looked at Katie and softly asked, "Think there's a chance for her and Billy?"

Katie marveled at how fast news traveled in a small town. "Sure. They just need to get on the right track and put in some hard work. How did you know?"

"Caroline called to thank me. She's excited that you can help. My niece is a sweet girl. I just wish that I had more time to spend with her. But after we close here, I need to go home to my husband. He's fighting cancer."

Katie reached out to squeeze Susie's hand. "We heard that. I've recently endured breast cancer myself."

"I thought so because of your hair. Plus, you're so thin." Susie turned uncharacteristically philosophical. "You know that a well-lived life is a series of joyful moments. Charlie and I have had a lot of wonderful moments. We're still having a few. Maybe..." her voice faltered as her eyes lost focus. Susie shook off an emotional moment and took out her order pad. "We need to put some weight on your skinny bones," she kidded. "What'll you have today? Our Christmas special is lutefisk."

"What is lutefisk?" Dave wanted to know.

"Lutefisk is a Nordic dish made from air-dried whitefish. It's part of the Christmas tradition for Scandinavians who immigrated to Minnesota. The legend is that the Irish tried to poison invading Vikings with dried cod soaked in lye. The Vikings liked the combination and took the recipe back home. Unless you're used to lutefisk, I wouldn't make it a full meal," Susie confided. The couple ordered a lutefisk appetizer and more familiar lunch entrees.

After Susie left, Katie told Dave about her meeting with Caroline. Dave clarified, "And this girl is a McReady?"

"No, she married a McReady," Katie corrected.

Shortly, Susie came back with their lunches including the lutefisk. Dave decided to probe for a little insight. "Is Caroline part of the extended McReady family?"

"Sort of." Susie explained, "During the war, Billy's grandfather volunteered for the navy, the only McReady to serve. Afterwards, he didn't join any of the family's businesses. He went to college on the GI Bill and became a dentist. Billy's father also studied dentistry and still practices in Winona. Like his grandfather, Billy went into the army right out of high school. He got a couple of medals in Afghanistan, I think. Then he got hurt by a roadside IED. They discharged him for injuries." Susie hesitated and added in a low voice, "Billy's the best one of the lot. I don't think he's involved much with the rest of the McReadys." Other customers entering the restaurant drew Susie away.

The lutefisk had come as a small gelatinous cake on a plate with a boiled potato and a spoonful of mashed green peas. The Scandinavian delicacy had an alkaline odor and sharply salty flavor with a strong hint of lye. "They call this an 'appetizer'?" Dave wondered aloud. The potato and mashed peas took most of the disagreeable taste from their mouths.

Katie asked, "How did your meeting with Mrs. Johnson go?" Dave repeated every detail from Mrs. Johnson. Katie could tell that the emotional story of Sam's disappearance had deeply affected her husband. "What do you think about it?" she asked.

His response, "I envy Sam," shocked her.

"What do you mean?"

"I spent thirty-six years looking at numbers and helping clients to minimize their taxes. Sam did something extraordinary with his life. I wish I could change my life or at least the color of it like that rabbit."

"You are a responsible husband and a great father. Do you realize how special that is? And on top of that you built a very successful business." Dave remained quiet in thought.

Driving back to Big River Dave tried to explain himself.

"Maybe 'envy' is the wrong word. Things you mentioned about responsibility are important. What I mean is that Sam was more than ordinary. I'd like to be like him once."

Katie had never realized this quality in her husband. They rode in silence a few minutes. Katie speculated, *Maybe Dave never realized this about himself.* She tried to encourage him, "Wasn't saving Lyle at the gas station more than ordinary?"

"Maybe that was a tiny bit above ordinary," Dave conceded. "But it wasn't much, really. I just wish that there had been sometime when I had acted heroically like Sam." Dave turned into the gate.

Maybe he's right, Katie thought. *Maybe something above ordinary is what we both need.* "What about me?" she started. When Dave didn't respond, she continued, "Maybe you're not the only one who wants to be more than ordinary."

"Sweetheart, you are a fabulous wife and mother. You were a great science teacher."

"I think that's a lot like what I said to you. My life sounds pretty ordinary to me."

After he had parked the truck, Dave promised, "I'm going to do my best to find out what happened to Sam."

"That is admirable. I'd like to help you, Dave." He nodded in appreciation as Katie paused then continued. "And I'm going to try to help Caroline."

"That sounds like a good plan. You can count on my help, Katie."

⏤◈⏤

"Mrs. Johnson, thank you again for meeting with me yesterday," Dave said over the phone. "I wanted to tell you that I'm going to start investigating Sam's disappearance. Maybe I won't find anything, but I plan to try."

"Thank you for trying, Dave. Even if you don't discover anything, I'll be grateful for your efforts."

"You are certainly welcome. Sam sounds like a wonderful man."

"He was."

"Mrs. Johnson, do you know anybody involved in the strike with Sam? Anybody who was there when the fight occurred or with him before he came home with the note?"

"Oh my. I think they're all dead now. I can't think of anybody who would still be living. Maybe some of the children whose parents walked on the picket line. Wait, that reminds me, one of the local boys had graduated from high school and gotten a job at the mill."

"Do you know what happened to him?"

"Yes. I used to see him at Sears whenever we went shopping in Winona. I'm sure that he worked at the store. I think he did pretty well for himself, a manager or something."

"Can you remember a name, first or last?"

"Let me see, his first and last names rhymed. Henry. Henry Henderson. That's it, I think. But I don't know whether he's still alive or not."

"Thank you, Mrs. Johnson. That's enough to get me started. If you think of anybody else, please phone me."

Dave stopped the pickup in front of a large home that faced the lake in Winona. "This is the right address for Henry Henderson." Several phone calls made by Katie and even a visit to the Sears and Roebuck regional office had located Henry. They gave Dave the address to which the company sent his pension check. Dave had called the Hendersons and asked for an appointment. He and Katie stared out the truck window at a two-story Federal style brick house with well-kept gardens and beautiful Christmas decorations. "They should be expecting us."

The couple walked up a brick walkway to a cut-glass door with a brass knocker. Before they could reach the front, a handsome well-dressed older woman opened the door. She smiled broadly. "You must be the Parkers. Henry is expecting you." She greeted them each with a gentle touch of hands and spoke softly, "My husband has never talked much about what happened in Washita. You will need to be patient."

Mrs. Henderson ushered them into a warm den where a man with a blanket on his lap sat in an easy chair facing a TV. The man looked at them and struggled to get out of his chair. Dave stepped forward quickly and extended his hand. "There's no need for you to get up, Mr. Henderson." The older man squeezed Dave's fingers tightly and settled back. "Thank you for meeting with us. I'm Dave Parker. This is my wife Katie," Dave continued as Katie received a finger squeeze.

"Call me Henry. This is my wife Mable," the old man rasped. "I've been a little under the weather."

Dave stood frozen with indecision about what to say next. Katie looked around and rescued him, "You have a lovely home."

"Thank you," answered Mable. "Won't you take a seat? Would you like coffee or tea?"

Dave and Katie sat down on a sofa and requested tea. "You don't talk like you're from around here," Henry said.

"We're from South Alabama," Katie answered and explained how house sitting had brought them to Minnesota. "This area is a lot different from what we're used to."

"A lot colder, I'll bet," the old man chuckled.

Dave talked a few minutes about the differences between Mobile and Minnesota and asked, "How long have you lived in Winona?"

"I moved here in 1950 to go to Winona State University. I worked as a night watchman to get through school. After college, I got a job at Sears and Roebuck and worked my way up to regional manager. I met Mable at Winona State when I was a senior and she came in as a freshman."

Mable returned carrying a tray with tea for the Parkers and coffee for herself and Henry. She placed two sugars in a cup of coffee for her husband then passed the cup and sat down nearby. He accepted the cup from her and turned to the Parkers. "What can we do for you today?"

Dave spoke carefully, "Mr. Henderson, I mean Henry, Mrs. Sam Johnson suggested you to us." Dave told about the meeting he had with her. "She said that you worked at the mill in Washita with her husband, Sam. We hoped you could tell us about the 1949 strike."

Henry seemed to deflate and suddenly looked much older. "I've never talked about that, even to Mable. I've thought about it though, nearly every day of my life." He sat quietly for a couple of minutes. "Why should I tell anything to you?"

"I believe a good woman like Mrs. Johnson deserves closure. A man like Sam should be remembered by his family as the hero I believe he was."

The old man nodded and rubbed his face. "Yes, she deserves that. Sam does too. But . . . "

Mable interrupted, "Henry do you want me to leave the room?"

"No. I shouldn't tell strangers anything I won't tell my wife of fifty-six years." Henry stared at his coffee as if into a view port to the past.

Chapter Thirteen

—•—

"Right out of high school I got a job at the paper mill to save money for college," Henry began. "They paid so little that I couldn't have saved a penny, if I hadn't lived with my parents who fed me. But I was lucky to get any job. A lot of men needed work after the war. Even though the mill made plenty of money in the post-war prosperity, the owners kept wages low. A worker could hardly feed a family, much less buy a house or an automobile. Maybe more important, the safety standards would give nightmares to today's workers. The mill's owners, a family of brothers, refused to even talk with the workers. We had to strike to make them listen.

"I remember that beautiful June day. Chilly air from Canada felt and smelled clean. I enjoyed the warm sunshine circling with the other picketers in front of the mill's gates. We carried signs saying 'Safety,' 'Decent Wages,' and 'Strike.'

Women carried signs too. A few of them worked at the mill. More were wives walking while their husbands rested. Some children played nearby while their parents maintained the vigil. The strike had already lasted for six weeks.

"Under a tree, Sam Johnson and several of the other strike leaders talked. Sam was tall, well built, and projected an attitude of determination. All the workers looked to him as our leader. Everybody knew Sam to be a decorated hero from the war in Europe. In fact, nearly all the men were veterans of the war. During the war, the mill owners made barrels of money selling paper products to the government.

"Across the road, I saw one of the mill owners and a teenage boy watching from a shop window. They thought we couldn't see them, but we could. The mill owner stood out because he dressed so well compared to everybody else. He and his family had never tried to conceal their contempt for the strikers. 'Filthy communists,' they called us.

"A stranger carrying a portable two-way radio entered the shop. He must have used the radio to call the strikebreakers. Because in a few minutes, three trucks showed up bringing tough-looking men and then left. All the police quietly disappeared. Later I heard the police chief had ordered them to leave.

"The stranger came out from the shop carrying a megaphone instead of the radio. The strikebreakers gathered around their boss. The hired men formed a line and approached us. Suddenly their boss shouted, 'Clear the trash from the gates!' through the megaphone. At these words, the strikebreakers rushed forward. They attacked everybody with clubs, chains, and brass knuckles. The women ran to protect their children.

"One of the strikebreakers came at me with a chain. I dodged him and ran. A lot of other picketers ran right behind me. Most of us stopped about fifty feet away and looked back. But Sam and the other men from under the tree pushed to the center of the melee and stood their ground. I saw Sam take a head blow from a club. When the goon raised his arm for a second blow, Sam blocked the descending arm and wrestled the club from his attacker.

"Insults and various obscenities came through the megaphone." Mr. Henderson's voice rose to mimic the orders they had received. " 'Teach the commies a lesson!' 'Show who's in charge!' They stepped over the workers who had been knocked down and beaten. I heard a woman shriek 'Aaaaeee!' over the noise. She threw a baseball-sized rock to hit a man beating her husband. Me and some of the smaller guys followed her example by picking up stones to hurl directly at the faces of the strikebreakers. They stopped moving forward.

"Then Sam started wildly swinging the club he had taken. 'Fight for your families!' I heard him shouting. The goons started to surround him." Henry paused and looked at Dave. "Have you ever been in a fight like that?"

Dave sat transfixed. He shook his head. "No."

"Well, when it happens, you lose your head. Dying or being hurt doesn't mean anything." Henry sighed deeply and looked back at his coffee. "Without thinking, I ran forward and tackled one of the strikebreakers as hard as I could. He was a lot bigger than me. But I was a good wrestler in those days. Before he could recover, I slipped behind him and got my arm under his chin. That's against wrestling rules, you know." Dave nodded understanding.

"In a few seconds, I had choked him out." For the women, Henry explained, "Without blood to his brain, he went unconscious." The old man continued, "Other men came back to the fight. All around me cursing and shouting workers fought alongside of Sam using their fists or the flimsy picket signs. Without weapons, many of the workers like me tackled their opponents to the ground where they grappled, gouged, and even used their teeth. Then I felt somebody pulling me away from the man I still choked. Sam jerked me up and shouted in my face, 'Don't kill him, Henry!' When Sam turned his back, I kicked the unconscious man in the face twice. But Sam himself had been aroused to fury by pain and anger. I watched him smash one man to the ground with the club. He moved forward and knocked another down. Me and other workers surged behind Sam and pushed the strikebreakers back.

"The goons started backing away. Enraged workers struck down several more as they tried to escape. Sam raised the club into the air in victory, and then he leaned over to throw up. Bloody men lay on the ground groaning or inert. I saw a couple of bit-off pieces of ears among them. We helped up our wounded and left the hurt goons to crawl away. I saw the man I choked stagger off. We all remained at the gates until every strikebreaker had left. Later I saw a car leaving with the well-dressed owner and teenager."

Henry looked up from his coffee that had gotten cold with tears in his eyes. His voice hesitated, "Except for Sam, I would have choked that man to death. Is that what you wanted to hear?" Mable came over and put her hand on her husband's shoulder. Henry patted her in appreciation.

Dave forced words from his mouth. "Do you know what happened to Sam?"

"Since I wasn't hurt much, I stayed at the gates all day. After a while, the police showed back up acting like nothing had happened. Late that afternoon the other strikers urged Sam to go home and get some rest. As he walked toward home, I saw a kid run up and hand him a note. Sam read the note and said something to the kid, who ran off." Henry's voice choked. "That's the last I ever saw Sam. A couple more men disappeared later too. The strike fell apart without leaders."

Dave started to speak again, until he felt Katie press her hand against his thigh in restraint. He saw Mable looking directly at Katie non-verbally communicating, "Enough."

"Thank you, Mr. Henderson," Dave heard Katie begin. "You have been a big help to us. You've honored the memory of Sam Johnson."

Mable showed them to the door. "Come back another time, please," she invited. "Henry would enjoy talking about more pleasant things."

Back in the truck, the Parkers rode in silence. Katie could feel Dave's outrage and determination. "Thanks for your help, Katie. I couldn't have done this without you," he commented.

"It's about time you figured that out."

⬤

Katie picked up the ringing phone. "This is Caroline. I talked to Billy. I asked him to meet with you and Dave as my Christmas present. He agreed to!" The girl sounded excited. "He's working graveyard shift from midnight until eight in the morning right now. Then he sleeps during the day. Could you meet with us tomorrow evening before he starts his shift, please?"

"Could we meet with you and Billy tomorrow evening?" Katie repeated loudly while making eye contact with Dave. Her husband signaled "okay" with an upward thumb. "Sure. How about we have dinner together?" Katie named a chain restaurant out on the highway.

"Just a second." Obviously, Caroline had her palm over the phone mouthpiece while she talked to Billy. "That will be great. Could we meet at six?" Katie affirmed that time and said goodbye.

Afterwards, Katie reviewed with Dave the things Caroline had said earlier. "I didn't sense physical abuse, or substance addiction, or infidelity issues. Not yet anyway. They're always arguing about everything. That leads to hurt feelings on both sides. They just don't know how to be married."

"Sounds like you did a good job," Dave encouraged. "But I don't see how I can help you."

"I need you to talk to Caroline's husband, Billy."

"What would I have to say to him?"

Katie became stern. "That dodge won't work. *You* told me to listen to Caroline and then share the things about marriage we learned in the discussion groups. *You* attended the same groups as me."

Dave suppressed a smile. "I learned that using the word 'you' in an argument isn't a good idea."

Katie added even more emphasis. "*You* know what I mean."

——◆——

The house phone rang about 2:00 a.m. Dave got up to answer it.

"How did you like that present in your driveway?" The male voice sounded low and tinged with menace. "You've been meddling where you shouldn't. There'll be worse, if you keep on." *Click.*

Dave returned to bed. "Our unknown garbage-dumping friend called again." They lay awake for a long time. Old Yeller, having been awakened by the phone, joined them.

Chapter Fourteen

———•———

On the way to meet Caroline and Billy, Dave stopped at the downtown bookstore. Inside, he and Katie looked for a favorite book on marriage and purchased two copies.

The Parkers arrived early at the restaurant and asked for a back-corner booth. Katie watched for Caroline. A couple of minutes before 6:00, she entered with a nice-looking, clean-shaven young man. Billy dressed in civilian clothes, but a slight bulge in his coat revealed that he carried a gun. Katie noticed that Billy walked with a slight limp. As he rose to meet them, Dave recognized Caroline. "I know you. You're the librarian. You stayed late to give me a library card." He extended his hand.

Caroline reached out to grasp his hand. "I remember. You're Katie's husband?"

Dave assured Caroline that he was Katie's husband while he and Billy shook hands firmly. Billy's body language revealed apprehension, perhaps even sullenness.

A waitress appeared. "What would you like to drink?"

"Tonight is our treat," Dave explained. "Would you like beer, Billy? Is six hours before your shift long enough?"

Billy perked up a little and nodded assent.

"Caroline?"

She asked for "pop." Asked what kind, Caroline chose Pepsi. Katie and Dave ordered their usual lemon water and unsweetened iced tea. While the waiter collected their drinks, Katie rambled a bit about her and Dave's positive experiences in Minnesota.

When the drinks came, they all ordered. Dave and Katie ordered first and each selected something on the expensive side so that Caroline and Billy would feel free to do likewise. After the waiter departed with their orders, Katie started the more personal conversation. "How did you two meet?"

They had met through a mutual friend. Katie responded by telling about meeting Dave at college and then continued to tell a story about their early life as a couple. "Dave and I married in the fall. I looked forward to our first Valentine's Day as a married couple and dropped some hints to Dave about making it memorable. He promised to pick me up after school where I taught and take me to eat seafood someplace special on the bay. I looked forward to an expensive romantic restaurant.

"Dave was used to seeing me dressed casually as a college student and then as a teacher. To surprise him, I took the money my grandmother had given me at Christmas and bought a tight, sexy dress and new shoes with three-inch heels. On Valentine's Day, I asked the hall monitor to watch my last class while I slipped into the girls' locker room. There I showered, fixed my hair, put on fresh makeup with red lipstick, and wiggled into the dress. A crowd of fifteen-year-old girls watched silently. But I wanted to please my husband. I didn't care.

"After the last bell rang, I waited on the curb for Dave to pick me up. A group of teenaged boys stared, although they tried not to be noticed. I heard one mother who was picking up her daughter ask about me. 'That's our science teacher,' her daughter explained. The mother asked, 'What science is she teaching?'

"Dave surprised me by arriving in his pickup truck wearing shorts. If he noticed my dress, he didn't say anything. I became suspicious when I suggested that we pull over somewhere private to start with a little romantic necking. Dave said something about the tide schedule and kept driving. As the sun set, he drove down a little-used and unpaved road to a remote beach. *Where is the restaurant?* I thought.

"From the back of the truck, Dave pulled out a long-handled net, a bucket, and a flashlight. 'Have you ever been crabbing?' he asked.

"I slipped off my heels and held the flashlight as we waded in the shallow water. Dave scooped up blue crabs the light from the flashlight revealed. Then he built a fire with driftwood and boiled the crabs on the beach. Too bad he didn't think to bring napkins.

"At first I felt unloved and heartbroken. But as we picked apart the crabs in the firelight, Dave explained that his parents had taken him crabbing as a boy at that place. He had tried to share a deeply meaningful memory with me. I had hoped our first married Valentine's Day would be memorable. That one certainly was memorable. Fortunately, the dry cleaners salvaged my new dress. But I could never put it on again without imagining the odor of salt water, wood smoke, and crab guts."

Everybody laughed except Billy. He did smile though, despite what seemed to be a resolution to participate as little as possible. Dave picked up the conversation. "I heard that you're in law enforcement, Billy."

"Yes sir."

"Do you like being a policeman?"

"Yes sir."

"What's your favorite part?"

"I like protecting people."

"Do you have any off-duty hobbies?"

"I love fishing."

Dave smiled. "Fishing is *my* favorite thing to do."

Billy perked up. "You've got to be kidding me."

Dave told a little about deep-south fishing and asked, "What's your favorite fish to catch?

Billy had relaxed a bit. "Muskies."

Caroline listened hopefully as Dave continued to chat with Billy.

Their food came. Dave knew eating would give Caroline and Billy something pleasant to do while he shared some ideas. "We," indicating himself and Katie, "appreciate you making an investment of your time by meeting with us tonight. Marriage can be one of the best things in life and is also one of the most difficult." Billy tensed up again. His knife and fork gave him something to do to cover his unease. "Do you know what is the most important thing in marriage?"

Billy had heard the answer from Caroline. "Commitment to a good marriage," he said without emotion.

"Right. That's why we so appreciate your commitment to meet with us. Do you know the second most important thing in marriage?" Neither Caroline nor Billy made any guesses. "The second most important thing is having a common plan for your marriage." Caroline and Billy sat perplexed. This meeting wasn't going the way either had expected.

Katie sat observing Billy. *He doesn't want his interpersonal limitations to be exposed*, she realized. *He is covering his fear.* She found it amazing how emotionally intimate relationships frightened many men more than facing danger in the army or as a policeman.

Dave continued, "A contractor needs a blueprint to build a house. When we get married, each of us starts with ideas about marriage. Both the husband and wife bring into their relationship a mental blueprint of how marriage should work. The problem is that newly married couples nearly always have different blueprints. Can you imagine two contractors working on the same house while using different blueprints?" Caroline and Billy listened, their food forgotten.

Katie started illustrating the ways her blueprint had differed from Dave's. "My father turned over all of the money he made to my mother. Mom paid any outstanding bills first and then felt free to spend all the remaining money before the next paycheck. But on our honeymoon, Dave created a strict budget for us, including aggressive saving. He insisted on sticking to that budget even when we had plenty of money in the bank. I couldn't understand why we had to save up for a new car rather than buy one on payments we could afford. We had a lot of arguments about money.

"Another issue was communication. The family I grew up in would argue about everything. That was our way to discuss things. Whenever Dave and I had a disagreement, he would completely clam up. Our dog communicated better." Dave assisted his wife with facial expressions and gestures to highlight her stories. Caroline laughed out loud and even Billy chuckled.

Dave took over the conversation. "Therefore, the two of you need a common blueprint. We have an early Christmas gift for you." He handed each of them a copy of the book they had purchased. "This book has a good blueprint for marriage. We're asking that you each make a commitment to your marriage by reading the book. Every relationship is unique. So, we don't expect that everything you read will apply to you right now, and you might even disagree with the author. But the book is a great starting point to create your own marriage blueprint together."

"We really do appreciate you meeting with us," Katie added. Then she changed the subject to the weather. "Do you think we'll get much more snow?"

"Wait! I thought we could talk about some of our problems," Caroline objected. At her comment, Billy visibly cringed.

Dave answered her, "Sorry, but we aren't trained counselors. If we start into the he-did-this and she-did-that stories, we'll only be refereeing your arguments. Read the book first. At the end of each chapter you'll find discussion questions that will help you to create a common blueprint without accusing each other. If after you've read the book, you disagree with each other about something in the book, we can help you to work through that." Dave picked up his fork and began eating.

"Whew." Billy audibly exhaled in relief. His mistakes would not be exposed or judged that night. With the threat of embarrassment removed, he became friendlier. Once relaxed, Billy revealed himself to be an energetic and amiable young man. He told about boyhood adventures growing up in the Washita area. Playing high school hockey had been his wintertime passion. His summers revolved around the Mississippi River, fishing, and boating. He and some buddies once built a flimsy log raft hoping to recreate Huck Finn's ride down the river. But their parents discovered the plan and intervened. In exchange for a promise to not attempt the river journey, Billy and his friends settled for a week-long canoe trip in Minnesota's northern Boundary Waters wilderness. Dave and Katie didn't need to fake genuine interest.

As Billy continued to talk, Caroline started flipping through the marriage book with a slight smile on her face. *Maybe this is what we both need to hear.*

◄◆►

On their ride back to Big River, Katie twittered with excitement. "Oh, what a nice young couple. I really hope we can help them." Dave could tell what she called her "happiness meter" was pegged out.

"Katie, you have a gift for loving and helping people. Maybe you could pursue more opportunities like this in our retirement."

"Would you help me like you did tonight?"

"*Absolutely* yes, sweetheart."

Katie grew serious. "Thank you Dave, I couldn't do this without you."

"It's about time you figured that out," he repeated her words.

Chapter Fifteen

Katie got up early to do some baking on Christmas Eve. After he struggled into breakfast, Dave announced, "Today, I'm making gumbo." While her baking cooled, Katie helped him collect the ingredients including Cajun spices brought from Alabama. To resist her temptation to hover while Dave cooked, she joined Old Yeller at his window seat to finish her mystery novel. The cat welcomed her company.

Two hours later she returned downstairs to find Dave trying to watch a college football game on the TV that he had moved into the kitchen. At the same time, he stirred his favorite Cajun dish on the stove. The roux, made from a mixture of flour and oil, had to be constantly stirred to avoid scorching. He had already spoiled one batch of roux during a goal line stand. He didn't welcome any additional distractions when his wife started, "I'd like to go in to town."

Her husband watched the pot while frequently glancing at the game. "What do you need?"

Katie ignored Dave's dual effort. "Nothing. I'd like to deliver some presents." She pointed toward the banana-walnut breads baked earlier. He reluctantly tore his eyes away from the game and the pot to look at her early morning work.

Dave added okra powder as a thickener to the roux. Soon he would cut in slices of hot sausage and put the mixture into a crock-pot. Before eating, he would add in shrimp with onions and diced bell pepper along with the Cajun spices. "Would you like to walk the rail trail into town, or drive?"

"Let's walk."

—◄+►—

An hour later, gentle snowfall greeted the couple on the trail. Katie thought Main Street looked like one of her Christmas movies. Last-minute shoppers scoured the stores for that special gift or, in some cases, any gift. Since Dave and Katie had finished their shopping, they simply enjoyed the atmosphere of Christmas.

Katie had packaged and decorated the banana-walnut breads with red and green ribbons. With Dave carrying the breads in a shoulder bag, they delivered the first to Mrs. Johnson. She insisted that they stay for a cup of tea. During tea, they duly admired her cats, all five of them. From taking care of Old Yeller, the couple had learned how to scratch under the felines' chins in a manner they enjoyed. Mrs. Johnson was excited that her son would pick her up late that afternoon for a big family holiday in St. Paul.

After wishing Mrs. Johnson a Merry Christmas, Dave and Katie distributed the breads to their new friends: Susie, Betty, Frank Pederson and the Williamses from the Historical Society, and two for Caroline at the library. Caroline whispered conspiratorially under her breath, "Billy has been reading the book!" The last dessert bread they left with the kindly older man at the post office. He handed them a heavy bag full of Christmas cards. The post box hadn't been able to accommodate all their mail.

Posters around town advertised a special Christmas Eve service at the Lutheran Church shortly after most stores closed at 6:00 p.m. Dave and Katie finished their deliveries in time to get a good seat. The gothic-styled sanctuary soon filled with parishioners in holiday apparel. Wreaths and a Christmas tree from which gifts hung for less fortunate children created a beautiful decor. The pleasant odor of hot wax from burning candles permeated the atmosphere. The choir director led the congregation in several Christmas hymns. A teenage girl read a poem about Christmas. A middle-aged woman told a touching story about a Christmas blessing she received as a child. The entire congregation seemed to hold their breath when an alto soloist filled the room with "O Holy Night."

To the Parkers' surprise, the same slender pastor who had introduced the Community Christmas Concert stood to speak. Standing before the audience he simply shared, "Hope is an essential element of a Christian's life. In the thirteenth chapter of the book of First Corinthians, verse thirteen, Apostle Paul lists hope along with faith and love. All of us know these three qualities are the keys to godly living.

Have you ever seen young fathers or mothers who weren't full of hope as they cradled their new baby? Probably not. At Christmas, all of us have a new baby: the baby Jesus. That baby is God's gift of hope for all of us, the essence of Christmas." He ended the service with a brief prayer.

As they left the service, many people greeted Dave and Katie. Frequently they made comments such as, "I hear you're house sitting at Big River," or "I'll bet this is colder than Alabama." The minivan mother Dave had pulled onto the road during the first snow introduced herself and her husband. "We're Lisa and Richard Christensen." Richard thanked them for helping his family. Another woman whom neither Dave nor Katie recognized shook hands and whispered, "I know what you're doing for Caroline and Billy. God bless you!"

Susie from The Blue Ox attended the service along with a frail-looking middle-aged man they presumed to be her husband. Well-wishers surrounded him. Dave and Katie waited their turn and then introduced themselves. Katie and Susie shared a hearty hug and wished each other a Merry Christmas.

◄◆►

After a brisk walk in the dark back to Big River, Dave added in the final ingredients to finish the gumbo while Katie made cornbread. Then her cell phone rang.

"Merry Christmas!" their son Jeremy greeted. "Turn on Skype. I want you to meet someone." Jeremy waited while Katie started her laptop. Immediately two people appeared

116

on her screen. A handsome young woman in a colorful summer dress stood next to her son. Behind them, waves crashed on a sandy beach on a warm sunny day. "This is Denyse," Jeremy introduced. Denyse said something unmistakably friendly, yet not understandable through her Aussie accent.

"Dave, get over here!" Katie demanded. Dave immediately came to appear on Jeremy's screen along with Katie. They chatted with Jeremy and Denyse about the differences between Christmas in Minnesota and Down Under. With attentive listening, Denyse's words became more discernable to Dave and Katie. Jeremy and Denyse shuddered at Dave's description of a Minnesota winter. After a while, Denyse excused herself, leaving Jeremy to visit with his parents.

Katie seemed quiet after the call. "Are you sad?" Dave wondered.

"I'm just remembering Christmases past. Remember when Jeremy was little? Those were magical Christmases. The last few years especially have brought so much change. Your job troubles, my cancer, the downsizing, and Jeremy in Australia. All our traditions are gone. Nothing stays the same. And . . . " Katie paused, " . . . I'm a little jealous that my only son has another woman in his life."

"Looked like a good one to have," Dave commented. That didn't help. Therefore, he simply gave Katie a long hug. Then they enjoyed the gumbo and cornbread. Afterwards, they snuggled on the couch watching the last movie on Katie's list with a fire in the fireplace and gentle snow falling outside.

In the middle of a sound sleep, Dave felt a nudge followed by words from Katie. "I hear something."

Dave mumbled a response. "That's the cat again."

"No, he's right here."

True enough. Old Yeller sat on the bed with them, staring intensely at the open door that led to the rest of the house.

Dave listened more closely. Noise *was* coming from within the house. He remembered Susie's warning about break-ins in their area. Suddenly, light filled the room. "Turn that lamp off!" Dave said more sharply than he had intended.

Katie did so. "Why don't you want light?"

"Light could help an intruder more than us. We know our way around in the dark better than they would. Also, if they're using flashlights we'll know where they are. They won't know where we are. So, keep your voice down." Dave slipped out of bed.

"Where do you think you're going? Don't leave me," Katie whispered.

"Stay here. I'll be right back." Dave soft footed quietly out of the bedroom. In a minute, he came back. "Hold these, but don't turn them on."

Katie felt Dave's big flashlight and her cell phone placed beside her. In the dark, she heard a metallic *click*, then a soft *thump, thump* followed by the *click* again. "What are you doing?"

"I'm loading the gun."

"What gun?"

"My old 20-gauge shotgun for cottonmouths. I usually carry it on the floor of the pickup's extended cab. After the threatening phone calls, I put it under the bed in the spare bedroom."

Katie's voice revealed her fear. "Are you going to shoot someone?"

"No, but I might scare them badly. Burglars won't stay around when they know somebody in the dark has a loaded gun. We're safe now."

Katie felt more secure as they lay on the bed in the darkness. Noises could still be heard from within the mansion. Old Yeller, next to Katie, listened too. She could feel his tail burred up like a bristle brush and twitching. "Should we call 911?" she whispered.

"Let's just wait. We don't want to send out a false alarm."

Louder sounds of ransacking came from the house. "How false does that sound to you? Our job is to protect the house." A crash added emphasis to Katie's words.

"I would expect burglars to be quieter. Follow me and leave the light off. But be ready to call 911, if we need help." Dave stood and quietly moved toward the door, pointing his double-barreled shotgun ahead of him. Katie reluctantly followed, carrying the flashlight and cell phone. Old Yeller followed too, staying well behind.

Slipping into the entertaining room through the formal dining room, the couple gingerly approached the sound of the ransacking. The cat suddenly hissed and snarled. A dark shape scuttled across the floor toward the basement stairs. Dave grabbed the flashlight from Katie in time to illuminate a bushy ringed tail exiting.

Katie leaned forward trying to see. "What was that?"

"That was a raccoon. It must have gotten in somehow

119

through the basement. Probably looking for food, or maybe just causing mischief." An overturned end table gave credibility to the latter purpose.

Dave opened the basement door and turned on the light. Old Yeller slipped between his legs and down the stairs. His bristle brush tail had receded. "I think the raccoon is gone."

"How do you know?"

Dave cracked open the breech-loading shotgun and removed the shells. "Did you see Old Yeller? Cats can't smell as well as dogs. But they smell a lot better than we do. He isn't perturbed anymore. Tomorrow we'll need to figure out how the raccoon got in."

They returned to the guest quarters where Katie commented, "Nights are really starting to be an adventure here." She then turned on the Christmas tree lights and brightly wished, "Merry Christmas!"

Chapter Sixteen

———•———

Katie made tea and brought out Christmas cookies while Dave built a warm fire. Old Yeller wandered up from the basement and curled up in front of the blaze. The sky glowed pink in the dawning sun. "Would you like your presents?" Dave asked.

"Sure, why not?" Katie went to retrieve the things she'd purchased for Dave. When she returned, Dave had gifts ready. They started opening packages, starting with the most utilitarian. Dave always welcomed gifts of gloves and socks. Katie loved gift cards from her favorite stores. Finally, only two gifts remained, surprisingly from the same store.

Dave opened his present to reveal a beautiful book featuring outdoor scenes from Minnesota. "Did you see me looking at this?"

"I did," Katie confessed. She then opened her last present to find a cookbook, *Recipes of Minnesota*. "You must have seen me admiring this." Dave *had* seen her admiring the cookbook.

Old Yeller had been watching the strange ritual of gift giving. The ribbons interested him the most. Then Katie brought out a cloth-covered catnip mouse and placed it before the cat. The feline sniffed the toy tentatively. He batted it first with one paw, then back and forth with two paws. Suddenly the cat tossed the catnip mouse into the air with his claws and chased after it. Gradually, Old Yeller became more excited as the couple watched in amazement. He dashed around the room with a crazed look in his eye. "If I didn't know better, I'd say that cat is drunk," Katie observed.

Soon the cat clutched and seriously chewed the catnip mouse. His molars would soon rip the cloth skin spilling the catnip flakes all over the floor. Before he could destroy his present, Dave took the toy away. "That's enough for now, big fellow." Old Yeller slowly settled down and returned to the fire's warmth.

Next Katie got out the bag of Christmas cards. They looked at the enclosed photos from people they knew and took turns reading the letters aloud. Afterwards, they settled in for a peaceful day. Katie busied herself in the kitchen making dinner featuring ham, sweet potato casserole, peas, a fruit ambrosia, and rolls. She even made Dave's favorite dessert, pecan pie with whipped cream.

Dave idly perused the ledger books from the former McReady Enterprises. Huge losses documented in the 1920s and '30s that somehow managed to disappear puzzled him. He could not find the source of the balancing revenue. He thought about the 1949 strike at the mill. *I wonder how they recorded those expenditures and losses?* A quick trip to the carriage house yielded ledgers from the strike period. There Dave found insights into the squelching of the workers' requests. Cost estimates of implementing safety measures and raising salaries had been documented. These had been compared to the short-term costs of hiring "security agents." *Say what you want about the McReadys, somebody kept thorough records*, Dave thought. Then he noticed a cryptic record:

Jones - $1,500 - Johnson
Smith - $1,000 - Rogers
Smith - $500 - McNickles
Jones - $1,000 - Carpenter
Smith - $1,000 - Miller
Smith - $500 - Eckerson

"$1,500 - Johnson" stood out to Dave. *Could this be a reference to Mrs. Johnson's Sam?* Listed under "Strike Expenses" in 1949, it could hardly be a coincidence. Dave concentrated so intensely that he hardly noticed Katie entering the room and sitting on the chair arm.

She interrupted his thoughts by asking, "What have you found that's so important?"

"I think I've found a reference to Mrs. Johnson's husband. Maybe he *was* bribed." Dave pointed to the ledger entry.

"But even if he did take a bribe, that doesn't explain his disappearance." Katie became adamant. "I don't think a man like him would abandon his family for $1,500." Katie bordered on belligerence at the suggestion of impugning Sam. "And who are Smith and Jones? Do you believe your own theory?"

"I don't know. Maybe . . . "

Katie interrupted, "Oh my." She covered her mouth with

her hands. "Could these could be records of payments for assassinations?"

"You mean murders?"

"What else do you think happened to Sam? Look, the payees are recorded as 'Smith' and 'Jones.' Do those sound like real names?" Dave put down the ledger in horror. Something in him recoiled at touching it. Katie continued, "Who were the other men who disappeared in 1949? Can you find out?"

Checking the phone book and picking up the phone, Dave called Frank Pederson of the Historical Society. "Frank, I know this is Christmas Day. But could you please answer just one question for me?" Frank was willing. "Can you remember the names of any men who disappeared about the time of the mill strike of forty-nine?"

"Let's see. Sam Johnson was the workers' leader. Then I remember Kirk Rogers, Terry Miller, Bill McNickles... There were a couple more. Are they important?"

"Maybe. I'm just doing some research." Dave ended the call with a rather lame, "Merry Christmas."

The ledger listed all the names Frank remembered. Having uncovered what could be several murders, the mood in the guest quarters became somber. Dave and Katie could not help thinking about Sam Johnson fighting Nazis across Europe, then coming home to be murdered.

Katie tried to lighten the mood. "Have you forgotten the raccoon?"

Dave had forgotten their early morning visitor. He put on his coat, boots, and gloves to go outside. Circling the mansion, Dave found raccoon tracks in the snow between the woods and a loose corner of the old coal chute. Fortunately, the tracks came from the woods and led back to the woods.

That confirmed the raccoon wasn't still hiding downstairs. Out of curiosity, Dave followed the raccoon's tracks to a hollow oak tree. Returning to the mansion, he blocked the animal's entrance to the coal chute with a spare board from the carriage house and a few nails.

After solving the raccoon issue, Dave wandered down to the bank of the still unfrozen Mississippi. A barge carrying shipping containers slowly moved upstream against the current. The river explained the likely reason why no remains of Sam or the others had ever been found. *Maybe ghosts do remain here,* he thought. *I certainly feel haunted.*

<hr>

Inside, Katie also felt overwhelmed with sympathy for those who lost loved ones. *We don't know for certain what happened. I don't want our holiday to be ruined,* she thought. She borrowed some fine dishes from a china cabinet. She poured a little wine found in the pantry into two cut crystal glasses. She and Dave didn't drink alcohol often, but the occasion needed something special. When Dave came in, the table had been set with candles lit in the formal dining room. Avoiding any mention of their disturbing discovery, the couple joked about the possibility of having grandchildren who spoke with an Australian accent.

Then they reminisced about past Christmases. "I remember you all dressed up for the office Christmas parties," Dave reminded Katie. "Every man envied me for the stunningly beautiful wife I had."

She touched her short hair. "I'm not so young and attractive anymore."

"Funny thing about that. When you truly love someone, you always think about them like the person you first met. You're still that sassy coed I fell in love with back at college."

"And you'll always be my heroic dinosaur and my best friend."

After a lovely dinner, they tuned into the news. Weather concerns dominated evening news broadcasts. The local weather forecaster direly predicted, "A tremendous storm is moving out of the Rockies now. Expect up to three feet of snow starting tomorrow night. High winds and drifting snow will create whiteout conditions. An arctic cold front should drop temperatures to minus ten, possibly as low as minus twenty degrees."

Soon after the weather report, the house phone rang. "Merry Christmas," Katie greeted.

"Katie, this is Susie. Have you heard the weather report?" Katie assured her that they had. "Well, we all know you're from Alabama. Once this storm starts, don't you go out into the blizzard. You need to stay put! In whiteout conditions, farmers have been known to get lost and die between the barn and their own house." After thanking Susie, Katie and Dave started to make lists of things to do and items to purchase before the storm arrived.

The phone rang again. Lyle warned them to prepare to sit out the blizzard for several days. "I'll plow you out after they manage to clear the main roads," he promised. After Lyle, the phone continued to ring. All their friends and even a few strangers called to warn them. All the messages were the same, "Get ready," and "Don't go outside once the blizzard starts."

Chapter Seventeen

———— · • · ————

The rising sun created a brilliant red sky. Dave remembered the old weather rhyme that ended in "Red sky in the morning, sailors take warning." He and Katie dressed warmly, got into the truck and headed into town. Minnesotans might have scoffed at a few inches of snow, but they knew better than to take chances with a major blizzard. More shoppers crowded the streets than before Christmas. Dave dropped Katie at the grocery store. Then he topped off the truck with gas after enduring a line for forty-five minutes.

Katie waited to check out with a shopping cart full of groceries. Several others with full shopping carts stood in line ahead of her. The line behind her stretched down the aisle. She felt relieved to spot Dave in the congestion. "Hold my place. I thought of a few more things." While Dave remained behind the cart, she struggled through jammed aisles to pick up a few last items. Empty shelves stood where milk, bread, and other perishables had been. Once Katie got back to Dave the checker had started processing their cart. The sky appeared ominous as they took their supplies to the truck.

Outside the grocery store, Minnesotans loaded fifty-pound bags of calcium chloride from pallets into pickups and car trunks. Dave wondered aloud, "Why do they need that stuff?"

"Calcium chloride is a type of salt. They use it to clear steps and sidewalks of ice."

"How does it work?"

"The same way regular salt works in an ice cream freezer. Salts lower the freezing point of water."

With the pickup loaded, the couple started back toward the mansion. To Katie's surprise, Dave pulled into the parking lot of the "Seed and Feed" store. "Are you planning on planting a garden?" she teased. Dave didn't answer but filled their cart with bags of sunflower seeds and shelled corn. Then he added a bird feeder. "You're thinking about birds?" Dave still didn't answer. Katie threw on a bag of cat food. A bitterly cold wind blew from the west as they headed home.

Back at the mansion, Dave unloaded the truck and left Katie to sort out their purchases. Next, he spent an hour moving firewood from the carriage house to the mudroom. Then he opened the mansion's garage doors. The Mercedes and Jaguar parked there had been undisturbed. Boxes and other storage items filled the third parking spot. He started to move these, even piling some onto the Mercedes and Jaguar, to make room. By 3:00 p.m. the snow had begun. But rather than beautiful flakes floating gently down, ice crystals blew in a cutting wind. Dave carefully pulled the pickup into the spot he had cleared and lowered the garage door.

When Dave got to the guest quarters, Katie waited with hot tea. He needed a hot drink. After several hours of working outside, the chill had penetrated every part of him. By 6:00 p.m., the blizzard raged against the mansion. From the windows, they couldn't distinguish snowfall from blowing snow. Never had either of them felt so isolated.

◄◆►

Through the night, the wind shrieked and shook the mansion. By daylight, temperatures outside had fallen to single digits. At times the phone rang with people checking on them. "Stay inside," everybody warned. Dave phoned Mrs. Johnson to check on her. No answer. Then he remembered that she had gone to St. Paul to spend Christmas with her son's family. Katie posted a photo of Dave and her in front of the fire and a description of the blizzard on Facebook. That got a lot of comments from friends back in Alabama. As she caught up with all her friends, she shared tidbits of news.

Dave played with Old Yeller. The catnip mouse still excited the feline. He also loved to play in a paper grocery sack, chase a string, or bat around a wad of paper. Even Katie had to marvel at his antics. After darting around a bit more, Old Yeller settled into his heated box.

Dave turned on a football game. The game couldn't hold his attention, though. He picked up one of the ledgers and started trying to solve the puzzles again. The losses, especially in the Depression, and expenditures versus the revenue still didn't add up. At one point in August 1935, the bank had written off $85,000 in bad loans. Yet the bottom line for the year remained unaffected.

Snowfall continued that night and all the next day. At least that's what the TV weather reporter claimed. From inside the mansion, the whiteout only looked like blowing fog. On the third day, light blue patches appeared in the western sky. The TV weatherman reported that over two feet of snow had fallen. On the ground, the storm seemed the same. The wind blew snow crystals into a "ground blizzard." Snow drifted into deep piles near any obstacle. Drifts halfway covered the first-floor windows on the mansion's west side. Temperatures outside plunged to minus fifteen degrees. Katie turned away from the window. "This is a whiter Christmas than I had expected."

The southerners filled time watching the storm and making up the most outrageous stories to explain Old Yeller's background. Katie suggested that he had been accidently left in New York when his family moved to Florida. Then the cat had set out on an epic journey to join them. He wound up in Minnesota because, as a male, the cat wouldn't ask directions. Dave thought he might have been a cat show star, but ran away to escape that glamor and glitz and live a normal cat life. Their favorite story had Old Yeller in training with US Customs to become the first drug-sniffing cat in a dog-dominated profession. But the feline washed out when he kept revealing travelers carrying catnip. Eventually, they agreed that an ordinary cat had become their housemate. Old Yeller refused to reveal the secrets of his former life.

—◆—

As the storm continued, Dave frequently analyzed the ledgers, putting together clues while Katie communicated with friends. The couple, along with Old Yeller, took long tours of the mansion, stopping to examine architectural features and antique items. By the fourth day, they knew the mansion well. Being snowed in had become rather dreary. Not so for the cat. Old Yeller enjoyed the couple's constant company and never tired of scouting for mice.

On one inside expedition, Dave stopped by the cracked door to the basement. "What about down here?" He had only gone downstairs occasionally to clean Old Yeller's litter box.

His wife grimaced. "Won't the basement be dirty?"

"Probably. This could be fun." He opened the door and punched on the button light switch. Old Yeller ran by his feet and down the steps. Dave followed the cat. Katie lagged, but joined them. The original windows in light wells had been painted over, leaving the basement dark except for the

131

electric lights. Brick pillars supported chimneys for fireplaces that originally heated rooms upstairs. A nearly new fuel-oil furnace on the right side of the stairs dominated the chilly basement.

Left of the stairs, the basement appeared more interesting. There old furniture, the stuff too good to be put into the carriage house, had been stored. Despite the accumulated dust and cobwebs, Katie found herself intrigued. "Let's get more light."

Dave went upstairs and returned with his big flashlight and an additional flashlight for Katie. As Katie continued examining the furniture, Dave shined his flashlight into the corners. In the darkest corner, he could see the old coal bin. Moving closer, he barely saw a pile of coal remaining. "Some coal could be useful," he speculated.

In the other corner, an old workshop remained intact. A backboard behind the workbench still held various woodworking tools. A large coal stove once used to heat the workshop connected to one of the chimneys. Having daily toured the upstairs levels, the basement seemed smaller to Dave. After an hour of exploring, the basement had chilled them thoroughly. "Let's go back to the kitchen and get warm."

"What happened to Old Yeller?" Katie wondered aloud.

"This is his area. He'll be fine."

"Aren't you curious what he's up to?" Katie started calling, "Kitty, kitty, kitty."

Having been challenged, Dave was a little curious. He

started shining his light into all of the dark recesses. Behind the newer furnace, a pair of green eyes appeared and then disappeared. Dave moved closer. Old Yeller had his back to them as, ever hopeful of a mouse, he stared at a crack near the floor between sheets of paneling. Presumably rodent odors emanated from the crack. And the crack did appear to have been created by rodent gnawing. "He's here looking for a mouse." To himself, Dave questioned, *Why would paneling have been installed on this side of the basement?* The couple left the cat on guard while they went upstairs to get warm.

Warming over a space heater, thoughts about the paneling continued to perplex Dave. He paced off the first floor. Returning to the basement, he found the open area approximately eleven paces shorter. The discrepancy in floor dimensions began where the paneling had been installed. He shined his light back to where Old Yeller remained on mouse watch. "Sweetheart!" he called up to Katie. "Would you come and look at something?" She came back down the stairs. He explained the discrepancy. She stood speechless. Dave walked over to the old workshop and returned with a large crowbar. "Please pick up the scourge of rodents."

His wife gathered Old Yeller into her arms. "What are you going to do?"

Dave tapped the paneling with a knuckle that created a hollow sound. "Let's see what's behind this wall."

"Shouldn't we check with the Swansons first?"

"They said we could explore. I'll put the paneling back after we're done." Dave inserted the crowbar into the crack and began to leverage the panel outward. Old nails squealed as they pulled free. The cat struggled to be released from Katie's arms. "Hold this in place," Dave pointed to the crowbar holding out the panel. Katie put Old Yeller down and pushed against the crowbar. Dave went to get another crowbar from the workshop and returned. "What happened to the cat?"

Katie pointed to the gap held out by the first crowbar. "He went in there."

"Unless we let curiosity kill the cat, we can't stop now." Dave took the second crowbar, inserted it above the first, and widened the gap. More nails squealed. Alternating crowbars, they worked up the panel edge until they had pried a gap wide enough to enter. Dave and Katie peeked into the opening.

Chapter Eighteen

Behind the paneling, they found a windowless room with a yellow cat sniffing around. Dave stepped inside the concealed room, followed by Katie. A calendar dated 1942 hung on the wall. An old printing press dominated one end of the room. Several solid oak desks lined the walls each with an old inoperable dial phone from the 1930s. Along with ashtrays with old cigar butts and empty liquor bottles, papers littered the desks and the floor. Dave picked a paper off a desk and shined the flashlight on it. He saw professional baseball teams listed.

Katie peered over his shoulder. "What is it?"

"I don't know." He picked up another piece of paper from a different desk. He recognized the names of football teams from the early years of the NFL.

The forms' purpose became apparent to Dave. "These are betting forms. This was a bookmaking operation! That's how the McReadys did so well during the Depression." Forms recording other types of gambling, especially on horse racing and boxing, also cluttered the room.

The couple continued to explore. One desk, larger than the others and less cluttered, held a different set of ledgers. Dates on these ledgers showed them to be from 1917-1942. Dave carried all the ledgers upstairs in several trips. Katie followed carrying Old Yeller and then put on water for tea.

Aroused with purpose Dave quickly cleared off the long table in the formal dining room. On one side, he arranged the ledgers from 1917-1942 he had found in the carriage house. These represented McReady Enterprises' legitimate businesses: the mills, tree cutting operation, and the bank that also handled the McReadys' other investments. On the other side of the table, he aligned the corresponding records found downstairs.

While the ground blizzard continued to obscure visibility and blow drifts, Dave studied and compared the two sets of ledgers. Starting with the bank ledger, he located the discrepancy in August 1935 that had puzzled him. Moving to the other side of the table with the bookmaking ledgers he found August 1935. There a cryptic note recorded, "Distribution to bank $85,000." The bank had written off the same amount in the same month without affecting their bottom line. Other distributions had been made directly to various family members.

He pointed out the $85,000 entry to Katie, but unlike her husband, she had not been an accountant. "What does that mean?"

"The entry implies that the McReady bank played shell games with money and came up with a pea under every shell." Katie looked confused. Dave explained, "The bank and other McReady businesses disguised illegal revenue. Today, we'd call that 'money laundering.' My guess is that illegal money also covered the bank's stock market losses during the Depression. Since the McReady family owned the bank, cash from the bookmaking operation kept them solvent."

"So, that's how they maintained their lavish lifestyles," Katie commented as she disappeared into the kitchen.

Later, she returned to stand by his seat. Dave turned to her. "To what do I owe this . . . visit?"

"You mean interruption?" When her husband didn't answer, Katie invited, "Supper's ready."

Looking out the window, Dave realized that the sun had set. On the kitchen table waited hot bowls of soup and warm homemade biscuits. At first consumed in his thoughts, Dave ate silently. Across the table, Katie also ate quietly, her face turned down. Soon he felt regret for neglecting her. "Sweetheart, this is delicious."

She looked up and brightened. "Do you really think so? I've never used wild rice before, especially in a soup. The recipe book explained that wild rice isn't a grain rice, but seed from a type of grass that grows along the edge of lakes. Native Americans collect the seeds by beating the grass over canoes. I like the texture and the nutty flavor," she explained. Then hesitantly she asked, "What have you found out? Anything more about Sam?"

"No more about Sam. But there's a lot." Dave started to summarize, "The McReadys used money from illegal operations to cover losses by their legitimate businesses. At the same time, the legitimate businesses acted as a cover for the illegal activities. Their bank covered the whole operation with transactions too complex and convoluted for me to follow perfectly."

Katie wanted a more thorough explanation. "What's your best guess?"

Dave spoke slowly putting the evidence into a story in his own mind. "During Prohibition, the McReadys started bootlegging to replace lost revenue after the old growth timber had run out. They could truck in liquor from Canada on logging roads then boat it down the river to St. Louis, Memphis, New Orleans, anyplace they wanted. Looks like they also bought liquor from Minnesota moonshiners and distributed that by the same network. They knew plenty of unemployed lumberjacks who needed work."

Katie interrupted, "I thought you mentioned gambling."

"Yes, I did. When Prohibition ended in late 1933, they converted from bootlegging to bookmaking. But starting in 1942, the mill and other businesses made plenty of money due to the war effort. They probably kept the room in case they needed to go back to bookmaking after the war. But the American economy thrived in the late forties and fifties. There was no longer the incentive to take those risks."

Katie had listened attentively. "Why do you think people around here seem reluctant to talk about any of this?"

"That's the worst part," Dave continued. "Records of payoffs and probably more murders are in the ledgers. They had a lot of public officials on their payroll or intimidated by threats of violence. The McReadys simply became gangsters of the worst sort. People learned to keep their mouths shut. I suspect that became a community habit."

"Have you noticed that Minnesotans use the term 'whatever' a lot?"

"Yeah, I guess so."

"Well, this sounds like the whole community took a 'whatever' attitude toward McReady Enterprises rather than investigate." Katie sat thinking while Dave marveled at his wife's insight. "Who are you going to tell?"

"I don't know. This all happened sixty to a hundred years ago. McReady Enterprises is kaput. The criminals are likely dead. Even if they aren't dead, the American justice system prosecutes individuals, not families. The ledgers don't implicate anybody by name. Every McReady can say that the others did it." Dave paused. "I don't know if we should reopen the wounds for people like Mrs. Johnson."

"Shouldn't she get closure? Shouldn't people know what happened?"

◄◆►

By New Year's Eve, the ground blizzard had blown out. Snowdrifts, many deeper than Dave's height, had collected around every obstacle. Yet the wind had scoured a few bare spots. The Parkers had been snowed in for five days.

Katie and Old Yeller watched from the window as Dave waded through the drifts. He scattered sunflower seeds and piled shelled corn in places blown bare. Next, he filled the bird feeder with sunflower seeds and hung it by the window. Close to finishing, he heard a *beep, beep.* Lyle's snow removal truck came up the driveway pushing snow to the side. Lyle wore a hat with earmuffs that tied under his chin. He waved Dave over. "Sorry for the delay. The town crews didn't get Riverfront Drive cleared until late yesterday. Some places the snow drifted nearly ten feet deep. Are you and Katie doing okay?"

"Sure, we're fine. How are folks along the road?"

"So far everybody's okay. Unless I see folks outside, like I did you, I knock on their doors to ask."

Dave gestured toward the garage where he had stored his truck. "Need any help checking on people?"

Lyle looked at the garage that had a snowdrift blown against the doors. "That truck of yours have chains?" Dave admitted that it didn't. "Thanks anyway. I'd just stay inside for a few more days. Wind chill is about minus twenty-five." Lyle turned his truck and headed back down the driveway, pushing snow to the other side.

The wind *was* cold. Dave's hands had stiffened despite his heavy gloves. After getting back inside, Dave kindled a large fire with firewood from the carriage house. Later he added hunks of coal from the basement. The coal burned cleanly and much slower than the firewood, plus it released more heat.

During a lunch of another Minnesota dish featuring Spam and eggs, Katie reminded Dave about the date. "Do you have any New Year's resolutions to make?"

"No, but I have a wish. I'm hoping that next year is less stressful than the previous several we've endured."

Katie had to agree with that. For herself she added, "My wish is to feel more settled and purposeful in our retirement." She thought for a minute and confessed, "I hope people will need me next year."

"You know that I need you."

"You need me more than you realize," Katie kidded back. "But you understand what I mean." Dave did understand his wife's feelings.

"Okay, as long as we're wishing," Dave said, "I hope to handle the information in the ledgers well."

"So, what are we going to do?"

Dave looked surprised. "*We* aren't going to do anything. This is my problem."

"You said you needed my help after we met with the Hendersons."

"Of course, I frequently need your help. But this could get nasty."

Katie felt flustered. "Why can't we face this challenge together as a team? We did when I had cancer."

"That was different."

"How?"

"We had been forced into a challenge, a purpose, a goal."

"Can't we choose to work as a team rather than being forced?"

Dave explained, "We've always been partners. I worked. You took care of Jeremy."

141

"I guess that's a type of teamwork. But now you don't work and I don't have Jeremy to care for. Our lives are different. If we don't try to work together, we could become isolated, no more than roommates. We can do everything better, if we work together using both of our strengths, even if danger is involved."

"You're pretty aggravating sometimes."

Katie smiled. "The best partners *are* aggravating sometimes."

Dave carefully considered his wife's words for a minute and made a decision. He slowly extended his hand across the table in a business-like fashion. "Partners with a purpose."

"Purposes," Katie corrected, reached out, and shook Dave's hand solemnly. She knew that a formal handshake was sacred to a man like her husband. Both knew that something had changed in their relationship.

Katie came around the table to sit in her husband's lap. A big kiss demonstrated that some things would never change. They would always be much more than roommates.

Before they finished kissing, a curious chattering sound came from the sitting room. "Ack, ack, ack."

Katie jumped up to investigate. "Dave, come look at this."

Old Yeller sat on the window sill staring out the glass. His jaw quivered. "Ack, ack, ack."

"Do you think he's having a fit?"

"I think he's just excited." Dave pointed to the bird feeder. A tiny chickadee perched on the feeder collecting a sunflower seed. The cat jerked his neck watching the bird as it flew away with the seed. Soon another bird landed. Titmice, cardinals, plus various sparrows competed with the chickadees.

"If he's watching birds, he's not catching birds," Dave pointed out.

The couple sat down in front of the fire. Katie asked, "What are you thinking about how to handle what we found out?"

"This situation is far beyond my experience. I really don't know what to do."

Katie prepped Dave for an idea. "Have you thought about this?"

"Probably not," he interrupted.

Undeterred, Katie continued with her idea. "Is there somebody you could ask? Anybody you trust?"

Chapter Nineteen

————•••————

Just like a woman, Dave thought. *When you don't know what to do, ask somebody; talk to a confidant.* But maybe Katie was right this time. "Maybe Frank Pederson at the Historical Society. He might have some idea how this would affect the community."

On New Year's Day, plenty of parades and college football games on TV took their minds off the dilemma. Dave didn't call Frank that day, or the following day. Katie didn't push her husband. Plus, she wasn't certain of the best course to take either. On the third day, she began, "This may sound like criticism . . . "

Dave interrupted her, "You want me to act on what we've discovered."

Katie nodded. Dave picked up and dialed the phone. "Frank, this is Dave Parker."

"Glad to hear your voice. How did the Parkers weather the storm?"

"We did fine. Thanks for calling to warn us, by the way."

Frank acknowledged the thanks. "That's what friends do."

"Uhhh Frank, I've been doing some research on local history. Do you remember my call on Christmas Day?"

"I've been wondering about that. What have you found?"

"I'd rather not talk about this over the phone. Things difficult to talk about are best done face-to-face. Is there a time we can get together to discuss some discoveries and how they might affect the community? A couple of hours could be necessary."

"Sure, anytime. Here's an idea. Ed and I and one other guy are planning on doing a little ice fishing Wednesday. You remember Ed from the Historical Society? Anyway, would you like to join us? There'll be plenty of time to talk in privacy." Frank waited a few seconds for Dave to reply. Then, not receiving a response, Frank added, "I know these men. You can trust them."

Rather than concern about the men, Dave remembered his experience breaking through the ice at the pond edge. He knew the water in the lake center would be much deeper—a nightmare to fall through. But trying ice fishing still appealed to him. "Isn't the lake covered in snow?"

"No, the wind blows the snow away. Besides, we'll be fishing inside a shelter."

"I would be delighted to join you. Thanks for the invitation." Frank instructed Dave to meet them at the boat launch on Goose Lake. "We're taking a boat?" Dave asked.

"No, the launch ramp is where you can easily drive out onto the ice."

Not long after Dave hung up, the phone rang. Katie answered. Nancy Williams spoke. "Ed told me that Dave is going ice fishing with the men." Katie affirmed that. "Well, when the men go out, we wives sometimes do, too. Would you like to have lunch with us on Wednesday? We're going to try the new café overlooking the river." Katie readily accepted. "Wonderful! We'll pick you up at eleven o'clock."

Dave found a snow shovel in the garage and spent the remainder of the day moving the drift that had trapped their truck in the garage. To his delight, Katie joined him dressed for the cold. The couple had been snowbound for a week. "Let's look around the property," she suggested.

If they avoided the deeper drifts, moving about the property wasn't difficult. Looking back at the house, they could see Old Yeller in the window watching birds. A snowmobile noisily passed on the edge of Riverfront Drive. Deer tracks circled the bare spots where Dave had put out shelled corn. Several sets of raccoon tracks by the shelled corn showed other recipients of Dave's generosity.

Continuing to survey their surroundings, the couple found the Mississippi River frozen bank-to-bank. Dave stood looking at it. "I guess that minus twenty will even freeze moving water—the surface anyway."

"We shouldn't be surprised," his wife answered. "Do you remember the *Little House on the Prairie* books? Laura Ingalls crossed the frozen Mississippi River in a covered wagon with her family on their way to Indian Territory. They started at the Wisconsin town of Pepin just across the river." She didn't remind her husband that the Ingalls family narrowly missed being in the middle of the river when the ice broke up.

Katie helped Dave replenish the sunflower seeds and corn. After caring for the wildlife, the couple returned to the door leading to the mudroom. Dave stalled there with his hand trying to turn the doorknob. "Oh no! We're locked out. Do you have the key?"

Katie's face expressed alarm. "No, I didn't bring the key. We only went outside to walk around. How could this have happened?"

"My guess is that Old Yeller locked us out."

Katie was not amused. "Very funny, big boy. Ha. Ha." She pushed by him into the door.

❧

"Get up, sleepyhead. Let's go into town. I need some supplies."

Dave blinked away grogginess. "Do you want to walk the rail trail to town?"

"In these temperatures? Don't be silly. We can take the truck."

After some hot tea and a Danish, Dave opened the garage door. Having been protected in the garage, the truck started easily. He backed the pickup out and closed the garage door. Katie, relatively lightly dressed for riding to town, hurried across the space between the mudroom door and the truck.

She shivered. "Next time how about warming up the truck first?"

A thin layer of packed snow covered Riverfront Drive even though the road had been plowed. In several places, the snowplows had cut through deep drifts and thrown the snow from the roadway onto the shoulders. This made the banks along the road even higher. Fortunately, ten-foot marker stakes protected the fire hydrants from being hit by snowplows. Dave tentatively tried the truck's brakes. The truck stopped normally. Packed dry snow gave surprisingly good traction. "I still wouldn't go too fast," Katie suggested. All the vehicles crept along on the snow-packed roads.

They collected more supplies at the grocery store and the Seed and Feed. Mountains of snow pushed up by the plows dominated every parking lot. Dave also had books to return to the library. Inside they greeted Caroline, who manned the front desk. "I'll bet things have been slow in here," Dave commented.

The girl feigned collapse. "No, just the opposite. Before the storm, everybody came in to check out videos and books. Then the library closed for three days. As soon as folks could get out, they came back picking up stuff to watch and read. It's been just crazy." Caroline turned away to check out some books for a patron.

Dave drifted into the fiction section to look for some of his favorite authors. Katie loitered near the front desk while Caroline worked. "Did you get a chance to read that book we gave to you?" she inquired when Caroline had a moment.

"Oh yeah, it's all really good stuff. I feel like the author has been inside our house the whole time we've been married. I'd never heard much of that stuff before."

"Did Billy read the book, too?"

"He finished it before me. He's on graveyard shift, you know. The police didn't get many calls during the storm. But there is one problem," Caroline confided. "We're having more arguments now than before we read the book."

Katie smiled and nodded. "That's absolutely normal. The reason is that you're dealing with issues now that you had avoided before. If you keep talking and apply what you've learned, things will get better. Did you read the chapter on 'Arguing without Fighting'?"

"Yes, we did."

"Are you following the rules? No 'you' statements, no threats, no bringing up the past?"

"Most of the time. Sometimes I just don't know what to say. Then I say something I shouldn't, Billy gets mad, and then we have a bigger problem." Caroline gestured bigness with her arms wide apart.

Katie reassured her, "Good communication takes practice. I'll bet you get angry sometimes, too."

"I get mad the most," the girl admitted.

"Dave and I will meet with you again, when Billy is ready."

Caroline wiped away a tear. "Thanks."

Dave then came up with an armload of books to check out. "Are you going to read all of those?" she teased him.

After leaving the library, Dave asked, "How about some lunch?"

"It seems like we haven't been to The Blue Ox in ages." Katie also missed seeing Susie.

Inside the restaurant, Susie brought their normal drinks and inspected the Parkers. "Looks like you survived the storm all right."

Dave picked up a menu. "How often do you have storms like that? Thanks for the warning, by the way."

"You betcha. A storm that big? Not very often. Maybe once in ten years. Lyle said that he saw you out in the yard."

"Has Lyle been plowing snow long?"

"About three years. Lyle is from Wisconsin. Leslie, his wife, is a local girl. They met at the University of Minnesota and got married. They moved here so she could watch over her mother. Leslie is her only child. Lyle studied horticulture. Now he's trying to get a landscaping business started. Everybody likes Lyle. His business will grow." Susie got out her order pad. "What'll you have today?"

Katie selected the club sandwich. She asked Susie about The Blue Ox's version of wild rice soup then added, "I made some wild rice soup for the first time the other night."

"This is the recipe my mom always made with a few variations," Susie said. "I think you'll like it."

"Ok, I'll have a cup, please."

Dave picked the fried walleye fillets. "These aren't Minnesota walleye though," Susie warned. Dave raised his eyebrows. "They import these from Canada. They call them 'pike' up there. Maybe you'll catch some Minnesota walleye when you go ice fishing tomorrow." She bounced toward the kitchen to get Betty started on their order.

Katie leaned toward Dave and whispered, "Does Susie know everything that goes on in Washita?"

"Apparently so."

As usual, the couple enjoyed a delicious lunch, especially Susie's mother's recipe for wild rice soup, which included chicken. After finishing, they signaled Susie for their check.

"No charge for you today. My thanks for looking after Caroline and Billy."

Katie protested, "Are you sure? We wouldn't want you to get into trouble with the owner."

"Honey, I am the owner." Susie laughed in her boisterous way and turned to greet someone coming into the restaurant.

Chapter Twenty

The next morning, Dave waited in his truck at the Goose Lake boat ramp at 9:00 a.m. Anticipating a day on the ice, he had dressed in many layers and had his ski mask ready. Frank pulled alongside in an old Chevy Malibu and rolled his window down. "Follow me."

Dave felt odd driving onto the ice. He kept himself poised to jump out of the truck, if necessary. Frank drove slowly and parked in front of a wooden shed mounted on skids. Dave felt even less secure when he left the truck. Out on the ice the sky seemed tremendous compared to being in town where trees and structures obstructed the skyline. Dave felt like he was in a boat on Mobile Bay.

Inside the shack, Ed prepared the fishing tackle. A man helping him looked familiar. "Dave, this is Reverend John Foster," Frank introduced. Dave recognized him as the Lutheran pastor from the church where they had attended the Christmas Eve service. He looked different without his clerical collar and dressed in a flannel shirt.

They shook hands. "Happy to meet you, Pastor. My wife and I enjoyed your Christmas Eve service."

"I go by John, please. Glad you joined us."

Ed used a scoop called a "skimmer" to clear the ice slush from three holes previously drilled in the ice. Each hole looked about eight inches in diameter. Accustomed to saltwater fishing in the Gulf of Mexico, Dave wondered what sort of fish they hoped to pull through that small hole. John set up three light-tackle fishing rods about two feet long. At the end of each line he tied a reflective jig. Baiting a jig with a grub worm, Ed explained, "This is what we call a 'waxie.' Outsiders call them wax worms."

Frank peered into a fish finder. Fifteen feet below, elongated shapes indicated a school of nearly motionless fish mostly near the bottom. Dave looked over Frank's shoulder. "How did you know where to auger the holes?"

"We can guess at the best areas. We've been fishing this lake for nearly fifty years. But with this new technology, we can narrow in on them. Yesterday, Ed came out and augured a dozen holes around the lake. He found a good spot." Frank tapped the screen. "Then Ed used his pickup to pull the fish house over the spot."

The others came to look at the screen. Dave stepped back to give them room. This gave him a chance to look around the floorless shed. The dimensions appeared to be about sixteen feet by sixteen feet. A plywood roof, which peaked at about twelve feet, covered the open space. On the wall opposite the door, shelves held tackle, coats, a few plastic dishes, condiments, and old bait containers. Folding lawn chairs hung on hooks. A glass window on the right wall had been cracked an inch. A gas grill was securely attached to the left wall along with a rack for several propane tanks. Dave began to feel warm and noticed that the other men had all dressed lightly. Then he realized that the propane grill warmed the shed. Dave quietly removed most of his winter gear and put it on a back shelf.

Soon the men pulled down the lawn chairs and arranged them around the holes. John handed Dave one of the rods with a waxie-baited hook. "We'll take turns fishing the three holes. You can go first on this hole. After you catch a fish, pass the rod to the next man who isn't fishing." Then sensing Dave's uncertainty, he added, "Lower the jig until you feel the bottom at about fifteen feet. You can gently raise the tip and let it fall back down."

Ed and Frank lowered lines into the other two holes. Dave watched them raising and releasing, then mimicked their motions. As he stared into the water and tried to "feel the bottom," John whispered, "I think you've got one." Dave glanced at the light rod. The tip quivered. Jerking up, he felt the fish pulling. After a few seconds of tussle, he pulled a narrow yellowish fish, about a foot long, through the hole. Dave experienced the familiar thrill he felt after catching any fish.

"That's a yellow perch. A nice one, too. Careful of its teeth when you take out the hook." John held out a pair of needle-nosed pliers to Dave. "They're very good to eat."

Dave took the pliers. "I didn't feel it strike."

"They bite gently in the wintertime."

Dave wrestled the hook out. "What do I do with the fish?"

"Throw it outside on the ice. It'll freeze in a few minutes." John baited the rod Dave had used and dropped the line into the water.

In another minute, Ed brought in a bluegill bigger than his hand. "Nice, a sunny," Frank commented.

"We call those 'brim,' " Dave commented.

"Don't you southerners call everything 'brim'?" Ed kidded him. "Except for bullheads?"

"What's a bullhead?" Dave wanted to know.

"Maybe you call them 'catfish.' We call them 'cat food.' " A lively discussion ensued on the merits of eating various fishes. Dave vigorously defended the culinary qualities of catfish.

Soon a rod returned to Dave's hands. Having already caught the perch, he knew what to do. But unlike the previous bite, this time the strike was unmistakable. The little rod bent double. The fish pulled line out against the drag. The other men holding rods quickly pulled their lines in. As Dave struggled with the fish, the men knowingly grinned at each other.

"Don't horse the fish. Wear it down," John coached. After several minutes, Dave had the fish near the hole until it took off again. Eventually, he brought the fish's exhausted head above the water. Frank stood near him. "Don't try to pull it all the way out. Let me help you." When the fish's head appeared again, Frank reached down with the pair of pliers, grabbed the fish by the jaw, and deftly pulled a long green fish out of the hole.

Ed complimented, "Nice little pike. Maybe one and a half pounds."

Dave felt as exhausted as the fish. "Pike? I had pike for lunch yesterday."

"You ate walleyed pike from Canada. This is a northern pike. We'll probably catch a walleye or two. You'll see the difference."

Dave carefully examined the long green fish and its mouth full of teeth. "Are northern pike good to eat?"

"They taste good. But they're full of bones."

This initiated a general discussion among the Minnesotans about northern pike. John told Dave that the aggressive predators sometimes attempt to swallow fish nearly as big as themselves. They might swim around for days with the prey's tail sticking out of their mouths as they digest their big meal gradually from the head. Dave marveled that thirty-pound northerns were not unusual. Then the men explained that a muskellunge, or "musky," is like a northern with a bad attitude and a lot bigger, up to sixty pounds. Dave could hardly imagine such fish living in the water below him, much less catching one.

Frank left his lawn chair and returned with four cans of Grain Belt beer. Then, as the men occasionally caught fish, they began telling the tales common among all fishermen. They described the monster fish reputed to live below the Mississippi River dams built by the WPA in the 1930s. All the men assured Dave that muskies occasionally ate small dogs swimming in the water.

John told an amusing story about river otters that stole his trout on a canoe trip in northern Minnesota. "All we found were fish heads still connected to the stringer."

Dave countered with a similar story about an alligator stealing his catch on the Tombigbee River flowing into Mobile Bay. "While we were having lunch on shore, a gator snuck up and swallowed a whole stringer of crappies. But the stringer was still attached to the boat and the boat was tied to a tree. We saw the boat straining at the rope as the gator tried to sneak away. None of us wanted to put our hands close enough to the gator's mouth to try letting it go. Eventually, the gator got so excited that it threw everything up. Our fish had been mixed with a mess of rotten turtles in the gator's stomach. Nobody wanted to take our crappies home."

The ice fishermen laughed. They loved hearing Dave's stories about deep south fishing. He told about alligator gars up to 100 pounds sometimes caught with a hook-less lure made from a nylon rope. After striking the lure, the fish would get the fibers tangled in their many teeth. The Alabamian also told about bluefish chasing mullet into the waves breaking onto the beach. Dave had seen people catch the fish by kicking them out of the surf onto the sand. Then Dave added the most amazing story about the periodic "jubilee" in Mobile Bay. When that happened, oxygen depletion forced crabs, shrimp, eels, and flounders to leave deep water and swarm into the beach. There they could be easily picked up or netted. The Minnesotans couldn't quite swallow that tale, but remained politely silent.

"How do you know when the ice is safe?" Dave asked, and told them about breaking through the previous time he had ventured onto a frozen pond.

"Four inches thick is considered safe to walk on, twelve inches to drive on," Frank responded for all of them. "Avoid the dark spots. That's where the ice could be thin. The safest thing is to follow somebody else's tracks." The men nodded in agreement. Then the stories turned to dramatic rescues of people, vehicles, and especially dogs breaking through the ice. Despite the warm air inside, Dave couldn't help but shiver.

After another round of beer, the conversation turned to the recent blizzard. The men retold stories of blizzards past. Everyone agreed that blizzards weren't generally as severe as in the "old days." To participate, Dave contributed a few hurricane stories. The men decided they preferred blizzards. The fish continued to bite. As Ed had promised, a couple of walleyes did come up through the holes. They looked like the yellow perch, only browner in color and three-to-five times as heavy.

Chapter Twenty-One

Back at Big River the phone rang. The caller identified herself as Nancy. "We're here. Could you let us in the gate to pick you up?"

Katie spelled out the gate code, "T-U-F-F-Y." A couple of minutes later, the front doorbell rang. At the door, two women in their seventies and one in her late thirties waited. Katie wore her favorite blue sleeveless puffer jacket. Starting to step out the door, she noticed the ladies curiously looking past her into the mansion. She stepped back and gestured toward the inside. "Would you like to come in a minute?"

"Oh yes!" Nancy answered. The three women walked in, their necks twisting as they looked around. Nancy introduced

161

the other women. "This is Helen Pederson, Frank's wife, and this is Ellie Foster," she indicated the younger woman. "She's our pastor's wife. He's out fishing with the other men."

Helen walked past Katie, scanning the mansion interior. "Isn't this lovely?"

Without asking, Katie began a tour of Big River. None of them had ever been inside the mansion before. The women admired all the paneled walls and the crown molding made from heavy dark wood. Thick wool carpets covered the lacquered hardwood floors that creaked charmingly as they walked through the quiet house. Nancy and Helen paused in front of the painting of the girl and horse that hung over the fireplace. "That girl seems familiar," said Helen. In addition to the painting of the girl and horse, other portraits, large landscapes, and English foxhunts covered the walls.

The women saw lavish Victorian furnishings filling every space like a museum rather than a home. Several windows had stained glass. Valance draperies and wooden paneling with bullseye molding made the house seem dark except for the sunroom. Katie led the women up the broad center staircase. The second floor had three large high-ceiling bedrooms including the one converted into Tom's office. The Swansons' master bedroom included a completely refurbished bathroom as big as a locker room and two separate walk-in closets. The women had never seen curtained beds in a functioning house. A large comfortable parlor with a fireplace and a big flat-screened TV connected to the master bedroom.

A narrower, yet still elegant, staircase accessed the third level. Seven smaller and less pretentious bedrooms finished that floor. Three modern bathrooms served them all. Two smaller sitting areas had couches, upholstered chairs, TVs, and tables for games. The back staircase leading down to the pantry had allowed servants to discretely access both upper floors. Katie finished the tour by coming down those stairs into the guest quarters where she and Dave stayed. Old Yeller sat at his window post chattering at the birds.

Nancy stroked his fur. "What a pretty cat." The feline politely responded with a purr while maintaining his vigil.

"He's just ordinary. I think they call his kind 'alley cats.' "

"Is this your son?" Ellie asked while picking up a picture of Jeremy. Katie confirmed Jeremy was their son and added a brief description of their Christmas Eve Skype call. She recounted their surprise at meeting Jeremy's Aussie girlfriend. This started a conversation about daughters-in-law and sons-in-law.

The group passed through the formal dining room and returned to the entertaining room on the way to the front door. Nobody noticed the old ledgers spread out on the table. At the front door, Katie picked up her coat and handbag. "I'd better set the security alarm."

In the driveway, a late-model Cadillac waited for them. Nancy drove with Helen riding in the front seat. Conversation shifted from in-laws to children and grandchildren. Since the women knew each other well, most of the talk related to current affairs of extended families. Helen, mother of six children, led the discussion. Katie had the least number of children. Ellie, the pastor's wife, had three still-at-home children including a teenager.

Nancy kept the speedometer on a steady twenty-five miles per hour over the snow-packed roads. The new café overlooked the river on the far end of Main Street. Unlike The Blue Ox, the café tables had been set with lace tablecloths, fine cloth napkins, and a vase of fresh flowers. Pastel floral wallpaper covered the walls around tables and chairs of white wicker. In the entry, a dessert cart proudly displayed death-by-chocolate cake, lingonberry pie, and a salted caramel ice cream brownie. The waiter seated the women in front of a large picture window facing the frozen Mississippi River. He distributed menus and took their drink orders.

Someone remarked on the frozen river. This initiated a new direction of conversation about hard winters. Helen took the lead. "Do you remember the Halloween blizzard of 1991?" They each did except for the Alabamian. Nearly three feet of snow had fallen. Twenty-two people had died and over 100 were injured.

Katie quickly got caught up in the "it-was-so-bad" game. She started to exaggerate summers in the deep south. "Ninety-nine and ninety-nine," she told them. "That's ninety-nine degrees and ninety-nine percent humidity. The early pioneers used to squeeze the air to get fresh water. Birds have to do a breaststroke to fly. Plants don't even need rain to grow." The last example, at least, accurately described the Spanish moss draping nearly every tree in South Alabama. The women began laughing at her wit and charm.

The waiter returned with their drinks. "The special of the day is a chicken salad croissant with a cup of leek soup."

"I'll try that," said Helen.

"Me too," said Ellie.

Nancy ordered the raspberry pecan turkey salad and Katie ordered the Greek chicken salad.

After each lunch had been ordered, the conversation took a more serious direction. "Did you hear that the Sandersons are getting a divorce?" Nancy started. Light local gossip followed to which Katie could not contribute. The women talked about relationship difficulties. Generally, they all sided with the wives of couples they discussed.

Helen turned to Katie. "I heard that you and Dave are marriage counselors."

Without trying to guess how Helen had heard that, Katie corrected, "Group leaders. We've led discussion groups on marriage."

"What did you teach?" Nancy asked, but all the women seemed curious.

Katie explained the two most important factors for marriage success. She described a few of the common problems young couples encounter and shared a couple of examples from her own early marriage. "We couldn't even agree on what type of Christmas tree to get. My family lived in Florida. Dad always bought northern fir trees for our Christmas. Dave wanted to go out into the woods and cut a spindly pine or cedar. That just wasn't Christmas to me." This started the older women sharing stories from their own marriages. Mostly their stories were of the he-was-so-stupid category. Ellie remained silent.

Their lunches arrived and slowed the conversation down. Still the women continued talking about local news and events. All of them expressed concern about the increase of crime and drug abuse reported on the local news broadcasts. Helen lowered her voice. "Do you think things are really that different from when we were young? A lot of bad stuff happened back when I was a girl. Only the newspaper didn't report anything and nobody would talk about much, if at all."

"That McReady clan was always in the middle of everything," Nancy whispered. "Nobody wanted to get on their bad side. If you opposed one of them, they'd all be out to get you."

"I think they're still in the middle of a lot that happens in this town," Helen suggested with a trace of bitterness in her voice.

An awkward silence hung over the table. Katie paused eating her salad to break the quiet. "How many of the McReadys are there?"

Helen waited for someone else to speak. Nobody did, so she started, "They're harder to keep track of since their family businesses failed back in the 1980s. They all used to live along Riverfront Drive. A few have left town. But dozens of them are still around. Some of the McReady women work. But Billy McReady seems to be the only one of the men with a regular job. After the army, he joined the police force and married that nice young girl . . . Caroline. She's Susie Holmquist's niece. Billy has made a good policeman. Conscientious, you know."

Nancy picked up the story. "Those three McReady cousins are the worst. All of them take issue with anybody they think is messing around with their family. They hang around together and look for trouble. I heard they've picked fights and nearly beat a couple of men to death. But witnesses don't talk or the McReadys alibi each other." Disgust tinged her voice.

Katie thought about the encounter she and Dave had with the three bullies at the gas station. She also remembered the threatening phone calls, and the driveway gift of trash they had received. Wondering if there could be a connection, she asked, "How old do you think the cousins are?"

"Let's see. The oldest is Jud, about mid-forties. Then the other two go by Bogus and Lars. They're somewhere in their thirties. All of them are big, strong, and have the McReady dark curly hair. They don't shave regularly. Women who don't know them think they're handsome. Folks who know them stay away and don't cross them."

The waiter broke the serious mood. "Who would like some dessert?" They ordered two desserts for the table and four forks.

Once again, the conversation changed. The women started talking about food and cooking and places to eat. Everybody agreed that Susie's place, The Blue Ox, had the best home-style food. When the conversation lagged, Katie started telling about some southern foods: shrimp and cheese grits, boiled peanuts, pecan pie, seafood gumbo, and jambalaya.

After splitting the check four ways, the women left the restaurant and walked up Main Street mostly window shopping. Ellie walked alongside Katie. "Is this the first time your husband has ice fished?"

"Yes, but he loves any kind of fishing. I'm so glad the

men took him." Katie then confided, "He misses going out in his boat to fish."

"You have a boat?"

"We keep a twenty-four-foot boat at the marina near where we live. While Jeremy was growing up, we spent lots of time on the water. Ruthie, our Labrador retriever, usually went along. In calm weather, we could venture into the Gulf trolling for king mackerel and occasionally even a tuna. Or we could reef fish for snappers and groupers. In rougher weather, we caught redfish, snook, and flounders inside the bay. Usually we went ashore on a remote beach for a picnic. Jeremy would catch blue crabs in a dip net. I boiled the crabs and shrimp on a portable propane burner."

Katie concluded, "We're enjoying Minnesota. But both of us are homesick." Ellie understood.

All the women picked up a couple of treats at Hansen's Bakery. Katie felt the cold more than the Minnesotans. She inwardly rejoiced when somebody suggested returning to the car.

After being dropped off, Katie put on the teakettle and wondered about Dave and the other men ice fishing.

Chapter Twenty-Two

————•————

Inside the fish house, the four men were having a lot of fun. Twenty-six fish lay frozen outside. About noon, Ed opened the grill that had heated the enclosure to put on brats and burgers. Bags of chips appeared. Frank issued more beer. As they continued, the tales got bigger. Ed claimed that a hooked musky had pulled his canoe all over the lake.

Dave told more stories about deep-sea fishing in the Gulf. While trolling with his father as a young boy, a big fish had pulled his father's best rod out of his hands. The rod and reel had been lost in the deep. Dave also described once catching a modest-sized sailfish. "It jumped more than six feet high in the air."

Frank kidded Dave, "I'll bet that sailfish was easier to catch than the northern you brought in earlier."

Dave had to admit that the northern on light tackle had been a handful. The men all challenged him, "Stay around for summer. We'll put you into some real fish." Privately Dave marveled at the fight catching a thirty-pound northern must require, much less a sixty-pound musky.

The fishing slowed. "Maybe we caught them all," Frank speculated. They all knew that couldn't be true. But they had put a dent in the ones clustered below them. "It'll pick up toward sunset, like all fishing," he predicted and passed out the last of the burgers.

Ed took several devices from the shelves behind them and rigged them to the fishing lines. "This is what we call a 'tip-up,' " he explained to Dave. "This flag will come up if a fish bites. That way we don't have to hold the rods all the time. Leaves our hands free for beer," he joked.

The men sat back in their chairs then. The food and the beer had a calming effect. Frank spoke to Dave, "On the phone you said that you'd found out something about the history here."

"Yes, we did. But Katie and I aren't sure what to do about it." Dave leaned forward and sighed. Although they appeared relaxed, each of the men listened attentively. He started by describing the discovery of old ledgers in the carriage house. "The ledgers didn't balance out with expenses versus revenue. I used to be a financial accountant, you know." The men didn't know that. Then Dave explained the cryptic notes with names and dollars that he had found. The names corresponded with men Frank knew of who had disappeared in 1949.

"What do you think is the significance of that?" John asked.

"Well, Katie and I think this might document murder of the strike leaders."

Absolute silence, except for the outside wind against the walls, filled the fish house. Such silence made Dave feel uneasy. Had he done the right thing by telling these men?

Frank relieved Dave by clearing his throat and speaking. "Everybody local always suspected foul play of some sort. But suspecting and knowing feel a lot different." The other men nodded their heads in agreement. "Is that all?" Frank asked.

The men sat forward now in anticipation. Dave sighed again. "No, I'm afraid not. Money from an unknown source appears to have been coming in to the legitimate businesses." Silence again dominated. Dave proceeded to describe their discovery of the hidden room at Big River. Trying to lighten the atmosphere, he told about the role of the cat. That didn't work. The men remained somber. "Inside the room, we found another set of ledgers, this time for bootlegging, bookmaking, and what they called 'enforcement.' By comparing the dates between the sets of ledgers, I correlated some of the discrepancies in the ledgers of the legitimate businesses. The public businesses acted essentially as fronts for racketeering and money laundering. I'm afraid a lot of people in the community helped the McReadys."

The silence continued for two full minutes as the men contemplated what they had heard. John, who wasn't originally from Washita, started to shake his head. "Is this a joke? This sounds like something out of a detective novel. Are you messing with us?"

Dave stared at a fishing hole. "I wish that I was."

Frank started speaking slowly. "Actually, this fits into a lot of what we already know. Everybody suspected that something wrong was going on, especially during the Depression. The McReadys thrived and built big houses on Riverfront Drive when everybody else just tried to survive. But they brought money and jobs into the community. I guess most folks didn't care how."

John spoke up again, "But if this is true, jobs don't justify bribery, extortion, and especially murder."

Ed spoke up, "No, they don't. But what can be done now? The men who committed these crimes are surely all dead. The oldest McReadys were just kids during most of that. The younger generation probably didn't even know about the room you found. If you reveal this, it'll tear the town apart."

Frank saw a different challenge. "Even if the guilty ones aren't dead, statutes of limitation would prevent them from being prosecuted."

"Murder doesn't have a statute of limitation," John argued.

Ed answered John with a bit of irritation in his voice. "No, but lawyers can say that their client didn't know or do anything. They'll all say that the other McReadys, the ones who are dead, did everything. There's no way to prove any individual wrong in a court of law."

"Even so, shouldn't the truth be told?"

"Better to let sleeping dogs lie. Somebody could get hurt."

Frank had been listening to this exchange thoughtfully. "Knowing what to do in a situation like this is tough. Some of this information is a hundred years old. The most recent is decades old. I suggest we think about everything carefully before we decide anything, and let's keep everything said between us."

Frank then somehow felt compelled to lower his voice. "Yes, these records are old. But what I'm wondering is, what have the McReadys been up to recently?" He had expressed what the others thought. Nobody had an answer.

—◄◆►—

An hour after sunset, Katie heard Dave parking the truck in the garage. She had a pot of seafood chowder with oysters and pepper jack cheese biscuits ready. She gave her fisherman a hug when he came into the guest quarters. "Did you catch anything?"

"Yes, we caught a good many. I brought home a few." He showed her some yellow perch, a nice walleye, and the northern pike. "I caught that one," he said pointing at the northern. "They say that this fish is a baby. He put up plenty of fight, though."

Dave seemed exhilarated and tired at the same time. Katie placed a bowl of chowder on the table. "Sit down and have some dinner. I thought something warm and familiar would be welcome tonight."

While they ate, Dave enthusiastically told Katie all about the ice fishing. She listened intently and occasionally asked a question. When he stopped talking, she asked, "Did you talk with the men about the discoveries we made?"

"Yes, I did." Katie could tell that the uncertainty of decision weighed on her husband. He continued, "They didn't know what to do about this either. The information

173

is so old. We decided to think about everything some more."
Dave seemed to finally notice the dish Katie had made. "This
is seafood chowder. It's delicious! You made my favorite.
Could I have another bowl, please?" Katie refilled his bowl
and added another biscuit to his plate. "Did you have a good
lunch with the girls?" he asked.

Katie gave a detailed recounting of who came, the tour
of the mansion, where and what they had for lunch, and
shopping afterwards. "All of them are very nice. Ellie is the
wife of John Foster, the pastor who introduced the community
Christmas concert. She's very sweet."

"I met John today. He went fishing with us. Seemed like
a good man. I think he invested his day double-fishing."
Katie looked puzzled. "He wanted to catch fish and knew
how. As a pastor, he also spent some time with the men in
his congregation and community." After another spoon of
chowder Dave asked, "Did you talk with the women about the
discoveries we made?"

"No, I thought that should be left to you right now. I did
get a little from them about the McReadys, though." Dave
listened as she told about the family, especially the cousins.
"Do you think they could be the same ones we tricked at the
gas station?"

"Sure does sound like them," Dave concluded. "And I
think people around here have good reason to be afraid of
them."

⚫

The next day Dave and Katie took a long walk away from

the town on the rail trail. All the snow piles had begun to shrink. "How can they melt when the temperatures are still below freezing?" Dave wondered aloud.

"They're evaporating in the sun. Sublimation is when the ice crystals turn into vapor without passing through the liquid phase." She received a look of admiration from her husband. "Don't forget, I used to be a science teacher."

Later that afternoon, Dave was relaxing and reading one of the books he had checked out at the library when the house phone rang. "Could I speak to Katie, please?" a female requested.

Dave passed the phone to Katie. The caller started, "This is Ellie Foster. I enjoyed our lunch yesterday." She and Katie chatted happily for a few minutes. Then Ellie explained, "The reason I called is that I'm interested in the classes you taught back in Alabama. You know, the ones about marriage. I was wondering if you could teach one for us?"

This request surprised Katie. "Probably yes. But we aren't members of your congregation."

"Oh, I didn't mean for the church. I meant for John and me."

"Maybe; did you have anything specific in mind?"

Ellie seemed nervous then. "We aren't about to get a divorce or anything. We have a plan for our marriage. But we just don't have fun together like we used to. John is a good man and we love each other. Sometimes I just feel like John has time for everybody except for me and the kids."

Katie laughed a little to relax the younger woman. "Well, pastors do have tremendous demands for their time. Plus, you have three children to take care of. Our one son was all Dave and I could handle. Couples with so many responsibilities frequently neglect each other. Maybe your plan just needs to be updated with a new 'How to Have Fun' chapter."

"Yes. That sounds perfect. Did you ever need a new chapter?"

Now Katie laughed out loud. "Absolutely, yes." Katie told about Dave's one-time obsession with his accounting firm. "During tax season, I felt like a widow. But we realized that we were missing some of the most important things in life, especially in our relationship. We worked out our priorities and set goals for spending time together. We became intentional about having fun as a couple and as a family."

"Could you help us to do that?"

"I think so. Have you talked with John about your idea?"

Ellie sounded deflated. "Not yet."

"Why don't you talk to John about the idea? Make certain that he knows this is about adding fun and romance to marriage, not fixing a struggling marriage."

"I think he'd like that." The women exchanged a few more pleasantries before hanging up.

Dave lowered his book. "Who was that?"

Katie told him about Ellie's request.

Dave looked thoughtful. "We'll see what happens."

Chapter Twenty-Three

The sound of breaking and falling glass startled both Parkers awake. They heard the sound of windows shattering in the sunroom and heavy thuds somewhere inside the mansion. An indistinct *pop, pop, pop* sound of gunfire came from the direction of the road. Dave rolled out of bed onto the floor, pulling Katie after him. "Get down!" he tersely ordered.

Katie could hear Dave groping under the bed for his shotgun. Then she heard the now-familiar metallic *click, thump, thump, click* of Dave's double-barreled shotgun being loaded in the dark. "What's happening?" Katie kept her voice at a whisper with difficulty. "Are those gunshots?"

"Yes! Somebody is shooting at us. Call 911."

Katie started to stand.

"No! Crawl." Dave pulled Katie down and positioned himself with the gun pointed toward the bedroom door.

She crawled over to the desk where she kept her purse and cell phone. She dialed 911. A male voice answered immediately. "What is your emergency?"

She shouted, "Somebody is shooting at us!"

"Please give your name and address." As Katie complied, the sounds of breaking glass and popping from the road ceased. "Where are you right now?"

Katie looked around to remind herself where they were. "We're on the floor in the bedroom."

"Stay there," the male voice ordered. "Units are responding. Is anybody hurt?"

"No one yet. Please hurry."

"Remain on the phone and lie on the floor. Don't go outside." The male voice paused a moment. "Our records show that address is a gated residence. Do you have an entry code?"

Katie spelled out "T-U-F-F-Y," then said, "The sound of shots has stopped."

"Stay where you are. Units are on the way."

The couple waited in the quiet darkness. Occasionally, the 911 operator would ask, "Are you okay?" and repeat, "Stay where you are."

Katie had crawled over to Dave who still guarded the door with the shotgun. His presence comforted her. Suddenly Katie remembered Old Yeller. "Where's the cat?"

Dave whispered, "I don't know much about cats. But I think the one thing they can be relied on to do is save themselves whenever there's danger."

True enough, Old Yeller had disappeared. Nevertheless, Katie felt chagrined at her husband's callousness. She risked a soft, "Kitty, kitty, kitty."

From under the wardrobe she heard, "Rrrow." That issue settled, she raised her head above the bed to look around. Faint blue flashes came through the window and reflected in the dresser mirror. Then a distant siren could be heard coming closer.

Long minutes passed. The blue flashing became brighter. The first siren stopped. After several minutes, they heard an additional siren. The 911 operator came back. "Police are at your location. Don't open the door until they identify themselves."

Additional minutes passed while the police carefully approached the mansion on foot. The front doorbell rang. "This is the police!" A loud male voice shouted. "Please open the door."

Dave stood, put away his shotgun, and started turning on lights. The couple disarmed the security system and answered the front door. Old Yeller, taking no chances, held his place under the wardrobe. On the front step, they found Billy McReady in uniform carrying a shortened twelve-gauge pump shotgun. A somewhat older policeman, also with a shotgun, stood back in the shadows. "Is everybody okay?" Billy asked with concern.

"Neither one of us is injured," Dave assured him.

Both policemen came inside and walked through, checking the entire mansion. A third siren could be heard coming down Riverfront Drive. "Better go and open the gate again," the older policeman said to Billy. The Parkers could see Billy's flashlight going down the driveway. Two squad cars with flashing lights still parked on the road. Billy opened the gate and waved an unmarked car with a temporary light on top directly through. The unmarked car came up the driveway. A man in civilian clothes, a little older than Dave and Katie, emerged.

"That's Chief Oleson," the second policeman whispered to inform them. The chief was somewhat heavyset, balding, and obviously no-nonsense. Billy also brought his squad car from the gate and parked by Chief Oleson.

The chief approached Billy and asked a couple of questions. Satisfied, he came toward Dave and Katie and asked with a graveled voice, "Are you the ones who dialed 911?" Both answered in the affirmative. "What happened?" Dave told the little they knew.

Billy turned the squad car spotlight onto the first and second floor sunrooms. Most of the glass of the sunrooms on both floors had been shot out. A few outside stone blocks showed cracks where bullets had missed the glass. While Dave answered questions, Katie stepped back and heard the second policeman remark to Billy, "Looks like somebody sprayed the sunroom with an assault rifle."

The chief summoned Katie to rejoin him and Dave. "Folks, this looks like a drive-by shooting. It could be random. However, can you think of any reason somebody would want to target this house?"

Dave and Katie looked at each other. There would be no withholding their discoveries now. Dave briefly told the chief about the ledgers. He added the threatening phone calls and the garbage in the driveway. The chief grunted. "You should have come to the police right away. Does anybody else know about this?" Dave responded that some members of the Washita Historical Society knew.

Chief Oleson grunted again. He called Billy over. "McReady, you stay here until morning, unless there's another emergency." To the second policeman he said, "Thomas, you can go home. We'll get a better look tomorrow morning." To both officers, he said gruffly, "Nice quick response tonight. You handled it by the book." The chief climbed back into his car, removed the light, and departed. Officer Thomas walked back down the driveway and left in his squad car.

—◆—

Billy turned off the searchlight. Dave and Katie suddenly noticed how cold they felt. In the excitement, they had forgotten to put on coats. "Billy, come inside. I'll make you something hot to drink," Katie invited. She hurried back to the guest quarters. The clock indicated 3:48 a.m.

With the sunrooms on both floors nearly glassless, cold air poured into the house. Billy followed Dave into the guest quarters where Katie had turned on the space heaters and the tea kettle. Being busy helped to calm her down. "Billy, would you like coffee, tea, hot chocolate?"

"Coffee, please ma'am." Dave asked for tea and headed for the garage.

Katie pulled out the French press she had brought from Alabama. "Regular or decaf? Medium or strong?"

"Regular please, and strong."

Katie put in two scoops of coffee grounds and poured in boiling water. After waiting fifteen seconds, she inserted the screened piston and pressed the grounds to the bottom. Fresh coffee passed through the screens, leaving the grounds. Katie poured a big cup for Billy. "Would you like cream or sugar?"

"Black is fine." Billy tasted the scalding, fresh coffee. "Wow, that *is* good! And you made this coffee nearly as fast as instant. Thank you." He looked at the coffee press with curiosity.

Dave returned with folded sheets of plastic he had found in the garage and a roll of duct tape. He propped a stepladder against the wall. Katie had hot tea ready for herself and her husband. "Thanks for coming so quickly, Billy. Is it okay to call you 'Billy' while you're on duty?"

"Sure, you can. Responding quickly is just part of my job."

"That's not what I hear. People say that you're a good officer and very conscientious," Katie passed on the compliment she had heard at lunch. Billy looked embarrassed.

Dave had finished his tea. "I'd better block the openings to the sunrooms before all of the heat is lost from the house."

Billy stood up with Dave. "Let me help you."

"You're on duty."

"I'll leave if the dispatcher orders."

Fortunately for Dave, the dispatcher did not call Billy away. Hanging the sheets of plastic over the broken doors between the mansion interior and sunrooms was a two-man job. The men chatted about police work and the destruction done to the house. Not only had the sunroom windows been damaged. Bullets had even broken through the interior doors and entered other parts of the mansion. They had splintered some of the beautiful wood paneling and damaged antique furniture.

Billy surveyed the damage. "Looks like someone fired hundreds of bullets. One weapon could have been on full automatic. See how the bullet holes climb the wall from the recoil? That could have been a Kalashnikov." Seeing Dave's confusion, Billy added, "That's the old Soviet AK-47 assault rifle our enemies have used in virtually every conflict since the Korean war. This could have been an original bought on the black market or a reproduction. Likely the other guns are any of several semi-automatic assault rifles available nearly everywhere. We'll know when they check ballistics."

"Do you see much of this in the States?" Dave asked while he taped down plastic held in place by Billy.

"Maybe there's some in the big cities. I've never heard of a drive-by like this in such a small town."

"You mentioned an AK-47. Did you learn about them in Afghanistan?"

"Yeah, I did. I learned to hate the sound they make, especially when anybody aimed them at us."

"I heard that you got some medals there."

Billy hesitated and spoke reluctantly. "I didn't do any more than the other guys would have done. They gave me a bronze star for covering my teammates when we withdrew from an ambush. Later I got a purple heart when a roadside bomb hit our convoy."

"I respect your courage."

"When your teammates are in trouble, you just don't think about the risks."

Suddenly Billy changed the subject to something of personal concern. "Thanks for the book on marriage you gave us."

"You're very welcome. Has the book helped?"

"Yeah, a lot. But talking things out is hard. Caroline and I are so different."

Dave chuckled a little. "Once people get married, they all find out that they are different from their spouse. But differences can make a couple stronger as a team because they each contribute different strengths."

Billy held up another sheet of plastic. "I can see that. Caroline is so much better than me at some things, like remembering names and birthdays and stuff."

"And you're better than she is at some things, too."

Billy had to concede the truth of that. "Some spots are still trouble for us. Would you meet with us again? We could talk about some of the hard spots."

"Certainly. Would you mind if we invited another couple or two as well? Their experiences might fit your circumstances better than ours. Also, I believe they could learn some things from you and Caroline."

That statement sounded ridiculous to Billy. "Learn from us? You've got to be kidding!"

"You would be surprised." Seeing Billy's disbelief, Dave added, "Try it. You'll see. Discussing issues with other couples is what helped my marriage to Katie the most."

"That sounds hard."

"Not as hard as facing an AK-47." Dave paused a moment and added, "Isn't your teammate Caroline in a type of trouble?"

Billy took a minute to think about that concept. "Yeah. You could put it that way. Okay. We'll try meeting with others. You've been right so far."

Chapter Twenty-Four

———•●•———

At 8:00 a.m., Officer Thomas arrived to relieve Billy. Katie protested, "We're all right now. Nobody needs to stay to protect us. But thank you."

"We're guarding the integrity of the crime scene, ma'am. Somebody has to stay until the detective arrives to document any evidence," Officer Thomas responded. Katie looked at Billy who grinned sheepishly.

"Come on in, then. I'll make you some coffee."

By 9:00 a.m., a tall, thin, middle-aged detective with a neatly trimmed mustache and wire-rimmed glasses arrived with a civilian lab technician. The detective introduced himself as Gary Hobson. He posted Officer Thomas at the front gate with instructions to keep the public back. Then Detective Hobson set up a sign-in log for all the investigators who might visit the crime scene. Katie, even under the circumstances, enjoyed preparing hot drinks and sharing baked goods with everyone.

Dave chuckled to himself and thought, *Only Katie would serve as a hostess at a crime scene.* A short time later, a news van from the local TV affiliate, KAAK, arrived. Officer Thomas did not allow it past the front gates.

While the lab technician worked inside, Detective Hobson thoroughly searched Riverfront Drive. He didn't find any casings. That made him think the shots had come from within a vehicle. But the technician did dig slugs out of the paneling behind each of the sunrooms. "These will tell us how many guns the suspects used and maybe help us to trace them."

At 10:30 a.m. Dave got a phone call. "Mr. Parker, this is Richard Christensen. I'm the District Attorney for Washita. Would you mind coming down to the Municipal Complex and having a talk with us?"

"Do I need an attorney?" Dave's cautious nature forced him to ask.

DA Christensen laughed a little and answered, "No, this isn't an interrogation. You're not suspected of any crime. We just want to hear your story."

"Should I bring my wife?"

"Please do bring her."

———◆———

Dave explained to Katie that they needed to go downtown to meet with the District Attorney. She collected her purse and cell phone, ran a brush through her hair, and joined Dave in the truck. A group of curious onlookers had gathered just outside the gate. As they drove onto Riverfront Drive, a KAAK cameraman focused on the truck as a female reporter shouted some unintelligible question.

When ushered into DA Christensen's office, Dave and Katie thought the dignified fortyish man looked familiar. "First," the DA began, "I'd like to thank you again for pulling my wife and kids out of a ditch during the first snow." Then the Parkers recognized him. They had met briefly when he and Lisa introduced themselves at the Christmas Eve service.

Dave smiled. "You're very welcome."

"But the reason that I asked you down here is that Chief Oleson mentioned you had found some records that might relate to the drive-by shooting. I've asked Chief Oleson to join us. Ah, here he is now." The chief entered wearing a police uniform, gave a taciturn nod to the Parkers, and sat down.

"Yes, we did find some old ledgers. But I don't see how they could relate to any current police matters. Many of the historical records are a century old."

"Just tell us what you've found, please, and include everything."

Dave talked for half an hour, telling all he and Katie had discovered in the ledgers and from members of the community. He carefully distinguished between what he knew and what he suspected to be true. Occasionally Katie interrupted to add something. At the end, DA Christensen and Chief Oleson looked at each other. Dave thought that he detected an invisible high-five passing between them.

"Thank you. There's another concern we'd like to inquire about," the DA continued with a smile that could have been interpreted as mischievous. "There's a story going around town about a late-middle-aged couple with southern accents who hoodwinked some bullies out at the gas station. Would you know anything about that?"

"Maybe," Dave answered carefully. "We haven't heard the town story. But we did pull a ruse on three troublemakers trying to pick a fight with a husband by insulting his wife." He added some details and reluctantly quoted some of the vile language the men had used.

"Hmmm . . . " The DA sat quietly for a few seconds then looked down at his desk for nearly a minute. To Katie the DA seemed to be trying to maintain a professional demeanor while enjoying a prank pulled on the bullies. Looking back up, the DA continued, "Did you get anything from their license plate?"

"No, I couldn't read it in the dark. Sorry."

"Mr. and Mrs. Parker, we thank you for your time. We'll do our best to find those who are responsible for what happened this morning." DA Christensen appeared somewhat winsome. "Oh, there's one more thing. We sure would like to examine the ledgers you've found." When Dave hesitated, he softly added, "I can get a warrant for them."

"Yes, you can see the ledgers. No warrant is necessary. Why do you think they're important?"

"Sorry, but we can't comment on an ongoing police investigation. Chief Oleson, would you please arrange for the ledgers to be collected and chain-of-custody to be established?" The chief nodded and left the DA's office.

Dave and Katie looked at each other. Their eyes said,

"Ongoing investigation?" They rose to leave as well.

"Could you stay just one more minute, please?" DA Christensen asked. They sat back down. The DA closed the door to his office and leaned back against his desk, facing them. "I really don't think whoever did the shooting was trying to kill you. They just wanted to scare you. Plus, I think the sunrooms with all that glass would be an absolutely tempting target for trigger-happy troublemakers. My advice would be to let them think they've succeeded. These could have even been the men you tricked at the gas station. If that's true, let them think they've gotten even with you. Don't talk about any of this around the community. Just lie low. Thank you again for your cooperation and your time." The DA personally escorted Dave and Katie out of the Municipal Complex.

Back at the mansion, Detective Hobson and the lab technician waited. Officer Thomas guarded the gate. "Chief Oleson called to say that you had some records for us."

Dave showed the investigators the ledgers that remained spread out on the dining room table. Then he led them down the steps into the basement. Crowbars he and Katie had used still wedged open the paneling that had previously concealed the hidden room. While the technician rigged up flood lights and a camera, Dave guided the detective to the carriage house where he had found the first ledgers.

Once the floodlights illuminated the hidden room, Chief Oleson arrived to supervise the search and signed into the crime scene log. After a little while, he called upstairs, "Mrs. Parker, there's a house cat down here getting in our way. Could you remove him, or should we bag him as evidence?"

Katie collected Old Yeller and took him upstairs. "I'll lock him in the pantry," she told her husband.

"He won't like that. I'll bring up his litter pan and lock it in with him."

"I won't like that." But neither of them could think of an alternative.

Dave and Katie busied themselves in the guest quarters and remained clear of the investigation. A gentle tapping brought Dave to the door leading into the kitchen from the formal dining room. There a clergyman wearing a collar stood waiting. Dave recognized Pastor John Foster from the fish house. "John! What are you doing here?"

"I'm the chaplain for the police department. Sometimes officers observe or experience things that need some counsel. Other times victims need some assistance. Could I come in?"

"Of course, please join us." Dave ushered John into the sitting room. "Katie, this is the pastor I met ice fishing."

Katie had risen from her seat. "Glad to meet you. I had lunch with Ellie the other day. Please sit down."

Seated, the trio exchanged some pleasantries mostly about ice fishing and the wives' luncheon. John asked a few polite questions about life in South Alabama. Then he started, "That must have been a frightening experience last night. How are you handling it?"

Dave awkwardly rubbed his face. "I don't know. Probably all that's happened hasn't sunk in yet." He turned to his wife.

"Katie, how about you?"

"I'm just in a daze. This is the kind of stuff that only happens in movies. Being part of an investigation is something I never would have expected. I'm trying not to think about the danger."

Dave continued, "John, on the ice we agreed to think about how to deal with the discoveries Katie and I had made. When the chief asked if we knew any reason somebody might do this, I had to tell him about the ledgers. DA Christensen politely asked to see them, but he had enough to get a search warrant. He took the decision out of my hands."

"I know. You did the right thing. Probably all of us would ultimately have agreed to approach the authorities. This shooting only made that happen more quickly. There's an ongoing pattern of crime and intimidation in our community. Maybe now the police can do something about it."

Dave sighed in relief. "I just didn't realize asking a few questions about history would bring such a reaction."

John asked, "Have you told others about finding the records?"

"Only the men we fished with. Katie, have you told anyone?"

Katie shook her head, "No."

Rising to go, John gave them his card. "If this hits you hard later or if there's anything you need from me, please don't hesitate to call."

As he approached the door to leave, Katie took a couple of quick steps toward him. "John, there is one other thing. I know this is an awkward time and I know how busy you are.

But Dave and I are considering starting a discussion group about relationships. I wondered if you and Ellie could spare a few evenings to come. You wouldn't need to come on duty as a pastor."

Her offer amused John. Katie didn't understand that pastors are never completely off duty. "Yes, Ellie was quite impressed by some of your comments. She told me that she had also phoned you. Our marriage could use a little spark, and I understand that you've done a good bit of this in Alabama." Dave and Katie nodded in affirmation. "I'm interested to see what you're doing. Marriages in our community could use some help. When do you plan to meet?"

"We haven't decided yet. When would be convenient to your schedule?"

John laughed out loud. "You would make a good pastor, Katie. Generally, Tuesday nights are good for me. Let me talk to Ellie. She'll give you a call."

Once John had left, Dave turned smiling to Katie. "You never miss an opportunity, do you? Even in a crisis?"

She grinned. "Well, the groups helped our marriage when we needed it. Plus, everybody enjoyed the discussions. Wouldn't we enjoy being involved with young couples again?"

Chapter Twenty-Five

Dave tried to place a phone call to the Swansons. The instructions Maureen left listed a number in Aruba. He thought about trying a good news/bad news joke. "Good news—your basement is cleaned up. Bad news—your home is a crime scene." After reflection, he thought better of that. His decision didn't matter in the end. The hotel reported that the Swansons had left with several clients on a sixty-eight foot sailboat. They hadn't expected to be within range of cell phone service.

After lunch, DA Christensen, along with a special agent from the state police, arrived to survey the scene. Neatly labeled bags of evidence lined the walkway between the driveway and front door. In them, all the ledgers and every scrap of paper found in the hidden room had been prepared for transport. The TV news crew from KAAK remained near the gate videoing the vehicles entering or leaving. The woman reporter tried to interview everybody she could.

By 4:30 p.m., the investigators wrapped up the evidence collection. Detective Hobson gave Dave a list of all they had removed. At 5:00, the last official vehicle left the front gate. KAAK followed the police into town. The mansion seemed quiet after the day's tumult. Dave let Old Yeller out of the pantry. The cat immediately raced downstairs to conduct his own investigation. The couple joined him. The formerly hidden room appeared as though a giant vacuum had sucked up everything. The entire basement had been searched carefully, as had the carriage house.

Katie headed back upstairs. "What would you like for dinner?"

Both Parkers felt tired and stressed. Dave answered his wife, "Anything edible. Don't go to a lot of trouble." In a minute, he heard the oven door opening and Katie sliding in a large frozen pizza. The aroma of cheese and pepperoni started to permeate the guest quarters. *Maybe I am hungry,* he thought.

With the hot pizza, the couple settled in front of the TV. Katie held the remote. "Let's see if the news reported the shooting."

KAAK had just started their broadcast featuring a man and woman anchor team. The woman anchor began, "Early this morning a disturbance was reported at the 'Big River' mansion on Riverfront Drive. Built by Thaddeus P. McReady in 1897, the thirty-one-room mansion is the only Washita building on the National Register of Historic Places. Police went to the location early in the morning and remained all day. What details do you have for us, Ramona?"

"This is Ramona Watkins at the Washita Municipal Complex. I interviewed Chief Oleson of the Washita Police Department earlier." A pre-recorded clip showed Ramona next to the chief in front of the Municipal Complex. "What can you tell us, Chief Oleson?"

"At approximately 3:02 a.m., officers responded to a 911 call on Riverfront Drive. Shots were fired in what appears to be a drive-by situation. There were no injuries to either civilians or police officers. I can't comment further about a police investigation."

"Chief Oleson, investigators stayed at the house nearly all day. Did you find drugs?"

"I can't comment about a police investigation," he restated.

"Was this a domestic altercation?" Ramona persisted.

"No comment at this time." The chief hurried away.

The newscast returned to Ramona broadcasting live. "The police are being very tight lipped about the circumstances surrounding this incident. A couple staying at the house, David and Katherine Parker, were subsequently summoned to the District Attorney's office." Another recorded clip showed Dave and Katie in the pickup headed into town. "Reports are that the Parkers have declined their legal right to counsel. I now have some neighbors of Big River." The camera panned back to reveal a middle-aged couple with several teenagers. Ramona extended the microphone before them. "Did you suspect trouble right next door?"

The mother spoke, "No. They kept to themselves and were real quiet. We never knew anything was going on over there."

Ramona took a couple of steps to her right. An older man whom Dave and Katie had seen having lunch alone at The Blue Ox came into view. "I understand that you've observed the Parkers around Washita. Did they seem like troublemakers to you?"

"No, they seemed nice. You know, sort of friendly. They always ate by themselves."

The camera focused back on Ramona's upper body. "So, there you have it. Highly suspicious activities right here in Washita. This is Ramona Watkins for KAAK. Back to you."

Dave and Katie sat transfixed at the broadcast. Dave started angrily, "That makes us look guilty of something. So much for us lying low."

He turned to Katie, who smiled and started to laugh. "Can you imagine how the ones who shot at us are reacting? They'll think that they have really intimidated us."

Dave began to relax. "Maybe this *could* work to our advantage. Haven't you always wanted to play a villainess?" He chuckled with Katie at the absurdity of the situation.

Katie repeated their neighbor's comment, "They kept to themselves and were real quiet." This started the couple laughing so hard that Old Yeller came in to check on them.

—◆—

Frank phoned the next morning. "I saw you made the news last night."

"Yes, we did. You don't need to believe what they implied about us."

"Oh, they're always looking for a story for the six o'clock news. If the police are tight lipped, they'll make something up. What really happened out there?"

Dave told Frank about the drive-by shooting and the police collecting the ledgers and other evidence. "Sorry, but I couldn't hold anything back from the police. But I still can't understand what we've done that would rile somebody up so much. You haven't told anybody what we talked about on the ice, have you?"

"No way! I can keep a secret. Ed can be trusted, too. I've known him since junior high school. John has only been in the community for a few years. But pastors know how to hold things private better than anybody." After a few more comments, Frank and Dave said goodbye.

A half hour later, the phone rang again. "This is Ramona Watkins for KAAK on a recorded line. Could I interview you about the shooting last night?"

Dave responded following Chief Oleson's example, "We really shouldn't comment on a police investigation."

Ramona fished, "Are you going to be charged with a crime?"

"Not that I know of," Dave said slowly in a clear voice.

"Why would somebody mount an attack like that?" the reporter persisted.

"Sorry, I don't know. Thank you for calling though." Dave hung up rather than be entangled in speculations.

A while later Dave answered a third phone call. A female voice asked, "Could I speak to Katie, please?"

As he handed the phone to his wife, he cautioned, "Be careful, this could be another reporter."

Katie took the phone, listened for a few seconds, and shook her head toward Dave. He could then hear her talking pleasantly with somebody. Soon she put the receiver back in its cradle. "That was Ellie, John's wife. They're on for a discussion group next Tuesday night. I asked them to come here to Big River early for a kick-off supper. I'll check with Caroline now."

After the call, Katie found Dave in the kitchen. "Caroline and Billy are coming Tuesday. Plus, they asked if they could bring another young couple. This will be so much fun." Next Katie phoned Lyle's wife, Leslie, to invite her and Lyle. "You can bring Elsie with you," Katie offered.

Dave detected Katie's hostess instinct re-emerging for the first time since her cancer battle. He could hear her humming and rummaging in the pantry. Anticipating her next request, he collected his wallet and the truck keys. "I'll need some supplies," she announced. "Would you take me to town? Or I can drive myself." Dave dangled the keys.

On the way, Katie asked, "Do you know the secret to hosting a successful dinner?"

"Relax and enjoy it?" Dave hoped.

"No, try again."

"Make thorough preparations?"

"Right. Then you can relax and enjoy it," she confirmed.

"Then I'm twice correct," he quipped.

"True, but in the wrong order." At the grocery store, Katie filled a cart with the necessities of hosting a dinner party while Dave looked at the magazines.

As they pushed the loaded cart toward the truck, Dave suggested, "How about some brunch?"

"Sure, why not? The Blue Ox, okay?"

Heads turned toward them as they entered the restaurant. "What have you two gotten yourselves into?" Susie asked loudly for everybody present.

Dave answered equally loudly for everyone to hear, "We don't know what's going on. We don't know what the police are looking for, either." Heads turned back toward their meals.

At their table, Susie fussed over them, "People are just curious, that's all. Lots of bad stuff has happened in this town. Unlike most people, you called the police." Susie gave them an appreciative look. "What'll you have today? We have another traditional special. It's called 'lefse.' That's a traditional Norwegian flatbread made with potatoes, flour, and cream. You'll like it better than the lutefisk."

"I'm in the mood for a big breakfast," Dave said. "I'll have the ham skillet with hash browns."

"That sounds so good," Katie said, "but I'll have the chef salad with blue cheese dressing. And I'll try today's special, the lefse."

Dave and Katie noticed people looking their way occasionally and whispering. Their food's arrival relieved them. As Katie had expected, the lefse looked similar to a pancake rolled up around a fruit filling. This Minnesota tradition tasted more pleasant than the lutefisk. As Dave and Katie enjoyed lunch, a few patrons dropped by their table to wish them well. Several introduced themselves, perhaps to get a closer look at the couple from the news. Even

Betty came out from the kitchen. "I warned you about that mansion," she reminded. "There's nothing good comes out from there."

Susie spoke quietly to the Parkers, "People think something big is happening around here. A lot of folks feel strongly that things should just be left alone. Also, there's this story being told about some sort of trickery out at the gas station that made some local McReady bullies look foolish. Please tell me you two don't know anything about that. No, don't tell me anything, or anybody else for that matter." She looked at them seriously. "You two need to watch yourselves and lie low."

Dave thanked her and asked, "Susie, can you tell us anything about Richard Christensen?"

"You betcha. Richard grew up in Washita. He was a popular boy and a leader, the captain of the high school debate team. He didn't show much interest in school work, though. Richard had a streak of mischief in him. A couple of times he even got suspended for pulling pranks, usually on some of the tough guys. He surprised folks when he attended the University of Minnesota and got a law degree with honors. The Minneapolis DA's office hiring him surprised people even more. He worked there for eleven or twelve years. When the old DA in Washita retired about two years ago, Richard ran for the office. Because he was a local boy who had made good in the city, enough people voted for him to win the election."

Susie paused, carefully considering what to say next. "There's been controversy since he took over the DA's office. A

200

year later, the police chief unexpectedly resigned. People say Richard forced the old chief out with evidence of corruption he'd found." Susie shrugged her shoulders. "Anyway, Richard recommended an outside man from Minneapolis. The town had always employed police chiefs from the local area. The Council voted six to five, with the mayor opposed, to hire Chief Oleson." Susie hesitated again, "I probably shouldn't tell you this, but a couple of the councilmen who voted for Oleson privately said that big money was offered to those who would support a local man."

"Where did the money come from?" Katie asked.

"You guess." In response to Katie's look of disappointment, Susie added, "Probably from some people who don't want the police to be too diligent. Besides the money, a lot of folks are afraid Christensen and Oleson will stir things up that people don't want to think about." Susie sternly finished, "Just you remember what I said about lying low."

Chapter Twenty-Six

---·•·---

"You're a good friend, Susie," said Dave. After she wandered back toward the kitchen, Dave figured their bill and added thirty percent. Katie put the money on the table. Quietly the couple slipped out lest Susie feel obligated to treat them again.

Arm-in-arm the Parkers strolled down Main Street in the direction of the bakery. Lots of people looked their way and a few nodded. Suddenly a van pulled up beside them. Ramona from KAAK jumped out, holding a microphone. A cameraman followed close behind her. "Can you comment on the police investigation related to the shooting at Big River?"

Dave glanced at the recording camera. Rudeness wasn't part of his southern upbringing. Accountants also know how to be diplomatic without saying anything of substance. "No, we could not comment on police activity. But we would like to thank the police department for their diligent protection." He smiled for the camera.

Ramona had obviously done some research. She moved the microphone in front of Katie. "Does this happen often in Alabama?"

Katie followed her husband's example. "I don't think this happens often in Alabama or Washita. But we would like to express our appreciation for the many Washita citizens who have welcomed us here. Thank you for your reporting, Ramona." Dave and Katie resumed their leisurely stroll down the street.

Ramona shouted after them, "Are you hiding something? Do you expect to be arrested?"

Katie ducked into Hansen's followed by Dave. After their time in Washita, the bakery staff knew the couple well. "The bismark flavor of the day is strawberry," the girl behind the counter volunteered.

"Sounds good," said Katie. "I'll take two of those, one of your amazing lemon bars and a half dozen of your iced sugar cookies." Then they hastened back to their pickup truck. There they found a long, deliberate scratch, perhaps from a screwdriver, on the passenger side door.

"I guess Susie knew what she was talking about," Dave commented.

—◆—

On the way home to Big River, Katie's cell phone rang. DA Christensen asked for Mr. Parker. Dave pulled into a parking lot and took the phone.

"Hello, Mr. Parker, this is Richard Christensen. I just saw the street interview you gave to that reporter from KAAK,

204

and I heard the recorded phone call they made of you earlier. Let me say that you both have handled yourselves well." Dave murmured thanks. The DA then continued, "Would you two be willing to come into the office again? Say, Wednesday at about 9:00 a.m.?" Dave agreed. The DA concluded, "Thank you so much, Mr. Parker. We appreciate your cooperation on the matter under investigation. You should probably expect to be here all day Wednesday. We'll have lunch catered in."

Clicking off the cell phone and returning it to Katie, Dave explained, "The DA wants us in his office all day Wednesday."

Katie stared at her husband. "What for?"

"He didn't say. But we will get lunch." Dave restarted the truck and turned back onto Riverfront Drive. Katie noticed a sick feeling of apprehension in her stomach.

When they got back to Big River, they found Old Yeller lonely and wanting attention. Katie gave him a few kitty treats she had purchased and his catnip mouse. While the cat played, she sorted out her purchases. Dave started work on their income taxes using Katie's laptop at the kitchen table. Finished with the sorting, Katie sat quietly nearby while Dave worked. Old Yeller jumped up into her lap. Stroking his soft fur relaxed her. Finally, she asked Dave, "Well, what do you think?"

"Think about what?" Dave replied, never looking away from the screen.

"About everything that's going on!" Katie showed anger then. The stress had caught up to her. She resented that Dave didn't seem to be fazed by current events at all. "What are we getting ourselves into? What are we already into?" Her voice trembled a little.

He hit "Save" and leaned back. "I don't know, Sweetheart. I'm trying not to think about it."

"Typical of a male," she responded with irritation in her voice. "Compartmentalize, compartmentalize, compartmentalize."

"What do *you* think about it?"

Katie started to talk and she didn't finish for a long time. All her fears came out. "We could be killed! Who is doing these things to us? And why? What happens if they come back?" Dave listened patiently and occasionally added his own concerns.

The computer timed out and shut itself down. Finally, they each sat in silence, every scenario having been discussed. Then Dave asked the big question: "Do you want to leave?"

Katie reacted in surprise. "You mean leave Washita?"

"Sure, we could just get into the truck and drive back to Alabama."

"Who would take care of the mansion?"

"This house isn't worth risking our lives."

"What about Old Yeller?" The cat still lay purring in her lap.

"We could take him along," Dave said.

"You mean steal him?"

"The Swansons don't care anything about him. Think of it as rescuing a cat that belongs to himself. Didn't Maureen even say not to worry if he got lost?"

Katie pondered those possibilities. "I really don't want to leave. What about Caroline and Billy? What about Ellie and John and the others? We're just getting to know them and I think they need us." Dave waited and listened until Katie asked him, "Do *you* think we should leave?"

"Leaving is certainly the safe thing to do, maybe even the smart thing," Dave conceded. "But what if we're here to do something important? I'd hate to wonder for the rest of my life what might have been accomplished if we had stayed. This has become much bigger than the disappearance of Sam Johnson."

Katie shook her head. "But we're not prepared for this. We're just an ordinary couple."

"Maybe this is our chance to be more than ordinary."

Dave and Katie sat in silence, pondering that concept. The cat's rough purring dominated the quiet. Katie broke the silence. "I think you're right. Let's stick this out."

—◆—

Katie enjoyed cleaning and preparing all day Tuesday. Dave propped open the front gate and did small tasks for Katie. Late in the afternoon, the phone rang. A man unknown to the Parkers spoke to Katie. "I heard that you're starting a marriage enrichment group. Would you have room for another couple?"

She assured him that they did and gave the address of Big River. "Can you come for supper at six?"

"Are you sure you'll have enough?"

"Certainly, please come."

Dave and Katie welcomed each couple as they arrived. All of them acted uncertain and even a little nervous, except for the Rogerses. Leslie, with curly red hair and lots of freckles, had a talkative, sanguine personality. Although they hadn't met any of the other couples before, she and Lyle instantly made friends with everybody and put them all at ease. All the women adored her baby girl, Elsie.

Caroline spoke with surprise, "Pastor John! You're here?" She and Billy attended his church, albeit infrequently. John looked a little uncomfortable, as if concerned that a rumor would start that he and Ellie had marriage trouble.

To relieve John's concern, Dave injected, "John wanted to see how we lead these groups. So, we invited the Fosters as observers. But they'll participate just like the rest of us." John looked more relaxed.

Tommy Bryant and Jane Jenkins were Caroline and Billy's friends and appeared to be even younger. "We're not actually married yet. I hope that's okay," Jane explained. Katie assured the couple of their heartfelt welcome.

Nobody knew the middle-aged, and undeniably apprehensive, couple who had called late. They introduced themselves as Rick and Beth Larson. During the polite introductions, Katie gently asked them how they had heard about the group. "My mother Betty urged us to come and offered to babysit," Rick responded. "She cooks at The Blue Ox downtown. Anything for a free night of babysitting!"

Naturally, all the guests knew about the drive-by shootings and felt some trepidation about meeting at the mansion. Curiosity had been an even more powerful attraction. The gunshot damage could clearly be seen. Billy explained bullet trajectories and penetration while they examined the broken windows and inside damage. "I don't know," he answered honestly to questions about the ballistic results. "But even if I did know, I couldn't say anything about a police investigation."

The couples also expressed curiosity about the mansion itself. Dave led a brief tour while Ellie helped Katie in the kitchen. She set places at the big kitchen table in the guest quarters. When Dave and the couples returned from the tour, they found large platters of food in the center of the table. Steaming hot red potatoes, corn on the cob, sausage, and shrimp had been mixed and boiled with Cajun spices. "This is what we in the deep south call a 'Seafood Boil,' " Katie explained. "Sorry that I couldn't find any crayfish to include. Everybody just find a place and help yourselves, please."

As the couples seated themselves, Dave described the traditional way to serve a boil in the summer. "A plastic tablecloth is placed over a picnic table. The cook simply dumps the boiled ingredients in the center."

Katie placed a large basket covered with a cloth on the table. Gingerly peeking under the cloth, Caroline found lumps of fried brown dough. "What are these?"

Katie smiled. "Those are called 'hush puppies.' They're cornmeal deep fried in vegetable oil. In the old days, the cook would give a couple to the yard dogs to quiet them during dinner. The name 'hush puppy' stuck. We have beer, iced tea, pop, as you call it, and water to drink. What would everybody like?"

While Dave and Katie brought the drinks, their guests served themselves from the platters. The men especially relished the simple, plentiful food. Everybody commented on how the flavor from the sausage and spices had penetrated the shrimp and vegetables making them unique and delicious. Each guest selected the components he or she preferred. Dave noticed that the men tended toward the sausage and potatoes, while the women favored the shrimp. When the platters got low, Katie replenished them from two stock pots still simmering on the stove. As they ate, Dave engaged everybody in polite conversation about food and cultural differences between the North and South.

Leslie brought up the gas station encounter with the bullies as a compliment to her hosts. Dave and Katie tried to shush her. The energetic girl didn't notice. The thespian in Leslie came out to reenact the entire drama for everyone with some humorous embellishment. All the couples laughed at her antics. Billy confirmed that if Lyle had struck first, he could have been seriously injured. "Some roughnecks deliberately pick fights like that. There's not much the police can do to them afterwards," he explained.

The couples visibly relaxed and enjoyed themselves. When everybody had eaten enough, Dave suggested that they move to the guest quarters sitting room. There he and Katie had arranged twelve comfortable seats in a circle. With the group seated, he passed out marriage discussion books he had ordered through the bookstore. Unfortunately, the late addition of the Larsons made them a pair of books short. Dave gave his book to them and promised to have an additional book by the following week.

Dave started by explaining, "This will be a discussion group. But we won't make anyone say anything. You can just listen, if you choose. We'll use the questions at the end of each chapter in the book. If you can, please read the chapter before the next meeting. But if you can't, that's okay. Also, this isn't a 'dump-on-your-spouse' opportunity. Therefore, don't anybody say anything critical of your spouse. Finally, everything shared in this group is confidential. *Do not repeat* anything outside of this group or even who is in the group." The last sentence Dave pronounced slowly with emphasis. Several of the couples looked relieved at the instructions. "Shall we begin?"

Chapter Twenty-Seven

Katie read the first question aloud. "What are some things that first attracted you to your partner?" Then she waited. The couples glanced around. Who would begin?

Caroline broke the silence. "Billy is just the handsomest man I ever saw." Her comment broke the tension and brought chuckles. Soon nearly all of them shared aspects of their early attraction to their spouse. Katie prodded them with her ever-present wit and shortly had everybody laughing.

Dave and Katie alternated reading the questions, which gradually became harder. Dave told about a difference in values between himself and Katie which had caused arguments in their early marriage. Billy, who had previously read the marriage book, repeated some important principles of compromise. John had been totally silent so far. Then he shared a serious story about a mistake he had made which hurt Ellie during their first year of marriage. Listening to John, Dave thought, *I like that guy.*

After John's personal confession, the group remained quiet. Katie could tell that all the group members had memories of occasions when they had hurt each other. She looked gratefully at John, then interrupted their thoughts. "All of us have done things we regret. So then, what are some ways each of us can avoid making mistakes like that again?"

The group seriously considered her question. Different participants suggested variations on the themes, "Don't take each other for granted," and "Think before you speak."

Billy added, "I liked what the book said about feelings. Sometimes I think what Caroline says about how she feels is silly. My mind says, 'She shouldn't feel that way.' But the point is that she does feel that way, regardless of whether she should or not. When you dismiss somebody's feelings, it's like saying, 'You're not important to me.' That probably hurts most of all. Part of loving somebody is acknowledging that their feelings are always important."

Sixty minutes of discussion had passed quickly. Each person had contributed and each person had learned. Dave wrapped up while Katie slipped out. "Thanks to each of you for joining us tonight. In the coming weeks, we'll talk about resolving conflict, communication, decision-making, and keeping fun and zest in our relationships. Please go on a date with each other this week. You can review the questions related to your specific circumstances. One last reminder: if you can, please read the second chapter."

Katie reappeared with a tray of dessert treats from Hansen's Bakery. "I have fresh coffee, loaded or decaf, in the kitchen, ready for anyone who wants some."

The couples with children politely declined and headed toward their cars. Dave and Katie walked them out and waved goodbye. The two youngest couples remained inside eating bakery treats and drinking coffee. Then Tommy and Jane needed to leave to get up early the next morning. Dave and Katie accompanied them to their car.

Returning to the kitchen they found Billy looking red and embarrassed. "Are you on shift tonight, Billy?" Katie asked and looked at Caroline with a question in her eyes. Billy murmured that he would be on duty. Without comment, Katie started filling a thermos for him with the leftover coffee.

"Billy's embarrassed!" Caroline playfully blurted out. "I told him how well he did tonight. Some men just don't know how to accept a compliment." Billy looked even more embarrassed.

Dave supported her. "Sorry, Billy. Caroline is right on this one. You did do well tonight. The couples learned from the comments you made."

"I just read the book."

"But you put helpful ideas in your own words in a real-life situation. That's always better than hearing something from a book. Plus, you set an example of a commitment to a good marriage. Tommy and Jane especially listened to you."

To divert attention from himself, Billy asked, "They live together, you know. Is that all right?"

Katie handed Billy the thermos. "Well, we would have guessed that from the examples they shared. Dave and I do think being legally married is best. But that's their decision.

213

We'll try to help them have a good relationship regardless of their status."

As Billy and Caroline drove away, Dave gave Katie a little hug. "Nice job tonight, sweetheart."

She responded with a big kiss. "It really felt good to have friends in our home again. Well, our temporary home. My happiness meter is pretty much pegged out right now. I couldn't have done it without you. Thanks, lover."

Dave thought, *That's the Katie I remember.*

━◆━

On Wednesday morning, Dave and Katie reported at the Municipal Complex. The receptionist issued temporary ID badges and ushered them into an interview room. There a tall, large-boned, and athletic-looking woman in her mid-thirties waited for them. She wore a dark blue police uniform with her blond hair knotted into a tight bun. Her size, no-nonsense attitude, and Nordic features made Dave imagine her rowing on a Viking ship. The police woman placed several albums of numbered photos in front of them.

Her deep voice instructed them, "I'm Officer Clark. Please tell me if you recognize anybody." She waited, watching them. "Take your time." The Parkers slowly turned the pages. Some features on one photo of a male seemed familiar. Katie placed her index finger on the picture as she and Dave turned their faces to the officer. She gave a nod in acknowledgment and repeated, "Take your time." A couple of pages later, another familiar face appeared, but again the couple couldn't quite place him. This time the officer smiled a little and encouraged, "You're doing fine." Near the end of the photo albums Katie recognized three faces, the men from the gas station. Dave couldn't remember any faces from that stressful encounter.

The Parkers finished the photo array without recognizing anybody else and leaned back in their chairs. The officer collected the albums and commented, "You picked out Officer Thomas and Detective Hobson. They came to your house after the drive-by shooting. I just put them in the collection to see how observant you are. Mrs. Parker, you also picked three other men. Can you tell me how you recognized them?"

"I saw them at a gas station."

The policewoman let out a long breath and looked at the Parkers with respect. "We've been wondering about who pulled that off. Do you know any names of the men you saw there?"

Katie shook her head, "No."

The policewoman continued, "Next I'm going to read you some names. I'd like you to raise your hand if any of the names sound familiar." She then proceeded, speaking slowly and distinctly. Dave didn't recognize any of the names. Katie raised her hand three times. After reading the list, the officer clarified, "Mrs. Parker, you've indicated Jud McReady, Bogus McReady, and Lars McReady." Katie nodded. "How do you know those names?"

Katie swallowed. "The women I had lunch with mentioned their names. They advised me to avoid them."

The officer grunted a little. "Can you name these women, please?" Katie told her. The officer recorded their names in her notes. Then she concluded, "Thank you for your cooperation. Would you follow me, please?" As they walked down a corridor she whispered to Katie, "Your friends gave you good advice. But unfortunately, those men are the same ones you tricked at the gas station."

She guided the Parkers into the DA's office. There Richard Christensen rose from his desk to welcome them with warm handshakes. "Thank you again for giving your time to assist us. Please sit down." He returned to his desk and initiated a little polite talk about their time in Minnesota. After a few minutes, he looked at them intently and began, "Mr. and Mrs. Parker, in the interest of full disclosure, you should know that we have inquired about you to colleagues in Mobile. They made some calls on your behalf. Mr. Parker, you have excellent credentials as a CPA and a reputation for integrity. Mrs. Parker, everybody likes you, and you've done a lot of work for the schools and community. We've asked you here today to solicit your professional input as consultants. This is a small department. We can't afford to hire a top-notch accounting firm. But we need some help."

"I'm a CPA and have thirty-five years of experience. But unfortunately, I'm not certified by the ICFA, the Institute of Certified Forensic Accountants," Dave protested. "Without that, I'm not considered a qualified accounting witness in court."

The DA shook his head. "That's no problem. What you'll be looking at is decades old. We're just trying to understand the background right now. More important, we're gathering information to use in interviews. But because this is a police investigation, we'll ask you to sign a confidentiality agreement." He pushed two sets of papers with ballpoint pens across the desk. "All this means is that you won't divulge anything you learn here without permission from this office until after the investigation is completed."

As an accountant, Dave expected and knew how to maintain confidentiality. He signed his papers readily and passed them back. Seeing his example, Katie signed her papers. A clerk they hadn't noticed before crossed the office, notarized the agreements, and passed them back to DA Christensen. The DA passed over another document to each of them. "And this volunteer form states that you agree to serve without remuneration." The couple each signed and returned the forms. The clerk then asked them to pose for photos, which she took with a digital camera.

The DA smiled and rose with a completely different demeanor. "Thank you. Do you mind if I call you Dave and Katie?" Without waiting for a response, he offered, "My friends call me Richard. Let's go." He led the southerners to the city council chambers where a uniformed officer guarded the door. "He's been here all night to ensure the legal integrity of the evidence," the DA explained.

Inside the council chambers, the chairs normally provided for an audience had been replaced with long tables. On the tables the ledgers and papers confiscated at the mansion waited. Three men and a woman chatted nearby. DA Christensen introduced them. "This is Darlene Clark." He indicated the woman officer who had showed them the photos. "She'll run errands and be your assistant. This is Special Agent Patterson from the State Police. This old guy is Professor Bernie Pearson from the University of Minnesota. I'll never forgive him for giving me a 'C' in Minnesota History."

The distinguished senior gentleman broke in, "I'll never forgive myself either. You deserved a 'D.' "

Wincing in good humor, DA Christensen continued, "Finally this is Detective Gary Hobson. I understand you fingered him in the photo array." They all laughed as the detective feigned a shocked expression. Then the DA turned serious. "I grew up in Washita. Bad things always happened that people just didn't talk or ask about. All of us know there has been an undercurrent of crime here for likely a century." He paused and took a deep breath. "As a teenager, I knew my own grandfather had been forced to 'buy insurance' from some gangsters to prevent them from damaging the hardware store he owned. When he couldn't afford to pay, somebody broke the front windows and threw in a gasoline bomb. After he complained to the local police, the bank refused to continue his credit line. He went out of business and lost everything."

The DA waited for the group to contemplate that, then continued, "We suspect that elements of criminal networks continue today, but we never get sufficient proof to convict the worst offenders. A few thugs have held this town hostage long enough. In this room, we have people with knowledge of both state and local law, the world's foremost expert in Minnesota history, and the accountant skillful enough and conscientious enough to identify serious financial discrepancies." He gestured in Katie's direction. "And we have the lady smart enough to see through the details and make a connection to a likely murder. You should be first-rate as a research and investigation team. Your task is to piece together, as best you can, the story of what has happened in Washita related to the McReady clan and their associates. The law officers will carefully document all evidence of specific crimes by individuals."

"What if the individuals are deceased?" Agent Patterson asked.

"That doesn't matter for now. We'll use the information to rattle some cages and get people talking. You'll see what I mean later. I'm due in court now, but I'll check on your progress in a few hours. Ask Darlene for anything you need. Darlene, when you're not busy otherwise, pitch in with the research."

The clerk returned with Police Department photo identification badges on lanyards for Dave and Katie. Their names had been printed above the title "Consultant."

"Welcome to the Washita Police Department," DA Christensen said as he passed the badges to Dave and Katie.

Chapter Twenty-Eight

———•—

Nobody spoke for a minute after the DA left. "Perhaps we should sit down and each of us outline who we are and what we know so that we're all starting in the same place," Detective Hobson suggested. "First off, I'm Gary Hobson. I've been on the Washita police force for twenty-one years, the last six as a detective." Gary described a pattern of drug dealing and racketeering suspected in the area. He produced a list of men and women who might have been involved going back into the 1940s. Jud, Bogus, and Lars McReady's names finished the list. "But we could never collect enough evidence for anything more than minor convictions."

"How about names of public officials being threatened or taking payoffs?" the state agent asked.

"They could be anybody. I personally have been anonymously offered inducements four times. Once an envelope came by mail with a newspaper article from Minneapolis about possible drug trafficking in our area.

Someone had stapled the article to an advertisement for a new boat. I went ahead as planned and busted a McReady in-law for distributing cocaine. I guess that I forfeited the boat." Everybody laughed.

Special Agent Patterson introduced himself and echoed Gary's comments. The State Police had suspicions including possible corruption among their ranks, but no specific leads. Darlene came next. "I grew up in this town. Everybody knew that some people you just didn't mess with." She pointed at Gary's list. "I recognize some of those names and remember some of the McReadys from high school. They always tried to pick fights with other kids. I never saw anything criminal I could testify to. But in this town, our elders brought us up to look the other way."

"How long have you been a police officer?" Dave asked.

"I served in the navy for fourteen years out of high school. I came back to Washita so that my daughter could be near her grandparents. The navy isn't a good place to raise a little girl alone. I've been on the Washita police force for nearly three years now."

"I'm Bernie Pearson. I've been at the University for thirty-six years. My specialty is Minnesota history." Bernie looked like a caricature of an old professor with long white hair, a scruffy beard, thick glasses, and a slouch. He outlined the area's history beginning with the 1800s sawmill years through the breakup of McReady Enterprises in the 1980s. He described ruthless and unethical business practices that had been common, but not illegal at the time. Other activities such as bootlegging and prostitution were illegal, but generally ignored. Bernie had compiled a chronological list of disappearances and unsolved murders of community members up to the current day. He had also brought a tree of the extended McReady family, several large volumes of public records, and online historical records from the University of Minnesota.

Everybody turned to Dave. "I'm Dave Parker and this is my wife, Katie. I worked as an accountant in South Alabama until I retired a year ago." He proceeded to explain house sitting as an adventure, then the legitimate and illegitimate ledgers, and the correlation explaining discrepancies in cash flow. Dave told about the phone threats, the garbage in the driveway, the scratch on his truck, and finally the drive-by shooting. He gestured toward Katie, "But my wife recognized how the facts came together as the most significant evidence we discovered."

The group's attention then focused on Katie. Although feeling a little nervous, she started by repeating what she had heard from various community members about the reputation of the McReadys and Big River.

"That confirms what Darlene said," Gary interjected. "But everything you've said is only hearsay in a court. What is the significant evidence?"

Katie selected and opened the ledger from the time of the 1949 mill strike. Everybody gathered around the ledger. She pointed to the list of names and dollar amounts. "Professor, would you please check your list of disappearances from 1949?" she softly requested.

Bernie took a few seconds to find the right time frame. "Look at that!" He laid his list by the ledger. His list included every name from the ledger. There could be no mistake. The names Katie had indicated from the ledger all represented unsolved cases, likely murders.

Detective Hobson looked a little weak in the knees and sat down. "This could be it," he mumbled. "This could be the loose thread that unravels the sweater. All we have to do is start pulling."

Bernie Pearson, the history professor, acted as if they had found a gold mine. He waved his arms around the room. "Look at all the ledgers! There could be dozens of loose threads. Where should we start?"

The accountant in Dave took over. "The beginning is always the best place to start. Let's make two lines of tables. We can put the legitimate business ledgers in order on the left and the corresponding ledgers from the illegitimate businesses on the right. That way we can compare entries by date. Bernie, could you put your public record references up at the head of the table? And Darlene, could you make each of us a copy of Bernie's missing person list and Gary's list of possible suspects?"

"I can do that." Darlene appeared nearly as excited as the professor. "Can I get anybody something to drink? Coffee? Tea? Pop?"

Nearly everybody ordered coffee. Katie asked for tea with milk. Dave said, "This is going to be hard work. I'll need caffeine and energy. Bring me a Coca-Cola, please."

The ensuing work required tedious attention to details. Dave and Bernie cooperated as a perfect team, methodically putting together the financial history of McReady Enterprises with historical facts. These could be useful to authenticate the ledgers. The investigators scoured the ledgers connecting names to records of real people. Katie asked a lot of questions. Everybody appreciated her questions, which helped them to understand much of what Dave and Bernie said to each other.

Unraveling the legitimate ledger history up until 1917 took only a couple of hours. As the professor had predicted, the McReadys used many ruthless and unethical business practices that had not been illegal then. Bootlegging documented in the ledgers from the hidden room began in 1917. These records became more cryptic and ominous, but definitely represented illegalities.

—◆—

The men hardly noticed when Darlene distributed lunch menus from The Blue Ox. Grudgingly, each picked something out, hardly caring what they ordered. As Darlene prepared to go, Katie asked, "Mind if I tag along?"

Darlene looked surprised, but responded, "Uhhh, sure. I could use some help. Let's walk."

The day remained still and cold as Katie and Darlene walked down Main Street toward The Blue Ox. Darlene, more than a head taller than Katie, strode purposefully along on her long legs. Katie hurried to keep up. "What did you do in the navy?"

"I was an MP. Maybe law enforcement is in my blood."

Katie's only knowledge of MP work came from old movies where MPs broke up bar fights. "Wasn't that rough for a

225

woman? How did you handle drunken men fighting?"

Darlene touched her belt where a Taser rested. "We tazed them all first and then sorted them out afterwards," she spoke with relish. "But I mostly did office work, which involved logging and controlling evidence. The navy brings in lots of people; most are good, a few are not. The military police use most of the same rules of evidence as civilians. But when a ship came home from a long tour, we all did enforcement."

"And you have a daughter?"

"Yes, she's eight years old. Her father was an ordnance technician and got posted to a carrier in the Persian Gulf." Seeing Katie's confusion, Darlene explained his job. "He handled explosives. We had planned on getting married, but he got killed in an accident loading Tomcats for strikes in Iraq. He never saw his daughter."

Katie reached out and touched Darlene's arm to stop her and looked directly into her eyes. "I am so sorry."

Darlene squeezed her lips, sighed, and resumed walking. "Thanks. He's a hero just like any of the army guys who got killed fighting on the ground. My daughter means everything to me. I left the navy for her. My parents take care of her while I'm working."

Katie shook her head in appreciation of Darlene's commitment as they entered The Blue Ox. Ever-present Susie met them with her usual vigor. "And why are you two together? Are the police bothering this gentle southern lady?"

Darlene put on her official face. "Sorry, Mrs. Holmquist. I can't comment on an ongoing police investigation," she stated for all the customers in the restaurant to hear.

"Darlene, you get off of your high horse! I used to babysit

you. I've changed your diapers." Everybody heard that as well.

Darlene couldn't help but smile. "That's true, Susie. But I still can't tell you anything." She handed her the food order.

"Well, you two just sit here and relax while Betty fixes this up." Susie returned in a minute with tea and milk for Katie and a Dr. Pepper for Darlene. "Here's something to drink while you wait. Katie, did you know that Darlene played on the boys' hockey team in high school? She was a good defenseman and started every game." Susie pointed to the state championship picture that Dave and Katie had noticed on their first visit to The Blue Ox. There a teenaged Darlene held one side of a trophy.

They had been sitting in the booth quietly for a minute when Darlene commented, "That was really smart, you know."

"What do you mean?"

"You figuring out the disappearances."

"Well thank you, Darlene. Can I call you Darlene?"

"Yes, of course, except 'Officer' is better when I'm on patrol." Darlene hesitated. "You know, being on this research team is a big break for me. I'd like to become a detective. In the Navy, I assisted commissioned officers who did most of the real investigating. I always thought, *I can do that.*"

Susie and Betty came out of the kitchen with the boxed lunches. Darlene picked up four of the boxes, leaving two for Katie to carry. "You have the department's credit card number," she reminded Susie, who held the front door open for the women.

On the walk back to the station, Katie asked, "Is there anybody special in your life now?"

"Sort of. I've been seeing this guy who was the star of our hockey team. He played some minor-league pro hockey after high school but never got called up to the NHL. A girl from a rich family married him when he looked like a future pro athlete. When he never made the big leagues or much money, she divorced him and married a banker. They never had any kids. But he loves my Sofie. She comes on dates with us."

Katie surmised that Sofie was Darlene's eight-year-old daughter and started to comment when a KAAK TV van pulled up. Ramona and her cameraman emerged. With the camera recording, Ramona demanded, "Officer, is Mrs. Parker under investigation?"

Darlene bypassed the reporter without slowing her pace. "No comment."

Undeterred, Ramona stepped in front of Katie, blocking her path. "Why did the police search your residence?" When Katie didn't answer, she continued, "Is it true that your husband is being questioned at the police station?"

"Do you understand the term 'obstruction of justice'?" Darlene had turned and stepped to within a few inches of Ramona.

Instinctively, Ramona took a step backwards, clearing the way for Katie. As Darlene and Katie continued down the street, Ramona shouted after them, "I understand freedom of the press."

Chapter Twenty-Nine

———•———

Back at the council chambers, the ledgers totally absorbed the men. Cross referencing revealed actual crimes even per the legal statutes of that day. Several more names from Bernie's list of the missing or murdered had surfaced. The records documented payoffs to public officials. The law enforcement officers had started a file on each crime along with the suspects and victims. They photographed and documented the pertinent entries from the ledgers and historical sources provided by the professor and the University of Minnesota's online sources.

None of the men turned from their work as Katie and Darlene put down the lunches. After a throat clearing "A-hem," by Darlene didn't work, Katie took charge. "Gentlemen, you'll work better on something more than caffeine. Take a few minutes for lunch, please." Reluctantly, the men came. Darlene got the drinks each wanted. Once seated, they seemed hungry and glad for the break.

"What are you finding?" Katie wanted to know.

Gary answered between bites of his burger, "The extended McReady family was definitely involved in racketeering. There's proof of bootlegging, prostitution rings, and extortion after 1917. That's how they kept their lifestyle and subsidized legitimate businesses." He took another bite of burger, chewed, swallowed, then continued. "Linking specific crimes to individual family members is impossible, but the victims and the collaborating officials are named. My guess is that the McReadys documented that knowledge to be used later for intimidation or blackmail."

Katie opened her own box lunch. "Aren't the criminals all deceased now?"

"Yes, but we're establishing a pattern. Facts we discover can be useful in questioning others. Darlene, we need your help. Can you search the online records for these names?" Gary handed her a list and took his last bite.

Darlene first glanced at Katie and winked before responding, "Yes, sir." Taking her lunch along, she moved to one of the computers.

The afternoon brought more difficult, tedious work. Katie quietly took over the assistant activities for Darlene. Between fetching drinks, making copies, and other errands, she asked questions and examined everyone's work. When the DA came in, Katie explained each person's activity and showed the accumulating information. He noticed Darlene busy in front of a computer screen and nodded approvingly. As the DA lingered, Katie commented, "I expected police work to be more dramatic."

"You mean like on TV?" He chuckled, "No, the best police work is frequently mind-numbingly boring. It'll get more exciting though, when we start to bring in witnesses and establish probable cause for warrants."

After the DA left, Chief Oleson visited as well. Katie made the same explanations she had to the DA. The chief seemed well satisfied. Before the chief left, the gruff man went to each person working and whispered something encouraging. To Darlene, he also gave a little pat on the back. Leaving he asked, "Mrs. Parker, could I show you something?"

He led her to a TV in the police department break room. "We recorded this about an hour earlier." He inserted a disc. On the recording, Ramona introduced a clip, "Here is Katherine Parker apparently being escorted by a member of the Washita Police Department. Her husband is currently at the police station." The clip showed Darlene in uniform and Katie in her sleeveless blue jacket walking down Main Street carrying lunches. Darlene's words about "obstruction of justice" had been conveniently edited out of their exchange by Ramona. Katie's first reaction had her wondering what her friends in Mobile might think if they saw that clip. She just shook her head.

The camera returned to Ramona who went on, "Confidential sources have informed us that Mr. David Parker was recently forced out as a partner of an accounting firm in South Alabama. Members of the community are questioning why he relocated to Minnesota. Our investigation continues. This is Ramona Watkins reporting for KAAK."

"Katie," the chief continued, "I can make a public statement that you and Dave aren't suspected of any crime.

Or I can call the station manager and warn him about interfering with a police investigation. But the truth is that the media focusing on you as suspects is a good smokescreen for the true investigation. The real suspects won't be as prepared when we start to move on them."

"Dave and I are doing alright for now. If the allegations get too ridiculous we might ask for your intervention." She paused a few seconds. "What I'm wondering is why Ramona is so eager to blame us."

"That *is* a good question," the chief said under his breath.

—◆—

At 6:00 p.m., DA Christensen and Chief Oleson, carrying several large pizzas, interrupted the work. They pried the researchers away from the ledgers and joined them for dinner. Each person gave a brief progress report. DA Christensen said, "You're all doing a great job. But you look exhausted. Let's break for the night and start tomorrow. Dave, Bernie, could you please give us another couple of days?" Each of them readily agreed. As they filed out of the council chambers, the chief posted another uniformed officer at the door.

Driving back to the mansion, Katie told Dave about the KAAK clip and Chief Oleson's comments. "What would our friends back home think if they saw that? What would Jeremy think?" The couple looked at each other. The thought of Jeremy hearing about his parents being questioned was just too much. The couple broke out laughing.

"Do you think Jeremy's girlfriend might dump him?" Dave added, renewing their laughter.

"Let's send the clip to her and see," the jealous mother retorted. Dave had to pull the truck over rather than risk an accident due to their mirth.

The laughter didn't last long after arriving back at the mansion, though. They soon fell asleep in their exhaustion. Old Yeller tried to protest their lack of attention for him, but they were too tired to care. He curled up between them and joined their sleep.

—•—

On Thursday morning Dave and Katie met the others at the council chambers at 8:00 a.m. Katie had brought her laptop and joined Darlene doing research online. Chief Oleson sent another officer to collect their lunches. During lunchtime, Katie found Darlene sitting beside her. They chatted about their experiences, men, and mostly the challenges of raising kids. Darlene showed intense interest in Katie's experience raising a boy. Katie guessed that she hoped to have more children.

As the team continued studying the records, the stack of files documenting crimes grew. The investigators steadily added names to lists of the collaborators and victims. In 1942, America geared up for WWII. The paper mill ran at maximum production making supplies for the military. Every one of McReady Enterprises' public businesses, which had done poorly during the Depression, made plenty of money. The bookmaking operation trailed off until activity stopped late in that year. The DA's research team theorized that the hidden room at Big River had been sealed off in late

1942, but preserved in case it was ever needed again. The six researchers broke for the day when they reached the final pages of the ledgers discovered in the hidden room.

On Friday, the DA's investigation team restarted their research where they had stopped the day before. Bernie speculated, "America was the only industrial power undamaged by the war. McReady Enterprises could easily make a lot of money legally in the late forties and fifties. I'll bet that the generation born after the war never knew about the hidden room and its contents."

But the records showed labor issues about safety and pay starting in the late 1940s. Even though she had identified the likely murder of Sam Johnson, Katie could hardly believe the blatant way the ledgers documented ruthless labor suppression. The names of ruffians who had been debt collectors in the 1930s reappeared as strikebreakers in the late 1940s. Fortunately, the latest records from the post-war years documented a few people who still lived or had been known by some still living. Darlene helped to make connections to those who could be interviewed.

Dave summed up what he had learned from the Historical Society about the demise of McReady Enterprises and added some context. "In the 1960s, major financial setbacks, legal fees, and a lot of extended family to support drained the wealth of McReady Enterprises. By then the paper mill could no longer compete with mills in the American South. McReady Enterprises filed for bankruptcy in 1983 and was dissolved to pay creditors. The new owners apparently stored the ledgers nobody wanted anymore in Big River's carriage house until we discovered them."

Darlene had also found public records revealing individual McReadys selling off personal assets such as houses on Riverfront Drive after the bankruptcy. "Apparently, these resources had soon been exhausted. Still the McReady clan continued to thrive in a disorganized fashion, albeit in humbler circumstances," she explained. "Fear in the community enabled many McReadys to continue nefarious activities on a lower scale, especially selling drugs. There have also been rumors of protection rackets and prostitution rings. DA Christensen's grandfather was a likely victim. Break-ins and burglary have been increasingly common."

"Significant convictions have been nearly impossible to achieve," Gary admitted. "Any witnesses recant their stories or disappear. Evidence is supposedly misplaced. Judges dismiss cases due to what they call 'inadequate police documentation.' I think we're just scratching the surface of Washita's corruption problem."

Relying on public and police records, the research team assembled files on a new generation of McReadys, possible victims, and collaborators. Darlene, having grown up in Washita, helped by adding personal details and explaining who was related to whom.

By Friday afternoon, everybody was exhausted. But a tremendous amount of background information had been documented. Real crimes had been uncovered. Linking them to living individuals with sufficient evidence would take a lot more work. DA Christensen and Chief Oleson came in to thank everybody. The DA asked Dave and Katie if they could remain in Washita for a while in case the investigation needed their consultation. They assured him that they would.

Chapter Thirty

———•———

That weekend Dave and Katie enjoyed doing a lot of nothing. They watched the NFL division championships, the final two games leading to the Super Bowl. The couple also played with Old Yeller and took walks into the country on the rail trail. Winter still dominated Minnesota. But the weather, unlike the blizzard and accompanying severe cold, remained mild by Minnesota standards. They called Jeremy and told him a little about their recent experiences. When asked about Denyse, Jeremy responded, "She's doing fine," but provided no other details.

Typical of a male, Katie thought.

For a change, Katie brought out a deck of playing cards. In front of a warm fire, she and Dave played poker for M&Ms. Katie could gradually clean him out every time. She could tell by watching him whether he had a good hand or bad hand. Trying to bluff resulted in disaster for him. Dave, like many men, didn't like losing consistently, so he eventually lost interest in the game. Instead he drove Katie to the grocery where he purchased the ingredients for a big pot of chili. While Dave made the chili, Katie made cornbread. They relaxed all weekend and the following Monday.

⏤◆⏤

On Tuesday afternoon, Katie prepared to host the marriage group. All the couples returned. Nearly everybody had read the chapter on communication. Beth, the wife of Rick Larson, whispered to Katie, "Rick has read the whole book. He seems different." Katie winked at her. Ellie also whispered to Katie, "John took me out on a date Friday night." Katie squeezed her hand.

The discussion stimulated all. Several of the couples shared humorous examples of instances where poor communication had caused conflict. Leslie and Lyle entertained the group by playacting a misunderstanding they had experienced the previous year. Everybody laughed and envisioned themselves in similar situations. Dave and Katie didn't mind that they could hardly get a word into the discussion. A couple of times someone from the group asked John what God's perspective might be about an issue. He answered succinctly with wisdom, without lecturing. Everyone showed disappointment when Dave drew the discussion to a conclusion. They all enjoyed the dessert Katie had prepared, chocolate mousse with raspberry sauce.

Several more uneventful days passed. Dave and Katie took a few day trips to nearby towns. They didn't want to risk running into Ramona. Eventually, without new public revelations, KAAK News lost interest. Another healthy snow, but not a blizzard, kept the Parkers mostly inside for a couple of days. Dave continued feeding the birds, deer, and apparently, a raccoon family as well. The marriage group met for another meaningful discussion the following week.

At times Dave and Katie talked and wondered about the police investigation. But mostly they just enjoyed the peace. A ringing phone interrupted that peace one morning. "Dave, this is Richard Christensen down at the DA's office. How are you and Katie doing?"

"We're getting some rest. Thanks."

"That's good. The reason I called was that the ballistics report from the state crime lab has finally come back on the bullets removed from your walls. The suspects used three assault rifles. One of them fired 7.62 mm bullets from a gun like an AK-47, probably on full automatic. The other two guns fired 5.56 mms. Those could have been semiautomatic AR-15s. Rifling marks have linked one of the AR-15s to an unidentified body found in the river by police in Dubuque, Iowa, last summer."

Dave spoke without thinking, "You think somebody from Iowa shot up the house?"

"That's possible. But more probable is that someone killed the victim near Washita. The body could have been dumped in the river and then floated downstream. I'm just reporting the results of the ballistics report and warning you to be extra careful." The DA paused before continuing, "Dave, we're starting to act on some of the information you helped us gather. Would you and Katie like to observe some police interviews? You'd be in a different room watching by closed-circuit TV. Nobody would see you. But you might notice something relevant."

"You would let us do that?" Dave felt surprised and thrilled at the same time.

"I have your confidentiality agreement. Hell, you're ad hoc members of the police department now. The officers will resume tomorrow morning at about 8:30, if you want to show up. If you don't, that's okay. You've already done plenty."

Dave thanked him and hung up to find Katie bursting with curiosity about the call. He told her about the bullets. "What does full automatic mean?" she wanted to know.

"That means the gun can fire a full clip, maybe sixty bullets, in a few seconds like a machine gun by holding down the trigger. The semi-automatics fire one shot with every trigger pull, about twenty shots in ten seconds." Then Dave told her about the DA's invitation and ended with, "What do you think?"

She swallowed hard. "I've always wanted to see how they actually do that." Katie bit her lip in thought. "Let's do it."

The next morning a little after 8:00 a.m., the Parkers presented themselves at the police department. The receptionist looked at their ID badges and made an internal call. Darlene came out to meet them. She shook their hands warmly and guided them to a sound-proofed observation booth. The interview room could be seen and heard on a large screen connected to a closed-circuit TV. Darlene had furnished the room where she had shown Dave and Katie the photo array with some comfortable chairs and a lamp. The atmosphere seemed less sterile, almost homey.

Darlene sat down beside them. "I'll be following the interview with you."

A few minutes later, the door opened to the room they watched on the screen. Detective Gary Hobson ushered in a middle-aged man. Darlene explained, "We do a lot of interviews in the field. But when they're willing, we encourage them to voluntarily come into the station. In here, we can video them. Once we arrest someone, that becomes an interrogation. Most suspects arrested ask for a lawyer. We can usually learn a lot more when we can conduct a nice, friendly interview. I also like the in-house interviews because I don't have to write such a long report."

Detective Hobson began, "Mr. Benet, I'm telling you clearly that you're not under suspicion of any crime. We're just trying to understand some things that may have happened even before you were born. Nevertheless, because this is a police station I must read you your rights. We once found an opossum raiding a trash can and read it the Miranda rights." Gary forced a laugh out loud. Mr. Benet made a feeble attempt to laugh with him at the poor joke. Gary then read the rights, "You have a right to remain silent, anything you say . . . " Afterwards the detective started reciting some of the history they had documented in Washita without revealing the names of any current suspects. Occasionally, he would ask, "Do you know anything about that?" Mr. Benet consistently indicated that he didn't.

"Gary is building credibility that the police department already knows a lot. He's also making Mr. Benet eager to cooperate," Darlene explained. "Gary looks like he's meandering, but he's actually following a script we wrote from the information you helped us to collect."

The interview went on for another thirty minutes with Gary doing most of the talking. Then Gary said, "Mr. Benet, we have found something else that is troubling. This old ledger we discovered seems to indicate that your grandfather, the judge, took bribes in 1953." He pulled out one of the ledgers and pointed to the judge's name alongside a list of payments. "Would you know anything about that?"

"Now watch this," Darlene whispered to the Parkers. "Mr. Benet may attempt to divert attention from his family by implicating somebody else."

Gary's question flabbergasted Mr. Benet and caught him off guard. He assured Gary that his grandfather would never have taken bribes. Gary gently demanded, "Then how can you account for his name here?"

"My grandfather was completely honest," Mr. Benet insisted. "And that was years ago anyway. But I can tell you about someone who is taking bribes now."

Both Dave and Katie looked at Darlene with admiration. She raised her arms in a touchdown signal.

"And who would that be?" Gary asked.

"Steve Collins bragged down at the Midnight Lounge that an undercover cop arrested him for dealing meth. He gave the cop all the money he had, about $3,000. The cop took the cash and told him to beat it."

"And you heard Steve say that himself?"

Mr. Benet nodded his head. "I sure did."

Gary couldn't help but glance at the camera where the others watched. He recorded whatever details Mr. Benet could remember, including others who had heard Steve's words.

Darlene grinned widely. "Steve's mother was a McReady. He considers himself part of the clan. That's enough for a warrant for meth. The warrant needs to be specific based on probable cause. A warrant can't be a vague, 'We think he did something wrong.' If we catch Steve with meth or if some of the others present confirm Mr. Benet's story, we can likely plea bargain Steve to roll over on the cop. Then we can get a warrant for the cop's financial records and we could be in business. The cop might give us bigger fish. Giving or taking a bribe is plenty to use leaning on them." To Katie's puzzled expression she added, " 'Leaning on' means pressuring them to implicate others of even more serious crimes."

A different voice startled Dave and Katie. "Eventually, we'll work our way up to the most serious crimes. This could take years. But we'll get there." DA Christensen had quietly slipped into the back and stood behind them watching. "Stay in here until Mr. Benet is gone. He doesn't know you, but he doesn't need to see you either."

Gary thanked Mr. Benet and ushered him back outside. In a few minutes, Gary opened the door to where the observers waited. DA Christensen held up his hand for a high five.

"Nice work! You're up next, Darlene. Mrs. Sara McReady Lancaster is in the lobby." The DA returned to his office.

Darlene left her chair to Gary. After she had left, Gary explained, "We're talking to the people who aren't suspected of crimes first. Since they probably aren't guilty of anything serious, they're more likely to talk. We don't want to spook the worst offenders by letting them know that we're after them."

In a minute, Darlene brought in a heavyset woman in her seventies. They sat down. Darlene offered her a cup of coffee. Mrs. Lancaster declined and said, "I remember you. You're the girl who played hockey." Darlene thanked her for remembering.

Then Darlene went through the same routine Gary had used previously. She even told the same lame joke about the opossum before reading Mrs. Lancaster her rights. Darlene began by asking about the woman's current life, children, and grandchildren. She bridged into the woman's upbringing by talking about the history of the mansion. "You grew up at Big River as part of the McReady family, didn't you?" Mrs. Lancaster's father had been one of the McReady grandsons. She had grown up at Big River and regretted that the family had lost the estate. Darlene recorded that Mrs. Lancaster had lived at Big River from 1941 until 1959.

Darlene asked seemingly innocuous questions about the mansion and the family. In a playful tone, the policewoman asked, "Were there any secret rooms in such a big place?" Mrs. Lancaster didn't know of any, but wished there had been some. Darlene didn't show her disappointment.

Darlene shared more of the history of the mansion and brought up the basement. "I never went down there," Mrs. Lancaster insisted. "I was afraid of spiders and rats."

"The basement would have been a good place to hide, when there might be danger."

"What sort of danger?"

Darlene spoke with a confidential tone and made a sympathetic facial expression. "Well, I heard that after the war some people down at the mill threatened trouble."

"Oh, you mean the strikers. Horrible people! Communists! I heard my father say that they would be taken care of shortly. Soon after that, the strike ended. My father died in 1991."

Darlene feigned a sympathetic expression. "Did anybody else talk about the strikers being, 'taken care of'?"

Mrs. Lancaster enjoyed chatting about the old days. "My older brother Fred was a teenager then. He swore the striker situation would be fixed and offered to help. Our father told him that they would take care of the problem together. Fred is still alive. You should ask him."

Then Darlene couldn't help but glance at the camera where the others observed. "Is there anybody else who might have overheard this?"

Mrs. Lancaster thought carefully for a minute. "We had this black housekeeper. Annie was her name. She might have heard them talking."

Chapter Thirty-One

After a few more polite questions, Darlene thanked Mrs. Lancaster and guided her out. Inside the observation room, Gary was jubilant. "Two for two already! Today's information could give us a dozen new leads. We'd never convict Fred McReady on her testimony, even if she would testify, which is unlikely. But we're finding out where to look." Katie surprised herself by speaking up. "Mrs. Lancaster seemed to genuinely regret that the mansion didn't have any secret rooms. That fits Professor Bernie's theory about the next generation not knowing. Otherwise they would have cleaned out that evidence before selling the mansion."

She didn't notice everybody looking at her in admiration of her ability to put things together. Katie thought out loud without realizing, "It would be interesting to ask that housekeeper about who else might have known about the situation with the strikers. I wonder if Fred has a son of his own?" She didn't see Gary making notes of her thoughts.

The third interview that day proved uninformative—
that is, uninformative for the police department. The process
fascinated Dave and Katie. They had truly learned a lot.

—◆—

Darlene received a summons to Detective Gary Hobson's
office. "A couple of patrolmen asked the men Mr. Benet
mentioned about Steve Collins' bragging. One of them had
a grudge against Steve over some woman. He confirmed
Steve talking about being caught dealing meth and paying
off the cop. That and Mr. Benet's recorded words gave us
enough for a drug warrant for Steve Collins' residence and
vehicle." Gary pushed the document across his desk toward
her. "Would you execute this? I'm covered up."

Darlene suppressed an internal cheer and answered
professionally. "I can do that. Who should I take along?"

"We're pretty thin right now. Chief Oleson gave me Pete
Thomas. He'll mostly be your backup and provide security.
You'll conduct the search."

Patrolman Thomas drove the squad car to the small
house where a tip reported Steve to be living. A poorly kept
woman opened the door in response to Darlene's knock.
Shown the warrant and faced with a formidable female in
police uniform, the woman stepped back. Darlene entered
the overheated house. Smells of tobacco and alcohol
dominated. She noticed the woman make a furtive sideways
glance at a decrepit couch.

"Are there any illegal drugs on the premise?" Darlene asked.

"Absolutely not! I promise there are no drugs here." The woman made a cross sign over her heart.

Darlene crossed the living room to the couch, bent down, and felt underneath. Her hands quickly found a canvas tote bag. The woman gasped as the bag appeared. *Easiest search ever*, Darlene thought.

She held the bag in front of the woman. "What's in here?" The woman remained silent.

Darlene unzipped the bag and inside she found maybe 300 doses of meth. "That's not mine," the woman insisted even before Darlene revealed the contents. "I didn't even know it was there."

"Then how do you know this isn't lollipops?" Darlene stared at her. "Where's Steve Collins?" The woman pointed toward a closed bedroom door.

"Pete, I need you in here," Darlene called Patrolman Thomas, who had waited outside. Without speaking, Darlene showed him the meth and then gestured toward the closed bedroom door. Both officers drew their handguns. Stepping close to the door, Darlene motioned Pete to flank her. She opened the door quickly and pointed inside.

There on a filthy looking bed a male lay asleep. "Sir, you need to wake up," Darlene ordered. She received no response. Darlene moved closer and shook the inert form. A slight stirring with a few muttered words followed.

"Ma'am, is this Steve Collins?" Darlene called back to

the woman. Without waiting for a response, she continued. "What's wrong with him?"

"He's just drunk."

"Drugs?"

"Liquor is all."

"Cuff him, Pete." She proceeded to read the inert man his rights.

Pete cuffed the man and called for an ambulance to circumvent any possible police liability regarding an inert man. Darlene rejoined the woman in the living room. "Are you Steve's wife?"

"Girlfriend."

"Turn around. You're under arrest."

"What for?"

"For lying to the police about the drugs for one thing. We also have the matter of the drugs themselves." Darlene cuffed her and read the rights for her.

—◆—

Two days later a sober Steve Collins sat in the interrogation room at the police station. Next to him sat a tired-looking public defender. "He's your bust, now you can follow through," Gary had said. Darlene entered the room and sat opposite the pair.

"Steve, we have maybe twenty thousand dollars' worth of drugs found at your house." She didn't mention the $8,000 in cash she had located after the paramedics had taken Steve away. That had legally become police property by civil asset forfeiture.

Steve shrugged. "That's my girlfriend's house. She must have been selling drugs. I was just visiting."

"But that's not the worst," Darlene continued. Steve looked a bit more interested. "We have an eyewitness accusing you of bribing a public official."

"I've never bribed anyone."

"Okay, stick to your story." Darlene appeared unconcerned. "I'm going to have you sent away so long that your mother will forget who you are."

"Just a minute," interrupted the public defender. "What sort of deal are you offering?"

"I'll ask the DA for only thirty years without possibility of parole, if your client will confess to everything."

"That's nearly the maximum sentence. We want to talk to the DA ourselves."

"Suit yourselves." Darlene left the room.

In the observation room, DA Christensen and Detective Hobson watched. Darlene entered. "Nice work, Darlene. You set him up well."

"What are you willing to offer?" Gary asked the DA.

"We're not sure of a conviction for Steve on the drugs. More important, what I really want is the identity of the cop who is corrupting the system. I'd give Collins probation on everything if that became necessary to get the cop. But maybe we won't have to." The trio conferred quietly. The DA left Gary and Darlene with, "Let them stew for a while. I'll be back in a couple of hours."

Three hours later Darlene and the DA entered the interrogation room. "Sorry for keeping you waiting," the DA lied.

"Thanks for coming," the public defender began. "The police have kept us sitting here all day."

The DA gave Darlene a harsh look in front of the suspect and his lawyer. Then he sat down opposite Steve. "I'm willing to offer you fifteen to twenty on the drug charge and ten to fifteen on the bribery to serve consecutively with a possibility of parole." Darlene audibly sighed and showed distress. She looked darkly at DA Christensen. Without seeming to notice, he continued, "But we want Steve here to testify against the public official he bribed."

Steve broke in, "I'll be glad to testify against any stinking cop."

"Wait!" the public defender insisted. "That's not a much better deal than this woman offered." He waved toward Darlene.

"Listen, I'm really busy today and need to get to court. I'll do probation on the bribery charge if you'll agree to the fifteen to twenty," DA Christensen responded.

"Are you kidding me!" Darlene stood and glared at the DA. "Are they paying you off, too?" She stomped out and slammed the door behind her.

The DA remained in the interrogation room with Steve and his attorney. DA Christensen looked frustrated and even fearful. "The offer is withdrawn."

"You can't withdraw an offer," the public defender protested.

"Sure, I can. You hadn't accepted yet. Listen," the DA confided. "I have to work with these hard-nosed police and not just her. They won't respect me if I cave in to you."

Steve broke in, "I'll take the deal."

"I don't know. We've already got the drugs and the cop's confession naming you. That's enough to get both convictions and consecutive sentences. We don't have to have your testimony."

"I can give you a judge, too."

DA Christensen answered, "How can I be sure you have something credible?"

"What do you want us to do?" Steve's attorney asked.

"You'll have to prove that your information is legitimate by telling me the name of the cop and the judge. Then Steve will confess to drug dealing and testify to everything. I'll probably regret this, but you can still have the fifteen to twenty on the drug charge and probation for the bribery."

"The cop is a state policeman, Willie Frankel. I don't know the judge's full name. Something Baker. Willie makes the arrangements with a court clerk or somebody."

DA Christensen nodded, left them, and entered the observation room. Gary and Darlene laughed as the DA sat down. Gary slapped him on the back. "You're a wily one! And you were right. We got the cop, a confession, and a lead on a judge. You could be a detective, if lawyering ever goes sour for you."

"We did all right," the DA admitted. "Nice acting job, Darlene. I almost believed you myself."

—◆—

Steve Collins' confession started the first dominos falling. Arrested and confronted with a maximum-security prison with the roughest inmates, Willie Frankel revealed thirteen others who had given him bribes to hide evidence. He had arranged nine payoffs to Judge Baker through an intermediary. The DA settled with Frankel for ten to fifteen years in a minimum-security prison for a full confession and testimony. The judge soon followed and accepted disbarment, a $100,000 fine, and ten years of prison time.

Chapter Thirty-Two

One morning Katie took the pickup truck to do some shopping and have lunch with Leslie Rogers. She dropped Dave at the police station to help the authorities examine financial records that had been subpoenaed.

Katie found The Blue Ox almost empty after she finished her shopping. Susie brought her hot water with lemon.

Leslie arrived a few minutes later. She had left Elsie with a local church who sponsored a Mom's Day Out. Susie knew Leslie, as she knew almost everybody, and brought her coffee. Both women ordered salads.

Katie and Leslie chatted a few minutes until Leslie commented, "I heard the police have arrested Steve Collins."

Katie remembered Steve Collins' name from one of the interviews she and Dave had observed, but didn't say so. "Do you know Steve Collins?"

Leslie looked disgusted as she admitted, "Yeah, I used to know him and those McReady cousins, too. I was sort of a wild girl after high school. I spent some time out at the Midnight Lounge," she confessed. "A lot of lowlifes congregated out there. If anyone wants to find out what's really going on in this town, they need to poke around at the Midnight Lounge."

"What happened for you to change?"

"The hurt look in my mother's eyes when I would come in late smelling of beer and smoke. She and my father were good people. I decided to start fresh by going to the U of M in Minneapolis. I met Lyle there. He seemed like a boy scout. I didn't know men like him still existed. I watched the type of girls he liked, friendly and wholesome. Then I started acting that way to get his attention. I majored in theater at college, you know. Act a role long enough and it becomes you. Then I found that I liked the new Leslie. My mother did too."

Katie nodded as though she heard such stories every day.

Leslie continued, "After graduation, Lyle started to work for a landscaping company in Minneapolis. Then my mother's health declined. She wouldn't leave Washita, and my father is deceased. So Lyle brought me back here. I had been afraid that I'd lapse into the old Leslie. But so far, I haven't. Lyle is trying to start his own landscaping company now. How did you and Dave meet?" Leslie wanted to know.

"We met in a student group at Auburn University. He finally took the hint and asked me out. After that first date, we spent a lot of time together until Dave graduated. Then he returned to Mobile to start an accounting firm. Mobile is only three hours' drive from Auburn. He came to see me nearly every weekend. Two years later I graduated and we got married the following fall."

Dave's business interested Leslie since her husband was starting a business of his own. "What was being the wife of a business owner like?"

"Dave had started an accounting firm with two classmates. In the beginning, the trio survived mostly doing individual income tax returns. Dave's accounting career didn't make much money at first. I made more those early years as a public-school teacher. But we both remember those financially tough years with fondness.

"Gradually Dave's new firm developed and gained larger year-round accounts. As the accounts became more complex, Dave's talent for details and integrity gave the firm a good reputation and attracted dozens of major clients. His partners didn't have as much skill as Dave. But both are personable men and able to socialize well with their clients, usually on a golf course.

"After three decades in business, Dave's partners wanted to cash in on the firm's reputation by expanding with an army of young, inexperienced associates. They charged substantial hourly fees for each employee. Dave found himself cleaning up messes the associates had created in the complex accounts. Heated arguments between Dave and his two partners led to them buying him out with a hundred-mile non-compete clause. He feels a bit lost now without the business he spent most of his life building."

"How about children? Don't you have a son?"

"We both wanted children, but conceiving didn't come easily for us. Jeremy didn't arrive until we had been married nearly twelve years. He changed everything. That's when I left teaching to be a full-time mom. I loved it. Dave's firm made enough money by then so that I no longer needed to work."

⟶◆⟶

At the police station, Dave studied newly subpoenaed financial documents. In those records, he found suspicious money exchanges. For example, a $10,000 cash withdrawal from a bank followed by a $10,000 deposit by a public official a few days later indicated possible bribery. In other cases, bank checks or large credit card expenditures listed the recipients. Dozens of individuals appeared to be connected in dubious transactions.

"One name seems to appear and reappear in the records," Dave reported to Gary, whom he found working at his desk. "Somebody called Clyde McReady receives a lot of payments and makes disbursements for what are called 'services.' "

Gary already knew a lot about Clyde. "That's Fred McReady's son. He owns a dive of a nightclub called the Midnight Lounge on a side road off Highway 61. There are a lot of fights out there, usually involving the three McReady cousins."

Dave elaborated, "That *dive* appears to average a profit of nearly $240,000 a month. Some of my accounting clients in Mobile made less money with the most popular restaurants in our area."

"Bars are always great covers for money laundering. It's hard to prove what goes on inside."

"And that's only the profit reflected in the records. If the nightclub is the hub of some illegal activities, the cash exchanges could far exceed what is documented."

258

"I doubt if we can get a search warrant based on this." Gary started tapping at his computer, which connected him to the database of outstanding warrants. "But look at this. We're in luck. Clyde has several outstanding traffic violations."

Gary and Dave went to the chief's office with their suspicions about Clyde. "Pick him up," the chief ordered.

In two hours, a patrol car returned to the police station with Clyde McReady manacled. Unlike the rough McReady cousins, Clyde appeared about Dave's age, well spoken, and dressed as a successful businessman. Without wasting time on the opossum baloney, Gary started to read him his legal rights. Clyde interrupted, "I want my lawyer!"

Gary finished the rights and asked, "Do you have a particular lawyer in mind?"

Clyde did.

An hour later, a grim attorney appeared. He had been phoned by a barmaid at The Midnight Lounge. As legally required, the Washita police gave them a private place to confer. The lawyer emerged demanding, "We want to talk to the DA."

The chief summoned DA Christensen. The DA and Detective Hobson met with Clyde McReady and his attorney in the interrogation room, which had been stripped of Darlene's home-like accessories. The chief, Darlene, Dave, and several others watching through the closed-circuit TV crowded the observation room. Katie arrived at the last minute and squeezed in next to Dave.

"Let's cut through the bullshit," the attorney began.

"We all know that you didn't bring my client in for some stinking traffic tickets." Clyde sat showing an alert yet wary expression.

DA Christensen shrugged in a non-committal manner. Then he baited the attorney, "Your client has been involved in some serious affairs. We're putting together a solid case. Looks like a life sentence without parole to me."

"What evidence have you got?" the attorney demanded.

Calmly the DA answered, "We have a speeding ticket, two red light violations, twelve unpaid parking citations, and a burnt-out tail light."

"You said my client had been involved in 'serious affairs.' "

"What makes you think we're not serious about traffic safety?"

"I said cut the bullshit." The attorney's voice had risen. "You're required to tell us what you have."

DA Christensen stared eye-to-eye at the attorney until his legal opponent looked away. "No. We're required to tell the judge at arraignment. Then it's too late for you to get the most favorable deal from me."

Clyde's attorney leaned over to whisper to his client. Clyde nodded and resumed his alert posture. He and his attorney had apparently already agreed to an offer during their earlier meeting.

"You'll give full immunity to my client, federal witness protection, and he takes with him all of the money in his possession."

The DA laughed. "That's quite a lot to ask on some traffic tickets. Maybe you should tell us what we'll be giving immunity from."

"Do you think I'm stupid?" The attorney struck the table with his fist.

DA Christensen rose and started to leave.

"Hold it. Hold it." The attorney gestured for the DA to remain seated. "Okay, I'm speaking hypothetically. You can't use anything I say."

DA Christensen nodded. "Okay, let's imagine."

"Suppose my client had handled various financial transactions for others? Some of them might have been conducting criminal enterprises."

"What sort of criminal enterprises?"

Clyde's attorney took a deep breath. "Maybe drugs, prostitution trafficking, fencing stolen goods, and possibly some influential incentives to business associates. My client could tell you who and what."

"What sort of incentives?"

"Maybe money. Maybe a little muscle."

"Does 'muscle' include murders?"

Then the attorney shrugged with non-commitment.

DA Christensen suddenly appeared friendlier. "We already have a lot of this about Mr. McReady. But here's what we'll do; you post bail on the traffic tickets and I'll talk to the Feds. Your client stays in town and keeps his mouth shut."

Clyde and his attorney appeared relieved.

—◆—

Afterwards DA Christensen pulled everyone who had observed the meeting with Clyde and his attorney into the police's shift meeting room. "These guys were eager to make a deal. They're scared by our investigation. I think we could be closer to breaking this situation open than any of us realized."

"Why did you release Clyde on bail?" Darlene asked.

"All we really have to tell a judge right now is the traffic violations. We couldn't hold him. Thinking about immunity may help keep him from leaving town."

Katie's curiosity overcame her reticence to speak up. "Would you really give Clyde immunity?"

The DA shook his head. "All I said was that I would talk to the Feds. After talking to me, the Feds will give a big 'No!' to any immunity or witness protection. In the meantime, we need to look for a loosely organized criminal network that connects at The Midnight Lounge. Clyde McReady probably serves as a cash bank and takes a cut of transactions he facilitates through his nightclub. He may have arranged any number of brutal intimidations, including murder. Guys like the McReady cousins, who probably shot up Big River's sunrooms and hang out at the nightclub, serve as contract enforcers. Don't worry. None of the worst offenders are getting any immunity from me."

Dave thought, *Richard does have a streak of mischief in him. I'm glad he's on the right side.*

Chapter Thirty-Three

———•—

After that meeting, DA Christensen started making phone calls. The state police sent three special agents to aid the investigations. Federal authorities sent an IRS investigator to consider tax evasion. An FBI agent came to consider racketeering. The DA's office started to file charges against individuals involved in the lesser crimes. Plea bargains and rollovers by peripheral suspects who wanted to avoid prosecution started to implicate more serious criminals. Several merchants came forward to reveal protection rackets that had plagued the town for decades. Clyde waited in town, expecting eventual immunity.

Ramona at KAAK downplayed the charges and arrests of anyone from the McReady family. The community itself became sharply divided. "Let sleeping dogs lie," many said. Other locals felt chagrined when the records tarnished their forefathers' reputations. One individual interviewed by Ramona asked, "What does it matter what happened so many years ago?"

Then in an interview by a Minneapolis TV station, Mrs. Johnson demanded, "I want the authorities to get to the bottom of this. My husband's disappearance was just part of the crime of that time. I believe the same crime continues in this community today. It's time we stopped looking the other way."

Other voices in the community supported her. Susie Holmquist stretched a banner with the words "Support Our Police" across the storefront of The Blue Ox. Some regular customers started to avoid the restaurant. The process of justice in Washita followed the old saying, "There is no action without a reaction." As the investigation widened, many in the community reacted. Some began a petition calling for a recall election. They wanted to remove DA Christensen from office. Others pressured the mayor and city council to fire Chief Oleson.

━◆━

An unusual notice caught Pastor John Foster's attention as he returned from visiting some shut-in parishioners. Posted on a town bulletin board where pet owners sought lost cats or dogs, the notice pictured an old brick. The caption stated, "Brick Found! Will the owner please claim their property in person at The Blue Ox?"

John's curiosity forced him to detour and stop at The Blue Ox. There he saw cardboard and tape covering a broken front window.

Inside the restaurant, Susie greeted him. "Hi John. Will Ellie be joining you?"

"No. I'm not here to eat today. I, umm, saw your lost-and-found advertisement."

"Is that your brick?" Susie teased him and pointed. She had cleared a shelf and posted a sign announcing, "Lost and Found Department." The brick pictured on the notice sat below the sign.

"No, Susie, that isn't my brick. Do you have any idea who could have thrown it?"

"There are plenty of candidates in Washita, I'm afraid. I'm going to leave it there and the window un-repaired for a while. I won't be intimidated by criminals."

Back at his study, John sat at his desk considering his weekly sermon. Susie's words and mute testimony of defiance tormented him. He understood the division and conflict in the community. *What is my responsibility as a pastor?* he pondered. *Is it my responsibility to keep the peace at all cost? Or, is it my responsibility to stand up for what I know is right? Pastor means Shepherd. Who exactly are my sheep? Just those in my congregation?* Privately he conceded, *The congregation pays the bills. Or*, he asked himself, *is the community my flock?*

On Sunday morning, Pastor John stood before his congregation. Fear had knotted his stomach; it wasn't a fear for safety, but fear of rejection. He began by quoting from the Bible, "Psalm eighty-two verse four tells us, 'Rescue the weak and the needy; deliver them from the hand of the wicked.' "

The congregation sat in anticipation. Where would their pastor go with this?

John continued by detailing some of the challenges the community currently experienced. He added, "I believe that most Christians lead lives of ordinary goodness. But a few times in our lives, God may ask us to do an extraordinary act of faith in standing up for our fellow man. When that happens, we should consider it a privilege and grasp it. I believe that this is one of those times. Our community is facing a crisis. I'm going to support the police efforts to end the reign of criminal activity and intimidation in Washita. I challenge you to join me. Please prayerfully consider how you should respond."

Pastor John sat down.

Members of the audience looked around. Was the sermon over? None of them had ever heard a shorter one.

After a closing hymn, some members of the congregation clustered around John giving encouragement; Richard and Lisa Christensen stood among them along with Susie. Other parishioners stomped out of the church. Slamming car doors announced their departures.

As the divisions in the community deepened, those known to be supporting the DA received thinly veiled threats. Sometimes cryptic and typewritten notes arrived by mail. Calls came from pre-paid and untraceable phones. Notes and phone calls weren't the only threats. Non-verbal threats such as the scratch on Dave and Katie's truck or punctured car tires became common. Dead animals appeared in strategic places. Someone dumped a dog shot through the head in front of the gates at Big River. The investigation had polarized the community between those who wanted justice and those who preferred to maintain the status quo.

John Foster received an anonymous call instructing him to "stick to church business." The caller mentioned the names of John's wife Ellie and each of their children. In response, the Fosters asked Ellie's parents to come to Washita, collect their children, and care for them at their home in Des Moines. Ellie chose to remain in Washita with John. The following Sunday, John began a series of sermons about the importance of standing up to injustice. Some members of his congregation didn't appreciate that emphasis and started avoiding Sunday services. Others had rallied to the outspoken pastor. Speaking invitations came to John from many groups in Washita, including several churches of other denominations.

A TV reporter asked John, "Is this part of your faith?"

John answered, "People use the word 'faith' differently. Sometimes I see a report when a tornado or other threat endangered lives. Almost invariably someone says, 'We put our faith in God.' I'm always glad that when faced with danger, people's thoughts turn to God. But in most cases, what choice did they have? I believe a greater faith is facing danger on behalf of others when you have a choice not to."

—◆—

The Tuesday night marriage group at Dave and Katie's started with tension that week. John and Ellie attended, albeit subdued by missing their children. Nobody had to ask why.

"John, everybody in town is talking about the sermon you preached on Sunday," Leslie said. "We didn't hear it, but Lyle and I admire you. Everybody needs to stand up for what they know is right. This town is a cesspool of wrong. All of us need to stand up for justice. The McReadys and that Midnight Lounge are in the middle of everything."

⸺◆⸺

The following afternoon, Leslie considered herself in the full-length mirror. Her figure wasn't as tight as it had been before having a baby. Still, she knew that men often looked her way. Moreover, she felt confident in her ability to act.

"Mom, I'm bringing Elsie over for a while. Would you watch her just until Lyle picks her up?" Leslie asked over the phone. She knew Lyle would be home from work soon. Leslie jotted down a note for Lyle, grabbed her car keys, and headed for the door carrying Elsie.

A half hour later she pulled into the gravel parking lot of the Midnight Lounge as the sun set. Using the rearview mirror, Leslie applied red lipstick, unhooked the top two buttons of her sweater and took off her wedding ring.

She had forgotten how hot and stuffy the interior felt in winter. The smoke and smells of sour alcohol made the air thick. "I'll have a draft beer," she told the bartender and took a stool.

She didn't need to wait long. A seedy, unshaven man sat down beside her. "You must be new here," he slurred.

"No, I've been here a lot. How about you?"

"I come here occasionally," her bar companion answered.

Leslie hadn't forgotten how to flirt. Added to that, her acting skills had taught her how to appear sultry. She accepted a second beer and asked, "What sort of work do you do?"

"A little of this, and a little of that," he answered evasively.

Suddenly two additional men appeared beside her. At a head gesture from one of them, her previous companion quickly picked up his drink and moved away.

"Well if it isn't Leslie." Bogus and Lars McReady sat down on the stools on either side of her. "We haven't seen you in here for a while. Where's your *husband?*"

I've hit the mother lode, Leslie thought. *This pair is surely part of all the rot involved with this place.*

"Sometimes a girl needs to unwind a little alone. How have you boys been doing?"

Getting them to brag about themselves wasn't difficult. *I can't believe I was once attracted to such immature pigs,* she thought.

"You guys making any money?"

Bogus pulled out a roll of $100 bills. "Yeah, we're flush. We're always flush."

"Then you can pay for my next drink." Lars signaled the barkeeper who brought whisky, not beer, for all three.

At a nearby table, Leslie noticed their older cousin Jud sitting with a woman who looked familiar. But Leslie couldn't place her. "Where do you get so much money?"

"You could call us contractors."

Bogus unexpectedly tipped over his drink onto the bar, stood up, and swore. Leslie turned to see what had happened. During the distraction, Lars poured something into Leslie's drink

"Drink up, girl. Let's see if you can still hold your liquor," Lars said as she turned back.

Lars and Bogus started telling Leslie about all sorts of supposedly successful money-making schemes. *They're lying. But if I keep them talking they'll eventually reveal something*, she thought and sipped her drink.

Leslie started to feel a little silly and surprisingly sleepy. "Drink a little more," Bogus said and held her glass to her lips.

As Leslie became more woozy and weak, she heard Lars lean near and say, "Did you think this act would work on us, girlie?"

Chapter Thirty-Four

---•---

Dave answered the mansion's phone. Lyle spoke with concern, "Do you know where Leslie is?"

"No, she isn't here."

"She left a note saying Elsie would be with her mother. Leslie's mom doesn't have any idea where she went. This isn't like her."

"Katie's in the shower right now. I'll ask her in a few minutes and call you if she has any ideas."

"Thanks."

In a few minutes, Katie came to stand by the fire as she dried her hair. Dave told her about the call. "That is unusual," Katie commented. "Where could she have gone?"

"I couldn't even begin to guess."

"Leslie has been upset about the community crisis. She also thinks the Midnight Lounge is the hub of all the trouble."

Dave seemed doubtful. "You don't think she would be foolish enough to go out there?"

"Maybe. Leslie is a bit impulsive, and she's confident in her ability to act. Maybe a little too confident."

"There's no need to call Lyle with speculation. Let's go and see." Neither one of the Parkers wasted any time getting to their pickup.

—◈—

Two men supporting an inebriated woman showed up in Dave's truck's headlights when he pulled into the Midnight Lounge's parking lot.

"That's Leslie!" Katie recognized her by her curly red hair. The men guided Leslie toward the jacked-up pickup Dave remembered from their gas station encounter.

"Stay in the truck and call 911. I mean it this time." Dave got out and left the keys in the ignition. Katie made the 911 call and one other.

Dave approached Bogus and Lars. "Stop. Where do you think you're going with that woman?"

"None of your business!"

"That's Leslie Rogers. Let her go."

"She said she wanted to go with us."

"Leslie," Dave spoke to her, "what are you doing here?"

From Leslie's mouth came a mumbling noise.

"There, I told you," said Bogus. "She wants to go with us. You heard her say so too, didn't you Lars?"

"Yep." The two men continued toward their truck.

Dave stepped ahead of them. "You're going nowhere with her." Dave kept his arms at his sides to prevent any appearance that he had started a fight.

Lars opened his coat to show a holstered handgun. "Who's going to stop us? *You?*"

Dave remained in front of them and stood blocking them from their pickup. The pair let Leslie collapse to the cold ground. Both McReadys approached Dave and looked at his face. "I remember you! You're that redneck yokel."

Behind him Dave heard the pickup start. Katie moved the truck closer and started to rev the engine. She aimed it at Bogus' big truck as if readying to ram. She started to lay on the horn with repeated blowing.

A few curious spectators emerged from the Midnight Lounge to watch the scene.

Lars moved so close to Dave that their chests touched. He started pushing Dave backwards with his bulk and the strength of his legs. Bogus moved around them to protect his truck from Katie.

"Beat it, you ignorant hick. She wants to go with us." Lars sneered into Dave's face and put his hand on the holstered gun.

"You're not taking her anywhere," Dave repeated and kept his arms down even though he couldn't help being pushed backwards by Lars.

A brief siren burst drew everybody's attention. Chief Oleson's unmarked car pulled into the parking lot. "You two separate," the chief ordered as he got out.

"Chief, this is Leslie Rogers, a friend of ours. These two are trying to take her." Dave spoke quickly.

Lars had closed his coat to conceal the handgun. "She agreed to go with us."

The chief walked to Leslie's mumbling form. "This woman isn't in shape to legally agree to anything."

Another car pulled into the parking lot. Katie's second call had been to Pastor Foster. John and Ellie left their car and hurried to Leslie.

Chief Oleson spoke to John, "Chaplain Foster, as a member of the police department, would you take custody of this woman until she is coherent and able to speak for herself?"

"Yes, certainly." Already Ellie urged Leslie to get to her feet. She and John helped Leslie stumble to their car.

"Go home right now, Mr. Parker," the chief said to Dave. He and Katie immediately and happily complied.

Chief Oleson said nothing to Lars and Bogus. He only stared at them until they returned to the Midnight Lounge.

On their drive back to Big River, Katie phoned Lyle with the barest of details and concluded, "Leslie is safe spending the night with Pastor John and Ellie. She's okay. But she won't be home until tomorrow."

Lyle wanted to see Leslie. "Should I go over there?"

"No, she's sleeping right now. Please just wait until tomorrow." Katie concluded the call, "Call me if you need any help with Elsie."

⊷⊶

"Ellie said that you rescued me. Thanks." Leslie spoke on the phone with Katie. "Would you be willing to come and drive me home? John said that he would, but I'd feel better with you."

"Of course we'll come. You're still at the Fosters', right?"

Leslie confirmed that.

"We'll be right over," Katie promised.

A little while later Dave parked the truck in front of the parsonage where John and Ellie lived. Inside he and Katie met Leslie, who still suffered from a massive headache. Ellie nursed her with coffee and soothing words.

Leslie gave a feeble smile to the Parkers. "I guess you think I'm the dumbest woman in Minnesota."

Katie gave her a gentle hug. "We think you tried to do a good thing."

Riding in the truck, Leslie told the whole story. "I didn't drink that much. They had to have put something in my glass." She repeated Lars' ominous words as the last thing she could remember and concluded, "I wanted to do something heroic."

Dave spoke kindly and yet firmly, "Leslie, you're a mother now. You can't afford to be heroic except for your family. Once you become a parent, your responsibility to your family outweighs everything else."

"That's what you told Lyle at the gas station, wasn't it?"

"Pretty close," Dave affirmed.

Leslie closed her eyes and groaned, "What is Lyle going to say?"

"We talked to him last night and early this morning. Rather than leading him to think you did something wrong, we told him that you tried to do something brave. He'll probably be relieved to see you, then be mad. You scared him badly. Take his anger as a sign he loves you," Katie answered. "And you'll need to tell him you made a mistake and ask him to forgive you. Promise him that you'll never do anything like that again."

"Okay," Leslie said through her headache.

"Leslie, how did you get to the Midnight Lounge?" Dave asked.

"I drove our car." Leslie then felt around. "I still have the keys in my pocket."

Dave turned toward the Midnight Lounge. "Why don't we just alleviate that problem by swinging by to get it." In the early morning, the parking lot remained empty except for a late model sedan.

Leslie pointed, "That's it. I can drive my car home."

"No, I'll drive your car. Katie will drive you in the truck."

"Thanks." Leslie slumped back in her seat before she sat back up temporarily. "I remember something else. I saw that TV reporter, Ramona something, with Jud McReady at the Midnight Lounge."

—◆—

Dave and Katie delivered Leslie and the car to her home. Lyle acted relieved and nurturing as Katie had expected. She knew that more serious discussions between the couple would follow in private.

As they drove back to Big River, Katie spoke to Dave, "Did you hear what you said to Leslie? You told her that responsibility is more important than heroics."

"I believe that's true."

"Well then, can you remember complaining about your years of being responsible to take care of Jeremy and me rather than having accomplished something more *heroic?*"

Dave drove in silence. Finally, he spoke, "I hate it when

you're right. But I love you more for it."

"I love you for being a responsible husband and father. And I respect you for admitting when you're wrong."

—◆—

The following Saturday morning dawned gray and overcast. The dismal day and discouraging circumstances even affected normally irrepressible Katie. Old Yeller had enough cat-sense to feel the couple's despondency. He disappeared into an unknown destination. "I feel an idea coming on," Katie remarked during their somber breakfast.

"With you, an idea is always coming on."

She ignored her husband's jest. "What we need is a party."

"I don't know where to find one."

"Then we'll have to organize one!" Katie spoke with determination. Thus committed, her creativity started taking over. "Isn't tomorrow the Super Bowl?"

That reminder perked up Dave a little. He had been looking forward to the Super Bowl. "Who would we invite?"

"How about your ice fishing buddies?"

"That could work. We could use the big flat-screen TV upstairs."

"We could make jambalaya, New Orleans style. That would be different for these Minnesotans."

Dave dialed Frank Pederson. The senior man enthusiastically responded, "I haven't been to a Super Bowl party in years. Shall we include the wives?" Dave heard Helen's voice expressing an opinion in the background.

Then Frank answered his own question, "I guess we will."

Frank promised to call the others. An hour later, Dave answered the ringing phone. "They're all in, and the wives as well," Frank reported. "Even John is coming. Ellie is visiting their kids in Des Moines."

By then, Katie had a list of supplies. Nothing energized her more than planning a party. Dave drove the truck to the grocery store. There Katie selected the sausage, rice, shrimp, garlic, tomatoes, and other ingredients needed for jambalaya. Dave picked out chips, dips, beer, soft drinks, and a surprise for their guests.

On Sunday morning, Dave and Katie attended services at John's church. Although not of his denomination, they felt like supporting his courage. Then Katie rushed Dave home to start party preparations. All afternoon she happily cooked and prepared for the party. Her decorations reflected the Mardi Gras tradition which had started in Mobile, not New Orleans, as most people thought. Their guests arrived an hour before kickoff. All of them wanted to see the damage done during the drive-by shooting.

Frank and Ed paused in front of the painting of the girl and her horse. Ed spoke with certainty, "That is Mary Johnson when she was a girl. I'm sure it is." Katie told the men Maureen Swanson had said the painting had come with the mansion.

Chapter Thirty-Five

The women raved about Katie's hors d'oeuvres. The men tried them but preferred the chips, dips, and beer. Everybody gathered upstairs in front of the Swansons' big flat screen TV before the kickoff. The men speculated on the strengths of the respective teams. A team from the South would play a team from the North. Dave took a lot of jibbing about southern football. "Did y'all know that we play Dixie before the games instead of the Star-Spangled Banner?" he responded. The northerners took a few seconds to realize Dave had kidded them.

Old Yeller showed up to pester everyone and sniff at the snacks. At the end of the first quarter, the wives brought steaming bowls from the kitchen. Katie set a basket of warm biscuits by the chips and dip. The spicy jambalaya momentarily distracted the men from the game.

During half-time, Dave disappeared to prepare the special treat he had purchased. Before the second half kickoff, he appeared with a basket of golden fried fish filets. Everybody tried them and marveled at their light taste and firm texture. "The key is to dry the fillets with a paper towel before lightly flouring them. That way they retain almost no oil," he explained.

The crunchy fillets had disappeared quickly when Frank asked, "What are these? Cod? Pollock? Tilapia?"

Dave spoke slowly for maximum effect. "These . . . are . . . catfish."

The northerners froze. Nancy wrinkled her nose. "Aren't they dirty bottom feeders?"

Dave assured their guests that the fillets had come from farm-grown catfish that had been fed pellets made mostly of soybeans. "But even the wild catfish prefer clean water and live food." Remembering their conversation about catfish while ice fishing, the men shook their heads in amazement.

During the second half, the wives turned on the game downstairs in the guest quarters and mostly talked about other things. The game ended with excitement when the northern team managed a fourth quarter touchdown drive to win the championship.

After the game, everybody thanked Dave and Katie. Ed had enjoyed too many beers and submitted to being driven home by Nancy. Frank and Helen lingered until the last. Frank got a little emotional. "You two are really special to us. Could we take a picture of you?"

"Certainly. Where do you want us to stand?"

"Right here in the kitchen will be fine."

Dave put his arm around Katie as they smiled for Frank to snap a photo on Helen's cell phone. The picture turned out well and was admired by all four. Then Katie took a picture of Frank and Helen before they too went home.

⚊◆⚊

For the next several weeks, the legal process ground forward. DA Christensen and Chief Oleson relentlessly sought justice despite opposition as the community remained polarized. Gradually a pattern of current-day crime and corruption became clear. Jud, Bogus, and Lars McReady's names came up repeatedly and could be linked to dozens of crimes. Still, they had covered their tracks well. Even search warrants based on specific tips had failed to produce hard evidence.

One morning Katie picked up the ringing phone. "Mrs. Parker?" A deep female voice spoke.

"Yes, I'm Katie Parker."

"This is Officer Darlene Clark down at the police station."

"Oh yes. Hi, Darlene. Do you want Dave?"

"No ma'am, I called to talk with you. I've located Annie."

"Annie?"

"Do you remember my interview with Mrs. Lancaster? She told us that Annie was a house servant of the McReadys at Big River back in the 1940s and 50s." With that reminder, Katie did remember. Darlene continued, "Annie Jordan is living in a nursing home in Rochester now. I'm going up there tomorrow morning to talk to her. Would you come along to help?"

"I'd be glad to go. I'm not sure how I could help, though."

"Well, I thought you might be good at talking to her."

281

"You mean because she's probably rather old?"

Darlene seemed bashful. "Yeah, partly. Mostly, I just think she'll trust you more. She'll see that you're nice. I can be scary to some people."

"Okay. Can I suggest something then? We'll probably do better if you're not wearing a police uniform and a gun."

Darlene laughed in agreement. "I can do that. Can I pick you up at 8:00 tomorrow morning?"

Katie promised to be ready and gave her Big River's gate entry code.

Promptly at 8:00, the doorbell rang. Katie opened the door to find Darlene smartly dressed in a pants suit with her blond hair in a waist-length pony tail. A patrol car stood in the driveway. Katie took the passenger seat. She noticed Darlene's police belt with a holstered pistol mostly covered by a blanket in the back seat. On the way to Rochester, Darlene explained how she had located Annie. A pay record for an Annie Jordan had been in one of the ledgers. Voter registration records had confirmed Annie Jordan with an address in a former lower-income neighborhood of Washita. After that, a lot of inquiries and computer searches had eventually placed Annie at the nursing home in Rochester.

Katie and Darlene chatted about all sorts of things on the drive. In addition to talking about her daughter, Darlene expressed interest in relationships. Katie asked about her former hockey teammate and suitor. Darlene would only admit, "He keeps hanging around."

In Rochester, Katie asked Darlene to stop at a florist where she purchased a vase of cut flowers for Mrs. Jordan.

Pulling into the nursing home parking lot, Darlene prepped Katie. "I called ahead. She'll be expecting visitors, but she doesn't know the reason for our visit."

Inside the nursing home, an attendant guided Darlene and Katie to a visiting room. The same attendant came back pushing a wheelchair. In the chair, a tiny and wrinkled African American woman sat covered with a knit blanket. The woman looked alertly at them with curiosity. They sat in silence for a moment. Darlene gestured with her head for Katie to proceed.

Katie started by offering the flowers and introducing herself and Darlene. Using her friendliest voice, she began to ask Annie a few questions beginning with, "How old are you?"

"Ninety-seven years old."

"You are doing well. Are you from Minnesota originally?"

"I came with my husband from Arkansas." Annie went on to explain that she and her husband moved in the late Depression looking for jobs. They had been sharecroppers displaced when the land owners started using tractors.

Katie listened intently, leaning forward to better hear Annie's soft voice. "Do you have children?"

"Nine, five still living, twenty-three grandchildren, eighteen great grandchildren, so far." The elderly lady enjoyed talking about her family.

Katie gently changed the subject. "Mrs. Jordan, we have some questions about when you worked as a housekeeper in Washita."

Annie looked amused. "I wondered when you'd get to the reason you had come to see an old woman. You and the police lady here." She tilted her head toward Darlene, who gave Katie an I-told-you-so look.

Katie reached out and clasped Annie's hand, then pleaded earnestly, "You could really help us, Mrs. Jordan. Do you remember working for a family named McReady at a mansion called 'Big River'?"

"Of course I do. They were a bad bunch. But my husband and I had kids to feed and we both needed jobs."

Darlene gently interrupted, "Mrs. Jordan, would you mind if I recorded this, please?" Annie didn't mind. Darlene started a small recorder and set it on a table beside her.

Katie continued, "Mrs. Jordan, did the McReadys ever talk about their businesses around you?"

"Sure did. Servants were just like furniture to them. They thought black people were dumb. I just did my job and let them think I *was* dumb."

"Do you remember them talking about or doing things that weren't . . . quite right? Things that might have been wrong?"

"Seems like everything they did was wrong to me." Then the elderly lady continued talking without hesitation. With only occasional prompting from Katie, she revealed a litany of McReady offenses. She unburdened years of stifled outrage at McReady corruption and abuses. Her harshest words concerned the thuggery used to squelch the mill employees in the late forties. Her husband had worked there as a laborer.

"Do you ever remember hearing any of these names?" Katie read the names of the men who had disappeared during those times.

"I only remember Sam Johnson. My husband spoke well of him. When some tools went missing at the mill, somebody accused my husband. Mr. Johnson spoke up and told the boss about the white man who had taken them. That didn't happen much back then."

Katie could hardly restrain her eagerness now. "Can you remember the McReadys ever talking about Sam Johnson?"

"They hated him. Called him a Communist. One night he came to the mansion. I let him in and took him to meet one of the McReady brothers and his teenage son, Fred. Mr. Johnson acted like he had never been in such a big house. I saw them take Sam into the basement to talk. That's where they did their 'private' business. Later that night, I saw them watching another man loading a heavy sack into a truck. I never saw Mr. Johnson leave."

"Are you saying they might have killed him?"

"I know they did!" The old woman was adamant. "When the McReadys came upstairs alone, I heard Fred say, 'That'll take care of him.' The next day a woman came to the mansion looking for Mr. Johnson. She said she was his wife. I felt sorry for her. But there was nothing I could do."

Katie could hardly breathe. "Mrs. Jordan. Did you ever tell anybody else about this?"

Mrs. Jordan became defiant. "Tell who? Everybody knew the chief of police had been picked by the McReady family and was in their pocket. And who'd ever have believed a poor black woman compared to those rich white folks? I had my kids to think about."

"Do you think anybody else knew about what happened to Sam Johnson?"

Annie thought carefully. "There was this boy who ran errands for the McReadys. He must have been about ten or eleven at the time. I saw Fred give him a note and tell him to take it to Mr. Johnson. A couple of hours later Mr. Johnson came to the mansion. The boy's name was Ed Williams. I remember, because a few years later the newspaper used to print his picture as a baseball player."

The elderly lady had become emotionally drained and tired. The nursing home attendant came to return her to her room. Katie could not speak, even to say goodbye. Darlene thanked Mrs. Jordan for both of them.

Back in the patrol car Darlene could not restrain her joy. "That is the first direct link we've found to the disappearance of Sam Johnson! And she gave us a lot of inside information." Then noticing Katie's silence, she asked, "What's the matter, Katie?"

Katie turned to look at Darlene. "Ed and Nancy Williams are friends of ours."

Chapter Thirty-Six

———•◦•———

"Darlene will be interviewing Ed Williams today, if you'd be willing to observe," Detective Hobson spoke on the phone, inviting the Parkers to the station. "Darlene mentioned that you are a friend of his. We completely understand if you aren't willing. But we think you might be able to fill in some missing pieces."

Reluctantly, Dave and Katie agreed to attend. They felt awkward like intruders watching on the screen as Darlene ushered their friend into the interview room. "This doesn't feel the same as when they interviewed strangers," Katie whispered to Dave. Detective Hobson observed with the Parkers. DA Christensen and Chief Oleson slipped in behind them.

Darlene started with the usual rigmarole about reading the opossum its rights. Once Ed had been given his rights, Darlene proceeded with the history of the McReady family and the discoveries at the mansion, the same as she had done for others. With a lot of practice, she had become quite eloquent telling the story. Ed had heard the gist of the story from Dave that day ice fishing. Darlene led up to the disappearance of Sam Johnson. Ed had also heard this. He became uneasy when she brought up the mansion's housekeeper, Annie. "I don't remember her," he stated.

"Well, Mr. Williams, she remembers you." Darlene played back a segment of the recording she had made of Annie Jordan talking about Sam Johnson and mentioning Ed.

Ed sat stunned. He took a deep breath while Darlene simply waited. His voice quivered, "I don't know why she would say that. I never went to the Big River mansion."

"Mr. Williams, we checked the records. You played as a standout shortstop for the Washita All Stars. That confirms her memory of you. Then we found this photo in the Historical Society's archives." The photo showed the McReady family in the late 1940s posed in front of the mansion. To the side, a boy stood watching. "Isn't this you leaning against the tree?"

Then Ed started to physically shake. Detective Hobson leaned forward in anticipation. Ed rubbed his face with his hands. "It was just me and my mother. My father was killed at Iwo Jima. Mom worked so hard to take care of my sister and me. Bringing in a little extra money made a big difference. She felt so proud of me. The McReadys gave me ten dollars some weeks just for running errands for them." The old man started to sob.

Katie started crying in sympathy for their friend. She looked up at Dave. Tears had also appeared on his cheeks. Darlene sat professionally quiet for five full minutes as Ed tried to compose himself. "Do you know what happened to Sam Johnson?" she softly prompted.

"The youngest grandson, Fred, gave me a note to deliver to Sam. I read the note on the way to find Sam. They asked him to come alone to the mansion. Sam had been a friend of my father's and knew me. I swear that I didn't know what they planned to do. He went into the mansion and never came out. I know because I waited outside all night. In the morning, Mrs. Johnson came to the mansion looking for her husband. They chased her away. I wanted to die myself then. I never worked for the McReadys again. A few days later Fred found me and told me terrible things they would do to my mother if I ever told anyone." Ed was sobbing again.

Detective Hobson leaned back to speak to DA Christensen. "We have him for lying to police and accessory to murder. There's no statute of limitations to murder, even if he was just a kid."

DA Christensen gave an audible sigh. Looking toward Dave and Katie he answered, "We're not going to prosecute the victims. But we are going to be as tough as necessary to learn what we need about the worst criminals." He stood and spoke quietly to Chief Oleson. Together the DA and chief opened the door to the observation room and walked around to the interrogation room. Ed visibly cringed as they entered. They both stood towering above him.

The DA spoke sternly, "Mr. Williams, I'm District Attorney Christensen. Do you know who this is?" He indicated the chief. Ed nodded that he did. "You need to tell us everything, and I mean *every . . . single . . . thing* you know. Then if your story checks out and you'll agree to testify, I'll give you immunity from prosecution for cooperating with the McReadys and lying to the police. Do you understand me?" Ed nodded again. DA Christensen leaned over and spoke more gently to the older man, "This will be okay, Mr. Williams. Just tell us the whole truth." The DA and the chief each affirmed Darlene's work with a nearly imperceptible nod to her as they departed.

Darlene discovered that she was holding her breath. She exhaled and started to breathe again. "Mr. Williams, before we continue, would you like to use the restroom? Could I get you something to drink? Coffee? Pop? Water?" Ed did need to use the facilities and asked for a Coca-Cola. She had a male colleague escort Ed to the men's room. Afterwards, the colleague waited with Ed in the interview room while Darlene consulted with detective Hobson. Then she reentered the interview room with a cold Coke for Ed. "Now please tell us all you can remember starting from when you first met the McReadys."

The DA had said "everything," so Ed complied, with only occasional questions from Darlene. Ninety-nine percent of what he said was irrelevant, hearsay, or related to those long dead. He did fill in a few details useful to the history, but probably not helpful in a court. After the murder of Sam Johnson and subsequent threat by Fred, Ed had stayed away from the family for decades. But then the next generation, Jud, Bogus, and Lars McReady, had somehow learned about his involvement in Sam Johnson's death. Most likely Fred had told them. They had started to periodically press him for information about members of the community and threatened to expose his past unless he cooperated.

Ed never revealed much of importance until the Parkers came to town. Somebody had tipped off the McReadys about Katie and Dave's snooping around and asking questions. From Ed, they learned about the Parkers' initial discussion with the Historical Society. The threatening phone calls to the Parkers and garbage in the Big River driveway followed. Later, Jud, Bogus, and Lars had all shown up at Ed's house with pictures of his grandchildren copied from school yearbooks. They demanded that Ed keep them informed. Ed had felt compelled to phone them after the conversations about the ledgers out ice fishing. In the McReadys' minds, this confirmed the Parkers as their primary threat. That happened just before the drive-by shooting.

After several hours of talking, Ed was drained of emotion and exhausted. "Mr. Williams, you are not under arrest," Darlene emphasized. "But we would like you to stay here overnight for your own protection while we review your story." She made her words sound like an invitation. Ed would have agreed to anything at that point. A uniformed officer led him away.

Darlene felt drained as well. She returned to the observation room. "I need to phone Mr. Williams' wife to tell her where he is."

"Could I do that?" Katie offered. "She knows me. Plus, I can reassure her." Darlene looked at Detective Hobson, who nodded his head. Katie used a police phone to call Nancy. Katie assured her friend that Ed was helping the police and not under arrest. "Ed will be home tomorrow," she promised.

"That was quite a day," Gary concluded as he prepared to go home to his own wife and kids. "I can't hate someone who tries to protect his family. Maybe I'd have done the same thing as Ed."

The tension of the interview completely exhausted Katie and Dave, even though they had done little but observe. Neither wanted to discuss Ed's role or victimization. They went back to the mansion and ate canned soup for supper without much conversation.

—◆—

The Parkers' phone rang the next morning. This time Chief Oleson called. "Mr. Parker, last night DA Christensen reviewed the tapes from yesterday's interview. He's asking the court for arrest warrants for Jud, Bogus, and Lars McReady on extortion and attempted murder for the drive-by shooting at Big River. Fred McReady is being indicted for the murder of Sam Johnson. I'm putting every officer available into finding them before they flee the jurisdiction. We'll arrest Clyde McReady as well and charge him as an accessory to a list of charges. I can put some men at Big River for your protection. But that would mean fewer men on the search. We just don't have enough officers to do everything right now."

Dave responded, "By all means arrest them before they get away. We have a security system here. We can call 911, and I have a double-barreled shotgun. We'll be all right."

"If you're sure, I'll put the officers on the hunt. The last thing is that we're releasing Ed Williams this morning. He's asking for you."

Dave promised the chief to come right down.

━━◆◆◆━━

Ed waited in the conference room the police used for shift meetings. He seemed like a crushed man. "I'm in a lot of trouble," Ed started. "And I need to tell you something."

"What happened?" Dave asked.

"When I was a boy, I helped the McReadys." Ed proceeded to briefly tell them about his part in the death of Sam Johnson and the attack on the mansion. "The McReadys threatened my children and grandchildren. I phoned Jud about our conversation ice fishing that day. I caused the drive-by shooting at Big River." The Parkers listened without revealing that they had watched the interview.

"I'm so sorry," the old man choked out. "I'd give my life to change all that's happened. I'm so thankful that neither of you got hurt."

Dave responded, "Ed, none of us knows what we might have done under the circumstances you faced." Katie put her hand on Ed's shoulder. "Can we drive you home? Nancy will be worried."

"Not home yet. I need to see Mrs. Johnson first. Would you take me there, please?"

"Certainly."

The three found Mrs. Johnson home and at first delighted to see them. Then their demeanor told her that this would not be a social visit. Ed sat on the edge of a chair and told her about her husband and his own part in Sam's death. Ed reviewed seeing her come looking for Sam the day after. The old man started sobbing again. "I'm so sorry," he repeated over and over again.

Mrs. Johnson sat motionless, forcing herself to breathe. She whispered, "I knew. I knew," repeatedly. "They killed him. They killed my Sam."

Dave then spoke to tell her about the circumstances and the threats to Ed's mother. The elderly lady listened until Dave had finished. She sat quietly for a minute and then spoke directly to Ed, "You were a good boy to try helping your mother. I was a single mother with a son myself. My son, Danny, wanted to play baseball like you. I remember when you pitched batting practice to him after some of your games." She hesitated and blinked as she looked at the ceiling. She forced words out of her mouth, "If you hadn't taken that note to Sam, somebody else would have. Thank you for giving me closure after so many years."

"One more question, please, Mrs. Johnson," Dave begged. "The Swansons have a beautiful painting of a teenage girl and a horse at the mansion. Several people have mentioned that the girl looks like you. Is that possible?"

The old lady looked surprised. "For my thirteenth birthday my father painted a portrait of me standing with my horse. My horse's name was Penny. I loved riding her. Many years later Danny needed money for a science project. I had to sell the painting to a local antique store. He won second place in the regional competition for that science project. What a joy it would be to see that painting again."

"I've seen the painting," Ed volunteered. "I think the girl is you. It's like your father has been looking over you from that old mansion all these years waiting for you to find the truth."

Mrs. Johnson looked at the floor. "I need to be alone now for a while, please."

"Are you sure, Mrs. Johnson?" Katie protested. "I can stay with you."

"That's sweet, honey, but I have my cats. Tonight, I'll need to call my son. What we always knew in our hearts is true. Everybody will finally know. I need to be alone now," she repeated.

Back in the truck, Ed rode subdued. His long-held secret had been exposed. Dave and Katie drove him home. Nancy met them halfway between the truck and house. Her anxiety showed. Inside the house, Katie privately suggested to Nancy to not press Ed for an explanation until he felt ready to talk. Dave reassured her that Ed had cooperated with the police and faced no charges. Not knowing what else to do, Nancy started making Ed's favorite lunch while he sat and contemplated the photographs of his children and grandchildren.

Chapter Thirty-Seven

———•———

What a pleasant dream Dave enjoyed. He and Katie had become college students on a Saturday afternoon date. They fished on the bank of a bayou on a warm spring day. Largemouth bass swam back and forth waiting to be caught. Suddenly in the dream, something soft touched his face. His dream-self tried to see what had touched him, yet could not discern anything. He felt the soft touch again. What could it be? The third touch came, and with this touch came painful pinpricks. Dave woke to find the pain to be real. A fourth touch came to his wakened self. His skin felt a cat paw clenching to force claws lightly into his cheek.

Dave shook his head and pushed Old Yeller away. The cat crouched tensely with his tail burred up. *What's gotten into this animal?* The old oak floors above Dave creaked subtly— not the creak of the wind, but the unmistakable sound of intruders' footsteps. Dave sat up and looked out the window. Faint glimmers of flashlights from an upstairs window reflected on the snow outside. He placed his hand gently over Katie's mouth. "Katie, don't make a sound," he whispered.

Katie awakened with a start but sensed the urgency in her husband's voice and lay quietly. Dave uncovered her mouth. "I think somebody is upstairs."

"You mean another raccoon?" she whispered back.

"No, not this time. Don't turn on the light. Whoever is upstairs doesn't know where we are. Do you have your cell phone?"

"The phone is in the charger on the dresser." Dave silently slipped to the floor and groped underneath the bed in darkness. Katie heard the *click, thump, thump, click* as Dave loaded the shotgun. He slowly took two steps, retrieved the phone, and returned to the bedside. "Come down here," he ordered from the floor by the bed. She quietly slid beside her husband. Old Yeller followed her and crawled under the bed.

In the stillness, they could hear stealthy footsteps upstairs. Dave pushed the phone into her hands and continued to whisper. "Have your phone ready, but don't turn it on yet."

"Why not?"

"It gives off light. I don't want to reveal where we are." Dave and Katie tiptoed into the kitchen and hid behind the counter where pots, pans, and ceramic dishes had been stored. Old Yeller followed behind them and crouched under the table.

Then they could hear low voices and creaks from the old boards on the main staircase. The intruders came slowly down the stairs. Peering over the counter, Dave and Katie could see glimmers from flashlights coming through the open door to the formal dining room. Katie detected a faint odor of alcohol and tobacco smoke. "Now call 911," Dave told her aloud. Katie started to dial. Then Dave shouted to the intruders, "Go away! I have a gun."

The couple first heard whispers. Then a harsh male voice came back, "We just want to talk."

Suddenly, a tremendous blast echoed within the confined walls and nearly deafened Katie. Dave had fired the shotgun through the glass of a window as a warning. Old Yeller bolted out from under the table and streaked through the open door past the intruders into the basement.

"What was that?" a guttural voice wondered about the cat.

The 911 operator answered Katie's call. "What is your emergency?"

"Somebody is inside our house," Katie began aloud. A series of explosions obscured her next words. Wood chips flew off the paneling as the intruders fired bullets through the walls. The din of gun shots and settling debris paralyzed Dave and Katie. But without knowing how to aim their shots, the intruders spread them widely. The kitchen counter and its heavy contents blocked some bullets that probably would have hit the couple.

The shots paused. The 911 operator came back demanding, "What is your location?"

Katie spoke the address. Her ears rang so badly that she could hardly hear her own voice. But she did discern another male speaking from the formal dining room, "Do you think we got them?"

"Maybe not. I think I heard something," the harsh voice answered. "Reload."

Dave grabbed Katie's wrist and pulled her behind him out

of the kitchen and into the pantry. There he opened the door to the service stairway and pushed her up the stairs. The 911 operator continued repeating, "Stay on the line. Assistance is on the way." Katie shut off the phone to silence the operator's voice.

As they climbed the service stairway to the second floor, the gunfire erupted again. Firing through the walls, the intruders systematically raked every part of the guest quarters. Out of the line of fire, the roar of continuous gunshots was less deafening. Dave and Katie hid in a bedroom on the second floor. Dave still clutched Katie with one hand and the shotgun in his other hand. "Call 911 again."

Katie touched redial on the phone. "What is your emergency?" the 911 operator answered.

"Somebody is shooting at us!"

"Is this the call about the intruder again? Try to hide. Help is on the way."

Dave and Katie could hear their assailants moving into the downstairs guest quarters firing at every spot that might conceal a person.

—◆—

Downtown, Billy McReady sat in a police car on Main Street trying to stay awake. The dispatcher came on the police radio. "Intruders reported at Big River Mansion on Riverfront Drive. Gunfire has been reported. Wait for backup. Then proceed with extreme caution."

In just three minutes, Billy got to the Big River gate. He entered the gate code T-U-F-F-Y that Dave had given to the marriage group. "Wait for backup. Then proceed with caution," the dispatcher repeated.

Billy looked toward the mansion; yellow flashes of muzzle blasts could be seen through the windows along with a muted popping sound from within the house. He thought about the danger to his friends. Billy pulled out his police shotgun. "The gate code is T-U-F-F-Y," he reported to the dispatcher, then headed up the driveway on foot.

"Wait for backup. Then proceed with caution," the dispatcher ordered more tersely. Receiving no reply, the dispatcher bellowed, "Billy! Billy! Are you there?"

The mansion's front door remained locked. Only sporadic gunfire could be heard now. Billy broke the glass and let himself in. Someone started turning on lights inside. Billy heard an unfamiliar male voice from the direction of the guest quarters saying, "Where the hell are they?"

"I'll bet they went up these back stairs," a harsher voice answered.

Billy quietly passed through the dining room into the guest quarters. There he found three large males in dark clothing in the kitchen looking through the pantry at the service stairs. Each of them held an assault rifle.

"Police!" he shouted as loudly as he could. "Put down your weapons."

The figures turned and recognized Billy. "If that isn't little Billy," the oldest man said. "Billy, you know us. I'm Jud McReady. This is Bogus and there is Lars. We're your family. Blood sticks with blood. You're one of us."

"I am the police!" Billy shouted. "Put down your weapons." Aiming the shotgun from his shoulder, he moved it back and forth slightly, attempting to cover the three intruders.

At his words, all three men started to bring up their rifles. A load of buckshot from Billy's shotgun hit Lars square in the face. Before Billy could fire again, he felt blows to his arm, leg, and shoulder. His leg, shattered by a bullet, crumpled under him. Searing pain blocked his mind. Involuntarily his throat gave a guttural cry.

Jud and Bogus walked over to Billy's prostrate body. Jud kicked Billy's shotgun out of his hands. "He's killed Lars. Finish him off," Bogus urged.

"Billy, you should have stuck with your kin," Jud said, and pulled a pistol from a holster. He casually pointed the gun at Billy's head. Billy closed his eyes.

"Stop!" a loud, angry voice demanded. "Don't turn around!"

Jud, still holding the pistol, looked over his shoulder. He saw a late-middle-aged man in his underwear pointing a double-barreled shotgun at him. Behind the man a terrified-looking woman in pajamas stood holding a cell phone to her ear. Dave and Katie had come down the service stairs.

Quick as lightening, Jud spun completely around and brought up his pistol. Fear and anger made Dave's reflexes faster. Another tremendous explosion stunned Katie's ears. Dave had fired without hesitation before Jud could get off a shot. The pellets hit Jud in the upper chest and knocked him backwards to the floor. The pistol and an AK-47 fell out of his hands. He writhed on the floor, screaming in pain.

Having been forced to shoot a man, Dave felt rage. "You want me to shoot you, too?" Dave yelled at the remaining cousin. He pointed the shotgun directly at his face and stepped closer.

Bogus could hear Jud's screams. He dropped his rifle and held up both hands. "No! No! Don't shoot. Don't shoot. I give up."

"I swear that if you move a muscle, I'll kill you!"

Dave glanced around the room while keeping his shotgun pointed at Bogus. One man lay dead in a pool of blood. Jud held his chest and moaned. Blood seeped through his fingers. Billy wasn't moving or making any noise. He was either dead or passed out. Dave shouted viciously at Bogus, "Move back and put your hands against the wall. If you try anything, I will blow your face away." Bogus did as instructed. "Now keep your hands on the wall and move your feet back. I'll kill you right here, if you don't."

With Bogus leaning against the wall, Dave moved forward. He kicked the rifles dropped by the McReadys behind him and picked up Jud's handgun. Dave fired a shot from the handgun into the floor. "Don't shoot. Don't shoot," Bogus begged.

Dave spoke viciously, "I just wanted you to know that I have the safety off. Move a muscle and I'll kill you." Dave sidestepped over to Billy. His upper arm spurted blood in gushes. An artery had been hit. The pulsing blood showed that he still lived. "Katie, help Billy. Use a towel. Hurry!"

Katie stood frozen, shocked at the scene and the transformation of her husband into someone she had never known. She heard her name shouted again, "Katie!" She opened a drawer and pulled out a clean kitchen towel. Dave kept the handgun pointed alternately at Bogus and Jud and told her, "Press the towel as hard as you can against Billy's arm where he's bleeding, and hold it there."

Unfortunately, she had trouble positioning the towel to stop the flow. Blood made Billy's arm slippery. The hot blood sprayed all over her before she could get a secure hold by sitting on the floor and clutching Billy's arm with both hands. Immediately the blood loss slowed and only trickled through the towel. Sirens could be heard coming from town. She looked at Jud, who writhed and moaned on the floor.

"Did you have to shoot him?"

"He would have killed Billy *and us*. Keep the pressure on Billy's wound."

"My arms hurt. I can't keep holding." But she did not let up the pressure.

In a few minutes, another police officer entered the mansion. After a quick look around, the officer entered the guest quarters swinging a shotgun back and forth. Dave recognized Darlene. He laid the handgun on the floor and stretched both palms out empty before her. Darlene understood the situation immediately. "Pick up the gun, Mr. Parker, and guard that man," she gestured toward Jud on the floor. Lowering her shotgun, she reached for her belt, pulled out a Taser, and immediately tazed Bogus, who still leaned against the wall.

Dave had picked up the handgun and pointed it at Jud. "Why did you do that?" he asked.

Darlene grinned wickedly as she cuffed the stricken man. "He's big and strong. I'm a woman. Can't be too careful."

From Katie, unaccustomed to the adrenalin surging through her body, they heard, "Sounds good. Let him have it again."

Darlene responded with a hint of regret, "Sorry, I've already cuffed him."

Chapter Thirty-Eight

While Dave continued watching Jud, Darlene assisted Katie in helping Billy. Darlene spoke into her portable radio. "Officer down. Emergency help needed. Multiple injuries."

But the dispatcher had already called for ambulances and alerted more police. Sirens blared in the distance. In only a few minutes, two ambulances and another police car arrived in the driveway. The first paramedics took over care of Billy. "Looks like we got here in time. Are you the one who stopped the bleeding, ma'am?"

Katie only nodded.

Another paramedic asked, "Are you hurt ma'am?"

Katie looked down at herself. Blood drenched her. Even her hair was matted down. Blood partially obscured one of her eyes. She shook her head, "No, I don't think so." She looked at herself again and wanted to cry, but couldn't. Dave said something, but she couldn't understand him.

"Ma'am, you're in danger of going into shock. Let us take you in for observation. Please lie down here," the paramedic indicated a stretcher.

"How about you, sir?" A different paramedic spoke to Dave. He assured them that he had no injuries. The first ambulance screamed away with Billy. Katie lay down to be strapped onto the gurney. The paramedic put in an IV that she hardly felt. In a minute, she was on the way to the hospital with Dave sitting beside her.

Nurses cleaned up Katie at the hospital. An emergency room doctor looked her over and found no physical injuries. A nurse injected her with a strong sedative. Soon she slept in a warm bed in a double room. Dave felt physically and emotionally drained. He took a shower in Katie's bathroom and lay down on the other hospital bed. He lay there awake for the remainder of the night in case Katie needed him.

◄◄✦►►

Katie woke remembering a terrible nightmare. In the nightmare, somebody had been trying to kill her and Dave. She opened her eyes to unfamiliar surroundings. She seemed to be in a hospital room. A familiar female voice spoke, "Wake up, sleepyhead. Are you going to stay in bed all day?"

Katie turned her head and blinked. Susie stood beside the bed. "Where am I?" Katie asked. Then she added, "What happened?"

"You're in the hospital. They say you were quite a mess when they brought you in. And you saved Billy's life."

A nurse walked into the room. "Good morning! And how are we doing?" Without waiting for an answer, the nurse checked Katie's vital signs. "You look all right. The doctor will be here in a few minutes." The nurse departed.

Katie spoke with a groggy voice. "Where is Dave?"

Susie answered, "He laid in that bed while you slept. This morning Chief Oleson came and picked him up. Dave asked the police department to call me to come and sit with you. You had quite a traumatic experience last night."

Katie started to remember. The nightmare had been real.

A resident doctor came in and looked at her chart. He listened to her heart, shined a light in her eyes, and asked a few questions. "If you feel able, you can go home now. Or to a hotel. I understand that your home isn't habitable right now."

"She'll come home with me," Susie told the doctor.

"That's fine. You should rest for a day or two," he said and left the room.

Katie still felt groggy. "How did he know about our home?"

"Honey, everybody knows. The shooting is all over the news. And I don't mean just local." Susie turned on the TV. A national news network had picked up the story. They described a home invasion that resulted in a bloody shootout between a policeman and members of his extended family.

Katie saw a clip of Chief Oleson giving a brief interview in front of several microphones. "We received a 911 call of a home invasion at 1:21 a.m. Arrests have been made. One of our officers was shot in performance of his duty. He is out of surgery and in intensive care, but expected to recover. Civilians were killed or wounded. We need to notify the families before we release any names. That's all I can say now."

The same nurse hustled back into the room. "We'll just start getting you ready for discharge." She disconnected the IV and pressed on the insertion point to prevent bleeding. After a minute, she secured a bandage to Katie's arm. Then she cranked up the bed so that Katie came almost to a sitting position. "Spend as much time as you need here. You might even want to take a shower before you go. Your husband sent over some fresh clothes and a few bathroom items. Just from me, what you did was really brave." The nurse hurried away.

Katie lay still a few minutes and suddenly wanted to leave the hospital. With Susie's help, she swung her legs to the floor. Standing wasn't as easy as she had expected. Her hair and skin felt slightly sticky. "I think that I will take that shower." Susie held her arm until Katie could grab onto the support bar in the shower.

"I'm leaving the door open in case you need me. Take your time," Susie suggested.

The warm water felt comforting. Katie put her head in the stream and noticed that the water entering the drain looked slightly pink from dried blood washing out of her hair. Liberally using the soap dispenser, she washed her entire body. Afterwards she stood in the hot spray for a long time. *This must be why Dave takes such long showers*, she thought. *It feels great.*

When she emerged, Susie smiled. "You already look a lot better." Katie felt a lot better.

An orderly brought in a lunch tray. Katie had slept through her breakfast, which apparently Dave ate before he left. Susie insisted that she take time to eat something. "This food isn't from The Blue Ox, but it must do."

Meanwhile, at the mansion, Dave sat in a chair in the kitchen answering questions about the early morning confrontation. DA Christensen and Chief Oleson watched with a video camera running as he explained the couple's experience to Detective Hobson. Dave told about hearing footsteps upstairs, firing the warning shot out the window, fleeing upstairs by the service stairway, and then coming back downstairs. "We heard Billy and them talking. Then they exchanged shots. We had to come back downstairs. They were going to kill Billy because he had shot one of them."

"Yeah, we know," Gary answered softly. Then he reverted to his official tone. "Mr. Parker, with what gun did you shoot the other suspect?"

Dave pointed to the double-barreled shotgun still lying where he had dropped it. Gary spoke to the chief and DA, "That accounts for the bird shot." Then he resumed the questions. "Mr. Parker, why did you drop your shotgun and pick up the suspect's handgun?"

"The shotgun was empty. I used one barrel to shoot out the window as a warning and the other barrel on the man who started to shoot me."

"You bluffed the last intruder with an empty gun?"

"I had no choice." Dave hesitated. "Maybe it was a good thing that the shotgun was empty. I felt so angry I might have shot the last man without thinking."

Gary glanced at the chief and DA. "Did you fire the handgun, Mr. Parker?"

"Yes, I fired once into the floor. I wanted to make sure I

had the safety off and discourage the last guy from trying anything."

"What happened next?"

Dave described Katie helping Billy and the other officer arriving. "That was Darlene. We knew her from the research team. She knew what to do. She was terrific."

"I'm still here, Mr. Parker." Darlene had come into the room behind the chief and DA.

"How is the man I shot?" Dave asked.

Darlene answered without any compassion, "He'll live. But they'll have a lot of trouble picking out all of that bird shot."

"One last question, Mr. Parker," the DA interjected. "Did you leave a ladder outside leaning up against an upstairs window?" Dave shook his head. The DA spoke to the others, "That's how they avoided the security alarm." Then he spoke to Gary, "Okay, turn off the camera."

The DA moved closer to Dave. "Dave, I'm so sorry that you and Katie had to suffer through all this. You'll be glad to know that we've got plenty of evidence on the ringleaders now. You should go take care of Katie. The hospital called and said she's awake and approved for checkout."

"One other thing before you go," the chief added. "What should we do with your cat? He came out from hiding after a few hours. He had probably been in the coal bin by the looks of him. We locked him in a bedroom upstairs because he was underfoot."

—◆—

The interview being over, Dave walked back through the

shambles the mansion had become. Crime scene investigators worked everywhere. The body and wounded men had been removed. But three large pools of partially dried blood remained on the floor. Debris from the bullet impacts littered the entire guest quarters. Clearly, his and Katie's house-sitting days had ended. One of their suitcases had several bullet holes but remained serviceable. Dave collected his wallet, truck keys, their bathroom items, Katie's purse, shoes, and a few undamaged personal belongings. He added spare clothes to the suitcase for each of them. Dave then found one of the plastic storage containers that they had used on the trip from Mobile with only minor damage. He cut several air holes into the sides using a kitchen knife and took their old comforter off the bed to pad the bottom. Upstairs, loud meowing from within a third-floor bedroom easily revealed Old Yeller's prison. There he found the cat dirty with coal dust and not very pleased. He placed the cat into the container and securely fitted the lid on. This wasn't to the cat's liking either, but Dave didn't ask him his preference.

Dave showed the items he carried to Chief Oleson. The chief waved him on. To the container with renewed meowing inside, the chief held both thumbs up. Darlene came to carry the suitcase to Dave's pickup truck while he carried the contained cat. They stowed both in the covered truck bed.

Outside, Darlene showed plenty of compassion. "I hope Katie is okay."

Dave looked at Darlene. "She should be. I'm going back to the hospital now. Thanks for coming to rescue us."

"Just part of my job. But I'd have done the same anytime for you. You two are amazing."

Did the tough woman's eyes have a couple of tears? Darlene looked around to see if anyone would notice. When she saw that nobody watched, she gave Dave a big hug, very unprofessional for a crime scene, before hurrying away.

━━◆━━

Leaving Big River, Dave passed several news vans clustered around the gate. Uniformed police officers kept them away from the crime scene. Gawkers from the community mingled with them. Ramona mixed with the crowd, interviewing anybody she could. Dave felt tempted to stop and see if she wanted to interview Old Yeller.

At the hospital, Dave found Katie just finishing lunch with Susie fussing over her. "Hi, sweetheart. Ready to get out of here?"

Katie emphatically assured him that she was ready.

"I was taking her to my house," Susie offered.

"That's very generous, Susie. But, if you don't mind, I think we'll just go to a hotel. We'll need some time to be alone."

"Sure. I understand. The doctor told Katie to take things easy for a few days," Susie told Dave.

Katie rose to go. She felt stronger and eager to leave.

"No, you have to wait for a wheelchair. Hospital policy," Susie added.

While Susie and Katie waited for an orderly with a wheelchair, Dave provided their medical insurance cards to the hospital. He hadn't had his wallet the night before. Then he pulled the truck up to the front door to find Katie waiting in the wheelchair with Susie standing beside her. Katie stood up and gave Susie a sincere hug. Dave gave Susie a hug too and whispered, "Thank you."

Chapter Thirty-Nine

———•◦•———

Alone with Dave in the truck, Katie wanted to know what had happened at the mansion. Dave described the crime scene investigation and the dismal state of their guest quarters. Then Katie noticed the meowing coming from the back. "You've brought Old Yeller?"

"He was underfoot, and besides, he may have saved us." Dave explained the wake-up he had received from the cat.

"Stop this truck right now! He'll be cold back there." Dave pulled over. Katie jumped out and brought the cat in the container up to the warm truck cab. She placed the container on the front seat between them. "You can go now." Old Yeller still wasn't happy in the container. But he stopped meowing.

They went to a hotel on the bypass near Winona. Within the room, Old Yeller appeared content to be released from his prison. He stalked around with his tail erect, sniffing everything. Dave phoned the police station in Washita to report their location.

Dave and Katie sat on the hotel bed and talked for a couple of hours about all that had happened. Katie could not help but tell Dave, "You surprised me back at the mansion."

"I just did what had to be done."

Katie razzing her husband showed the beginning of a recovery. "You mean like the snowshoe hare changing his color when he needs to?"

Dave smiled. "Maybe so."

Afterwards they each felt relieved. Katie decided that they needed some supper. Leaving Old Yeller locked in the bathroom, they went to a grocery store on the bypass. Each picked out some comfort food to eat back in the room. For the cat who saved them, Katie purchased several cans of tuna and a litter pan. Back at the hotel, the three of them enjoyed their respective dinners and then went to sleep all cuddled together.

―◆―

The hotel provided a convenient breakfast including hot water for tea the next morning. The headline of a courtesy newspaper read, "Heroic policeman out of intensive care." The front page featured a photo of Billy.

"I'm sure that we'll want to read this someday," Dave speculated and picked up a paper. Katie symbolically covered her eyes.

In their room, Dave suggested, "We might as well get this over with," and turned on the news.

A national TV anchor reported that Billy remained in the hospital but had been released from intensive care. They praised his courage and emphasized his wartime military record. "Wounded Twice," the caption under his picture said. A statement by a hospital spokeswoman detailed his injuries and promised a full recovery after a period of rehabilitation.

Chief Oleson gave an update report, "Today two suspects were arraigned for attempted murder and assault of a police officer. A police officer killed a third suspect during their apprehension. Weapons found at the crime scene have been tied to numerous other crimes. Other charges are expected. The court has denied bail." To a shouted question, the chief confirmed, "Yes, the injured police officer is a relative of the suspects. He did his duty in full accordance with the law." The chief had apparently decided to overlook Billy's violation of police procedure by not waiting for backup.

After listening to the national news, Dave switched over to the local affiliate, KAAK. A live shot showed uniformed Darlene guiding Ramona and her cameraman through the mansion. For the first time, Katie could see the devastation caused by hundreds of high-powered bullets fired indiscriminately. Truly they could hardly recognize their home of several months. She did recognize their favorite portrait of Jeremy completely smashed on the floor.

"Don't worry, we have the photo file backed up. We can reprint the picture," Dave reassured his wife.

Then Ramona's report took an unexpected turn. The cameraman swung the lens to reveal a well-dressed and familiar couple. Tom and Maureen Swanson had seen the news on CNN. A redeye flight had brought them home. The camera showed the Swansons seeing the damage to their home for the first time. Maureen's mouth gaped open in astonishment.

Ramona, sensing an opportunity, asked, "Are you the actual mansion owners?"

Tom first stood stoically surveying the destruction, then assured the reporter that they owned Big River. His words became angry. "Where are the ones we hired as house sitters? They're responsible for this." Unable to speak, Maureen's mouth remained opened.

"During your absence, the police questioned them numerous times," Ramona said. "We presume they are in police custody now. Didn't you know?"

"Know what? That criminals were living in our house? They'll pay for this." Maureen remained transfixed, staring at the damage as Tom walked away. "Come on, Maureen! We need to call our lawyer."

Katie looked at Dave in astonishment. "Can they blame us for this?"

"I don't know. The law is a funny thing sometimes." Dave tried to sound confident. "We'll be okay."

Katie wasn't so certain. She commented a bit bitterly, "They didn't even ask about Old Yeller. They don't care about him, didn't even care if he got 'lost or something,' like they said when they left him with us. He's our cat now."

"No, he's his own cat. But he's part of our family now."

"Dave," Katie suggested, "call Tom Swanson and ask him for our $200 a week house-sitting fee."

"This might not be the best time," Dave laughed. "Let's get out of the room and drive around a bit." After driving awhile he asked, "Where would you like to have dinner?"

Katie's response, "How about Paris?" told Dave that she had fully regained her ginger.

Dave pointed toward an upscale Italian restaurant. "Would you accept Italy instead?" They enjoyed a mid-afternoon Italian meal before returning to the hotel.

—◆—

The next morning, Dave and Katie finished breakfast at the hotel when they noticed DA Christensen and Chief Oleson entering the lobby. This surprised Dave, who waved them over to the breakfast area. "Are you looking for us?"

"Is there a place we could talk privately?" The DA asked.

The Parkers offered their hotel room and led the officials upstairs. In the room, old Yeller came to rub against the chief's legs. The chief leaned over to scratch him behind his ears, which made the feline purr. "My wife has three cats," he explained.

DA Christensen first asked Dave about how he and Katie had recovered from their ordeal. Dave assured him that they would be fine and asked about the investigation. Chief Oleson filled them in on the growing mountain of charges, including a couple of murders, against Jud and Bogus and the deceased Lars.

The DA took over. "We'll ask for the death penalty to scare them. But eventually we'll accept life in prison without the possibility of parole, if they'll implicate all those involved over the years. They had quite a network of criminal associates." DA Christensen paused and grinned. "Not that we need much help. People who haven't even been accused of anything are calling in to offer testimony in return for immunity from prosecution."

The DA looked directly at the Parkers. "Dave and Katie, the chief and I are here with a serious suggestion. Although Jud and Bogus aren't getting out of jail, there are plenty of others around who feel threatened. Some may want revenge by their primitive code of retribution. We need all the police manpower we can get to work through all the leads and evidence. Trying to protect you would make our job more difficult. The reason that we're here today is to warn you and ask you to leave town. Go home to Alabama, today."

"Go home to Alabama, today?" Dave repeated. The DA and chief nodded.

"Will we need witness protection?" Katie sounded fearful.

"No, this isn't a sophisticated syndicate of criminals. These are just local thugs and drug dealers, but a lot of them are still free. Some are likely as vindictive as Jud and Bogus. Eventually they'll figure out that Dave is the one who shot Jud."

"Don't you need us to testify?" Dave asked.

"Maybe later. But we expect plea bargains for nearly all before the actual trials. We can phone you whenever we have questions. Go home. You've done enough here. Just to be on the safe side, don't communicate with anybody in Washita except us until the investigation is completed."

The couple didn't know what to say. Chief Oleson spoke up, "Are there any personal belongings at the mansion that you can't replace?"

"My laptop?" Katie suggested.

"You could have that. But several bullets hit the computer. It's worthless now."

"How about my old shotgun?" Dave wanted to know.

"That's evidence. Maybe we'll release the gun in a few years."

Katie looked hopeful. "My cell phone?"

The chief reached into his pocket, pulled her phone out, and handed it to her. The outer case still showed dried blood. "I picked this up off the floor where you dropped it while helping Billy. Technically we should keep a phone. But we already checked it for evidence. I know you have important numbers and addresses inside."

Katie took her phone and smiled. "Thanks."

DA Christensen resumed, "Probably you've seen that the Swansons are back in town. Being the owners of the mansion, they've been making lawsuit threats. Not as a DA, but as an attorney, I advise you to avoid them for now. Let your lawyer deal with any issues."

"How can they sue us?" Katie wanted to know. "We didn't do anything."

"They're saying that the McReadys didn't go there to attack the mansion. They can contend that the confrontation was a personal matter between you and the McReadys. They could try to convince a jury that without your meddling, the mansion would not have been damaged. The police reports will include Dave's warning shot. From that, an attorney can even claim that Dave fired first. I know this is all unfair baloney. Get your own attorney and let him handle any litigation."

"Thanks, Richard," Dave responded. "You've given us good advice. There's nothing else at the mansion that we absolutely must have. We'll leave town immediately."

After taking the Parkers' Alabama address and contact information, the chief said, "Thanks. And by the way, you pulled off quite a bluff with that empty shotgun."

Katie broke in, "What? Dave can't bluff. I always beat him when we play poker."

"What man can bluff his own wife?" the chief rhetorically asked. The men all laughed.

The DA paused by the hotel room door. "Thanks again, Dave and Katie. You've helped us to break up a century-old criminal network. You've made a difference to the people of Washita for generations."

Dave responded modestly, "Any competent accountant could have done the same."

"Yes, that was important," Richard agreed. "But I meant what you two did as a team. You used your individual skills together in a way I haven't seen before, truly exceptional. That's what enabled you to have such a significant impact here."

—◆—

After the DA and chief left their hotel room, the couple looked around. There wasn't much to pack—one suitcase and a cat. A gentle snow started to fall from the back side of a low-pressure front, what Minnesotans call a "clipper." Soon they drove up out of the Mississippi Valley. Unlike when they arrived, snow covered the hills. Back on the interstate, the couple started east on I-90. Katie let Old Yeller out of the container into the truck cab where he curled up in her lap. His furry warmth comforted her.

"Did you hear what Richard said?" Katie gently chided her husband. "He called us 'exceptional.' Is that good enough for you?"

"Yeah, it is. The amazing thing is that our teamwork did it. We met the challenge together." He drove for a few minutes while continuing to think. "Would you be up for some more challenges for two, sweetheart?"

Katie flippantly replied, "Whatever" before exclaiming, "Absolutely, yes!"

Then she transferred sleeping Old Yeller from her lap into the open container on the seat beside her. She shifted the container to the truck's passenger side door and scooted herself to the center seat. After riding in silence a few minutes, she asked, "What are we going to do with a cat?"

"We can let him do what he does best, be an ordinary cat."

"He was ordinary, until he needed to be more than ordinary."

"Isn't that a pretty good definition of a hero?"

"You betcha." Katie reached for the truck's CD player and inserted the old Lynyrd Skynyrd song "Sweet Home Alabama." They both sang along as they rode toward home.

—◆—

In the early afternoon of the fourth day, Dave and Katie arrived back at their comfortable house on a beautiful, dry, seventy-degree spring day. Spanish moss and blooming azaleas red, white, and purple welcomed them home. That downsized house hadn't seemed like home before

Thanksgiving, but they certainly felt happy to be back there. The couple left the "heroic" cat exploring his new residence and walked under the live oaks to the marina.

An armadillo scurried out of the path as they approached. At the marina, they strolled up and down the docks looking at the fishermen's catches. Dave asked, "Would you like to have dinner?"

Katie liked that idea. Their favorite seafood restaurant contained large saltwater aquariums displaying gulf fish. Outdoor tables under gentle fans overlooked the water in the bay sparkling from reflections of the late afternoon sun. The air had the faint odor of decomposing barnacles and sawgrass roots exposed to air at low tide. Seagulls stalked between the tables. Sailboats slowly returned to their berths as the sun set. A mockingbird sang to express its joy somewhere nearby. In the bay, a school of mullet suddenly jumped. Black-finned backs revealed a pod of porpoises chasing the baitfish.

"It's great to be home. There's no place I'd rather live, and I do love the fishing." Dave poked at his shrimp without eating many. "But now I just feel restless somehow." Katie listened with interest as her husband continued, "Adventures aren't so bad. We're as free right now as we are likely to ever be. So, what would you like us to do with ourselves next?"

"Anything with you. But next time let's pick an adventure without the blood and gunfire."

Epilogue

Three Years Later

———⋅◆⋅———

Katie waited in the late afternoon sun while Dave finished securing their boat in its slip at the marina. At her feet rested a large ice chest with three king mackerel inside. Fish tails stuck out from under the cooler lid. They had caught the fish trolling just off shore in the Gulf. Her cell phone rang. "Hello," she answered.

The graveled voice of an older man spoke. "Katie, this is Buddy Oleson."

"Buddy?" *We don't know any Buddys*, she thought.

"You used to call me 'Chief Oleson' in Washita."

"Oh, Chief! I'm so glad to talk to you. We haven't heard much from Washita for years. We kept up with the investigation online for a while and answered questions from the DA's office a few times. We received some Christmas cards in return for those we sent. But nobody ever says much."

"That's because Richard Christensen and I discouraged everyone from communicating with you for your protection. But I'm not a chief anymore. That means this isn't an official call. I retired from the police force and moved with my wife to Santa Rosa Beach in North Florida last month. We just stopped at Bellingrath Gardens in Mobile on our way to visit New Orleans. I thought that I'd give you a call as we passed through."

"That's wonderful. Could we treat you to dinner?"

"No, no, thanks anyway. We've got hotel reservations in Biloxi tonight. But I just wanted to tell you a little about the status of things since you left Washita. We had some busy years following up all that happened. After Jud and Bogus accepted the plea deal for life in prison, the local resistance to the investigation pretty much crumbled. We got forty-two major convictions from the work you started. Convictions covered everything from murders to drug dealing and even a state judge taking bribes."

"What about Clyde McReady?" Katie wanted to know.

"He hung around the area counting on immunity until we collected enough evidence to arrest him. Jud and Bogus testified that Clyde served as a cash bank and go-between for the criminal network. We found $420,000 in cash when a warrant allowed us to search his nightclub. Since the money was part of a criminal enterprise, we could keep it as a civil asset forfeiture. That money helped to pay for the investigation and the prosecutions. Eventually, a judge gave Clyde twenty years before any possibility of parole. I doubt he'll live that long in prison. Things have quieted down now, though. You could go back to Washita to pay a visit sometime."

"Chief, I mean Buddy, are you saying that we would be safe now?"

"I believe so. That young DA, Richard, cleaned up Washita. Working with him was the best part of my entire career. You know, he's acting district attorney for the state of Minnesota right now and running unopposed for the elected office of state DA. I think he could be governor someday. Just keep a low profile visiting up there. All the folks would be glad to see you. Oh, how's that cat of yours doing?"

"Old Yeller? He's fat and sassy. He loves the warm climate here. On another trip, please stop to see him. Dave and I could take you out fishing."

Buddy promised to do just that and hung up.

Dave came up the ramp from the dock carrying the bag of supplies from their day on the water. At the fish cleaning station, he started filleting the mackerel. As always, huge brown pelicans converged to take the scraps he threw into the water.

"You'll never guess who I just talked to," Katie teased.

"The president of the United States congratulating us on our catch."

"Close. But not right. That was Buddy Oleson."

Dave threw the last scraps into the water. "Buddy?"

"The police chief in Washita, although he isn't the chief anymore." Katie told Dave about the rest of her conversation. She concluded with, "He suggested that we visit Washita. I really want to go."

"Visiting Washita would be fun. And I still wonder why the Swansons dropped their lawsuit. But our schedule is pretty full right now." Dave washed the fillets with the marina's water hose and dropped them into a plastic bag. He dumped the ice and rinsed out the cooler. One pelican grabbed an ice cube and immediately spit it out.

Word had spread among police departments about Dave's part in the Washita cleanup. He had received several requests to aid in investigations related to financial records. To serve civil authorities better, he had obtained his certification as a forensic accountant. Mentoring a loose association of marriage enrichment groups in the Mobile area kept Katie busy.

"What would you think about two months from now?" Dave asked.

"Early June could be perfect," Katie answered. "Would we take the truck or the car?"

Dave put everything into the empty cooler. "Let's take the car this time. The gas mileage is better and we won't need four-wheel drive." With Dave carrying the cooler, they walked to their truck and drove back to their house. Old Yeller slept in a warm box there. Katie picked him up and squeezed him with affection. Back on the floor, he stretched and started nosing around the fish fillets. Dave selected a fillet and held their catch before the feline. He sniffed it, but like most pampered cats, he wouldn't eat raw fish.

"What about Old Yeller?" asked Dave.

"I think he'll be happier here for a couple of weeks. Our neighbors, Caleb and Jordan, will take good care of him."

On a June afternoon the Parkers descended again into the Mississippi Valley. Early summer had come to Minnesota. Under a bright blue sky on a seventy-degree day, Dave and Katie found Washita alive with summer tourists wearing shorts and bathing suits. Boats coming and going from the Mississippi River made the marina busy. Luxuriant flowers filled window boxes and hanging baskets all over town.

Katie wanted to see Big River first. To their surprise the gates rested wide open. On the gate column, a new sign advertised:

Big River Historical Museum
National Register of Historic Places - 1897
Operated by the University of Minnesota

The couple pulled up the familiar driveway. More than a dozen cars parked in a newly paved parking lot. Inside the front door and past the foyer, an enthusiastic female receptionist greeted them, "Welcome to the Big River Historical Museum. Admission is twelve dollars per adult. The museum features the history of the McReady family. For a hundred years, they dominated this region as gangsters and criminals. Our local police broke up the gang. There was a hidden room and a shootout with police right here at the mansion. Have you heard the story?"

Dave paid the twenty-four dollars without answering directly. "We'd like to see the museum, please."

The girl took their money and handed them each a map.

"Go up the stairs to the third floor and work your way down. The shootout area has been preserved and is on this floor. The hidden room is in the basement. Here's a short background by a professor from the University of Minnesota." She gave Katie a staple-bound booklet and waved toward the main stairs. Katie pointed Dave to the name on the booklet, Professor Bernie Pearson.

On the third floor, bedrooms had been converted into exhibit areas featuring the history of pioneer Minnesota, the logging industry, sawmills, and the timber barons. Walls and cases displayed photographs and artifacts. One room showed pictures of the early McReady family. A plaque on another bedroom door read:

Office
Washita Historical Society

Dave knocked and then cautiously opened the door. Frank Pederson looked up from some paperwork. He didn't look any older. His eyes blinked, trying to place the two familiar faces before him. "Can I help you?" he started. Then he realized to whom he spoke. "Dave! Katie! What brings you here? I hardly recognized you. Katie's long hair threw me off. How do you like our museum?"

They shook hands warmly. Frank waved his hands around him. "Can you believe this place? The Historical Society bought the mansion, and we got a grant from the Historical Preservation Foundation. We're partners with the History Department at the University of Minnesota."

Dave asked, "How could the society afford to buy the mansion?"

"Washita conducted a big 'Save Big River' fund drive. Susie Holmquist served as the campaign manager. Everybody contributed. We raised over a million dollars in six months."

"Why did the mansion come up for sale?" Katie wanted to know.

"Probably you remember the previous owners, Tom and Maureen Swanson. He's a big hedge fund guy in Minneapolis. Rumor is that the police investigation turned up that Tom's daughter had been busted by an undercover cop for drug distribution. Tom had paid off the policeman. Maybe there wasn't enough evidence for a conviction. But DA Christensen and Chief Oleson went to talk with the Swansons, and the next day the mansion came up for sale 'as is.' We had to scramble then to get the money. But the Swansons deducted $350,000 after they kept the insurance payoff. That helped. And we wanted the mansion 'as is' anyway."

Dave looked at Katie. That explained the lawsuit being dropped. "Could you show us around?"

This request delighted Frank. "Yes, I would be honored to show you two around our project."

The second floor highlighted the criminal activities of the twentieth century. Recordings of local people described their victimization. Katie selected one titled "Mrs. Sam Johnson." They immediately recognized her voice. A woman, probably one of Bernie's graduate students, gently asked her about her husband, the war, the labor unrest, and finally her husband's disappearance. A picture of the newly married Johnsons from the early 1940s was displayed beside Sam's war medals. Next to the medals sat a photo of elderly Mrs. Johnson posed in front of the painting of herself as a teenager with her horse.

"Mary Johnson died last year," Frank spoke reverently. "She wanted to be cremated and her ashes sprinkled in the Mississippi, where she always suspected her husband's body went."

They descended the servants' stairs to the pantry. "This is what the tourists really want to see," Frank reported. Dave and Katie walked through their former quarters on mats cordoned off by thick ropes. Every part of the damage by bullets to the walls and floors had been preserved.

Katie noticed a large display case containing items damaged by the bullets. Many things they had originally brought from Alabama. The glass case held her laptop, which had been destroyed by bullets. A mannequin displayed her favorite blue sleeveless jacket, having been riddled by bullets. *That could have been me*, she thought.

Another large two-sided display case showed blown-up photos of Billy and Darlene on one side and Jud, Bogus, and Lars McReady on the other side. "We all suspect that you were more involved in this than we had realized at the time," Frank explained in a low voice. "The police never revealed much about that for your safety. DA Christensen and Chief Oleson suggested that we downplay your role. They feared that someone out there might still be dangerous."

In the basement, the hidden room had been set up like a bookkeeping operation of the 1930s. Photographs of mobsters decorated the walls. Display cases contained some of the evidence collected in the room, including one of the old ledgers open to a spot documenting odds and bets. The rest of the basement had been cleaned up and converted into a carpeted meeting room.

"The University of Minnesota brings history classes down here every semester," Frank explained. "The Criminal Justice Department of Winona State conducts classes here as well. We also get a lot of groups from local schools." Dave noticed that the coal bin had been converted into a secure storage locker for records.

Moving back upstairs, they found that the museum had closed for the day. Only two cars remained in the parking lot. Frank offered to take them out to dinner.

"Thanks, Frank," Dave demurred. "This has been quite an emotional experience for us. We'll be around for at least a week and will see you more later. Right now, we just need to get a hotel and absorb some of this. You guys have done a remarkable job here. This is all wonderful."

Outside, Dave and Katie walked over to the carriage house that still appeared derelict. The windows remained dark and dirty. Dave felt for the key in the light fixture. The key remained in its place, but he didn't retrieve it. Frank had locked the museum and headed for his car when he noticed them. "We hope to start restoring the carriage house next year," he called.

Pulling out of the mansion driveway, the couple noticed the rail trail that they had used so often. "Care for a walk?" Dave offered. Katie did. They parked their car and walked the familiar path toward the town.

Minnesota in June had a dramatically different feel than in winter. Lush green vegetation dominated the landscape they knew as gray and white. Deciduous trees leafed out made the trail seem hemmed in. A myriad of wildflowers bloomed on both sides of the trail. Butterflies covered the flowers. One lavender-colored bush attracted their attention. Up close its fragrance smelt heavenly.

"Those are lilacs," Katie said. "My favorite as a kid." The air had a crisp dryness like most northern June days.

Twenty minutes of purposeful walking took them back into town. June days are long in Minnesota. Eight o'clock had passed with the sun still well above the horizon. Nearly all the downtown shops had closed, even The Blue Ox.

Katie had an idea. "Let's try the library. It's open until nine. Maybe we'll find Caroline." At the library, the Parkers were disappointed to see that Caroline wasn't there.

They asked another librarian about Caroline. "Caroline McReady? She decided to stay home with her children. She hasn't worked here in two years. I don't think she even lives in Washita anymore. Her husband, Billy, became a famous police hero here a few years ago. He got shot and everything. Then Billy received a full scholarship to study criminal law at the university. He wants to be a DA."

Dave and Katie walked slowly back through the darkening town. The air felt chilly compared to South Alabama. Dave gave his shivering wife a little hug and suggested, "Let's get going." He broke into a fast walk back to the car. Soon they had another reason to hurry. Twilight brought out mosquitoes, hordes of them. Although small compared to southern varieties of the pest, they far outnumbered even bayou mosquitoes. Katie forged ahead as the insects started to bite. Warmth from the fast pace provided them a little consolation.

The couple checked into the same hotel where they had stayed after the final confrontation at Big River. Then they had supper at the restaurant where they had first taken Billy and Caroline. Nobody noticed or recognized them. That felt like good news and bad news. Their conversation mostly recalled people they had known in Washita.

The next morning, Dave and Katie headed to the police department at the Municipal Complex. There nearly everybody recognized them. As they shook hands and greeted people, the receptionist came to them. "The chief would like to see you in his office."

Dave looked at Katie. "The chief?" They thought he had retired to Florida.

The receptionist led the way to the chief's office. There Gary Hobson rose to meet them. "I think you've met Detective Anderson," he said gesturing toward Darlene who had also waited for a more private meeting in the office. Gary quickly closed the door. "We have an image of decorum to maintain," he explained with a smile. Then they shared hugs all around. Katie asked Darlene about her family. She had married her ex-hockey teammate and taken his name, Anderson. Together they had a little boy. Her daughter, Sofie, doted on the new baby, and her husband doted on them all.

For the next couple of hours, Gary and Darlene described the recent years. Fred McReady, who had participated in the murder of Sam Johnson, had died of old age before his trial. Jud and Bogus McReady had accepted life sentences without possibility of parole for implicating many others. The process had been long and arduous. Gary could not help gloating a little. "Forty-four capital convictions."

"Chief Oleson told us forty-two convictions," Katie protested.

"We got two more convictions last month," Darlene added.

Katie asked Darlene, "Whatever happened to Ramona at KAAK?"

"Leslie Rogers revealed that she had been dating one of the McReady cousins. That's why she acted so accusatory toward you. KAAK quietly fired her when that came out."

"You two pulled the loose thread that did indeed unravel the sweater. Washita can never thank you enough," Gary concluded. Darlene bear hugged Katie for nearly a minute as they departed. Katie had trouble breathing. That woman was strong.

From the police department, the couple headed for The Blue Ox. Several tables had been set up under an awning in front of the restaurant on Main Street's sidewalk. An unfamiliar man seated them and asked for drink orders. Dave asked for iced tea, Katie for hot water with lemon. When the man brought back the drinks, Dave commented, "We're looking for Susie Holmquist."

"Well, you've got the Holmquist part right. But I'm not Susie. She's my wife. I'm Charlie."

"Could we ask where Susie might be?"

"She's at the Municipal Complex on some sort of business. The mayor has to do that."

"Susie is the *mayor?*"

"She's been mayor nearly two years now. Folks didn't forget how she backed the police during the troubles three years ago and elected her in a landslide. Everybody already liked her anyway. She'll be running for the U.S. Congress next fall." Obviously, Charlie felt proud of his wife.

"You used to be the high school principal, right?" Katie remembered.

"That's right. Then I was diagnosed with cancer. Susie nursed me through the treatments and supported us both with this restaurant. An experimental treatment has made me cancer free for two years now. How did you know I had been a principal?"

"We used to be friends of Susie's. I'm cancer free for four years now myself."

"You must be Dave and Katie Parker from Alabama! We heard you had come to town. Wait just a minute." He disappeared without having asked for their lunch orders. Dave and Katie could hear him using a phone. "They're here."

A few minutes later, the front door burst open and Susie came in puffing from having run from the mayor's office. She almost looked unrecognizable in a woman's business suit. Susie cried as she clutched their necks in turn. After the warmest of greetings, Susie put her hands on her hips, "Well, what'll ya have?"

Washita's mayor waited on Dave and Katie. As always, the food tasted delicious. "This is on the house," she insisted.

"Okay then, I've got a campaign contribution for the fall." Dave passed her a check for a thousand dollars. They shared more hugs. "Oh, I forgot to ask, are you a Republican or Democrat?"

"Neither one, honey; I'm an Independent."

Why is that not a surprise? Katie mused to herself.

During the next several days, Dave and Katie enjoyed a Minnesota summer and saw everyone still in Washita. They took Frank and Helen and some others from the Historical

Society to dinner at a Minnesota supper club. Nancy attended, but not Ed. Frank explained, "Ed died of a stroke a year after we got the mansion. Too many years of hypertension, the doctors said. He was instrumental in setting up the museum, though. A TV station in Minneapolis ran a documentary. Ed and Mrs. Johnson each told their stories. After that Ed solicited a lot of big donations from outside Washita to help buy the mansion and set up the museum."

The following day, Frank took Dave and Katie fishing in Minnesota's fish-infested waters. Dave enjoyed being in a boat rather than on the ice. Katie shrieked while catching an eleven-pound northern pike. Dave caught several smaller ones. "They're tougher than a big mackerel," Dave admitted to Frank.

The marriage group except for Billy and Caroline reunited for a potluck dinner to honor Dave and Katie. John had presided over the marriage of Tommy and Jane Bryant, the unmarried couple in the original group. They showed a picture of twin sons. Rick Larson, Betty's son, who had come to the group with his wife Beth, reported that Betty had traveled to England to visit extended family members. Susie and Charlie had given her the trip for her twentieth anniversary of cooking at The Blue Ox.

The Parkers didn't know most of the couples who attended the dinner. Lyle and Leslie Rogers had assumed leadership of the group. Leslie had then developed a series of humorous sketches demonstrating marriage foibles and highlighting the differences between men and women. She and Lyle frequently performed the sketches for groups all over the region. The

Rogerses' enthusiasm and personalities had brought scores of couples to be involved in marriage enrichment groups. Many of those couples had come wanting to meet the ones Lyle and Leslie called "The Founders."

—◆—

Finally, only one day remained in their visit to Washita. Frank had asked them to come to the Big River Museum to see a new exhibit. "Come after all the tourists have left, about 6:00 p.m.," he instructed.

Unexpectedly, Dave and Katie found the parking lot full of vehicles. A bigger surprise waited inside. All their friends had assembled in the former entertaining room on the first floor, including Susie and her husband Charlie, John and Ellie, Lyle and Leslie and the others from the original marriage group, the Historical Society, Gary and Darlene with their respective families, and other off-duty police officers.

Richard Christensen, the former local DA, had come from the capital. Professor Bernie Pearson attended accompanied by several graduate students. Danny Johnson had come to represent his mother. Plus, a lot of others attended whom the Parkers didn't know or couldn't remember, but each had played some role in the events that changed the community. Finally, the Parkers saw Billy and Caroline. Billy held a small boy by the hand, while Caroline cradled an infant. They grabbed each other with wild hugs and tears. Dave and Katie discovered that there's no reunion like a reunion of people who have saved each other's lives.

As Dave and Katie went around the room meeting and greeting with hugs and memories, they couldn't help but feel overwhelmed for the way everything had turned out. Although house sitting had been a dangerous adventure that they hadn't anticipated, they had found each other in a new life. The people with whom they had shared that adventure had become cherished friends.

Eventually, Frank quieted the crowd. "Follow me to the new exhibit." He led the way into the old guest quarters. There in the large display case between the photos of Billy and Darlene, a photo of Dave and Katie in the Big River kitchen had been placed. Frank had taken that photo during the Super Bowl party. In front of the photo lay Dave's old double-barreled shotgun.

Everybody then moved to the basement meeting room where refreshments waited. A portable microphone passed from person to person. Many people talked, praising others and the Parkers for each person's part in the investigations. The microphone finally came to Dave's hands. Overcome with emotion, he couldn't speak. Katie took the microphone from his hands. She struggled as well. "I just want . . . I just want . . . every one of y'all to come visit us in Alabama!"

Authors' Note

———•———

All the characters in this novel are purely fictional and created in the imaginations of the authors. Likewise, the town of Washita in Minnesota is fictional. However, we confess to one amazing coincidence. Although we had visited Minnesota many times, the basic story had been written including the town description before we visited the area in the southeast along the river. To our chagrin, we discovered the Minnesota town of Wabasha nearly in the exact place we wanted Washita and much like our fictional depiction. Our fictional Minnesota town of Washita is a compilation of many charming towns we have visited.

The historical references in the novel accurately represent the eras in which they are depicted. The spelling of Washita was taken from a small hamlet near our home in Arkansas. The name is a derivative of the Ouachita Native Americans who originally inhabited our area of Arkansas. Washita and Ouachita are pronounced the same. The Washita River in western Oklahoma was named after the Native Americans after they had been relocated. There was a battle, or massacre by Custer, at the Washita River. Winona, Minnesota is a real town near where the fictional Washita would be located.

All cats are unique in their own way. However, the characteristics of Old Yeller are typical of many cats. The cat tactic of putting a paw on a sleeping face to wake up a person is true. But the usual reason is because the cat is bored or hungry. Communicating an alert by that method could be possible.

More from Kit and Drew Coons

Challenge Down Under
Challenge Series Book Two

"Challenge Down Under is a gripping story of the rawness of life when desperation hits and of the power of love in the most difficult of circumstances. I couldn't put this book down as I wanted to see justice win the day. I'm a born and bred New Zealander, and I love how the Coonses captured the heart of both city and country life Down Under. You will fall in love with the colorful characters and be intrigued by where curiosity and love can take a person."
Jill Rangeley of Auckland, NZ

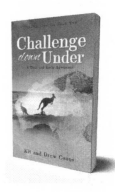

Dave and Katie Parker's only son, Jeremy, is getting married in Australia. In spite of initial reservations, the Parkers discover that Denyse is perfect for Jeremy and that she's the daughter they've always wanted. But she brings with her a colorful and largely dysfunctional Aussie family. Again Dave and Katie are fish out of water as they try to relate to a boisterous clan in a culture very different from their home in South Alabama.

After the wedding, Denyse feels heartbroken that her younger brother, Trevor, did not attend. Denyse believes her brother may be in trouble. Impressed by his parents' sleuthing experience in Minnesota, Jeremy volunteers them to locate Trevor. Their search leads them on an adventure through Australia and New Zealand.

Unfortunately, others are also searching for Trevor, with far more sinister intentions. With a talent for irresponsible chicanery inherited from his family, Trevor has left a trail of trouble in his wake. Can Dave and Katie locate him in time?

Challenge in Mobile
Challenge Series Book Three

"Adventure finds Dave and Katie even at home. Mobile and the Gulf Coast are the sultry setting for the couples' latest foray into a world of corruption, extortion, and racial tension. Thick southern charm and potential financial ruin swirl about them as they strive to serve those they love. A fast-paced and engaging story with colorful characters. A great read!" Leslie Mercer

Dave and Katie Parker regret that their only child Jeremy, his Australian wife Denyse, and their infant daughter live on the opposite side of the world. Unexpectedly, Jeremy calls to ask his father's help finding an accounting job in the US. Katie urges Dave to do whatever is necessary to find a job for Jeremy near Mobile. Dave's former accounting firm has floundered since his departure. The Parkers risk their financial security by purchasing full ownership of the struggling firm to make a place for Jeremy.

Denyse finds south Alabama fascinating compared to her native Australia. She quickly resumes her passion for teaching inner-city teenagers. Invited by Katie, other colorful guests arrive from Australia and Minnesota to experience gulf coast culture. Dave and Katie examine their faith after Katie receives discouraging news from her doctors.

Political, financial, and racial tensions have been building in Mobile. Bewildering financial expenditures of a client create suspicions of criminal activity. Denyse hears disturbing rumors from her students. A hurricane from the Gulf of Mexico exacerbates the community's tensions. Dave and Katie are pulled into a crisis that requires them to rise to a new level of more than ordinary.

Jeremy's Challenge
Challenge Series Book Four

"This is a novel you'll want your children or grandchildren to read. You'll enjoy it yourself." Drew Coons

Who has the bigger challenge—a teenager growing up with old-fashioned parents or parents trying to raise a modern teenager? Before their other exploits, Dave and Katie Parker had the challenge of raising a son—a son with an adventurous spirit. At an early age, Jeremy perceives the ordinariness of his parents' lives and resolves that he can do better.

Disappointment, bullies, alluring girls, peer pressure, and surging hormones combine to challenge Jeremy. His questions— Who do I want to be? What will I do with my life?—remain unanswered. Amid rich deep-south and Cajun-influenced culture, Jeremy explores routes to a future different from the heritage he received. Personal problems experienced by Dave and Katie complicate Jeremy's dilemma.

Into the uncertainty of Jeremy's world comes an irresponsible and beguiling older woman. Tara is a vagabond and a practiced con artist. To Jeremy, the street-smart and philosophical woman holds the secret to life. She offers him a path with her to a young man's dreams: adventure, passion, freedom. All Tara asks is that Jeremy bring his college fund with him.

Challenge in the Golden State
Challenge Series Book Five

*"The most fast paced and entertaining of all the
Dave and Katie novels."* Kit Coons

While on vacation with her husband
in California, Katie Parker discovers two
victims of a prescription opioid overdose. A
man is already dead. The other—a teenaged
girl—barely survives. The small town of
Redwood Hills, situated among giant trees
between California's rugged coastline and
picturesque wine country, has suffered an
escalating rash of tragic overdoses.

Sympathy for the girl draws Dave and Katie into an investigation
to discover the source of illicit drugs. Criminal elements of the
community are threatened as Dave and Katie find evidence of a
wicked scheme. The crooks fight back in nefarious ways, including
the use of poison and planting false evidence that leads to Dave
and Katie's arrest.

With no one to trust, the Parkers summon their son and
daughter-in-law for assistance. But Jeremy and Denyse are each
facing their own crises and need help, too. As Dave and Katie
pursue truth and exoneration, they must decide if they can place
their trust in an unexpected and unlikely source.

The Ambassadors

"The Ambassadors combines elements of science fiction and real-life genetics into a story that is smart, witty, and completely unique. Drew and Kit Coons navigate complex issues of humanity in a way that will leave you pondering the implications long after the book is over. If you're ready for a compelling adventure with humor, suspense, and protagonists you can really root for, don't miss out on this one!" Jayna Richardson

Two genetically engineered beings unexpectedly arrive on Earth. Unlike most extraterrestrials depicted in science fiction, the pair is attractive, personable, and telegenic—the perfect talk show guests. They have come to Earth as ambassadors bringing an offer of partnership in a confederation of civilizations. Technological advances are offered as part of the partnership. But humans must learn to cooperate among themselves to join.

Molly, a young reporter, and Paul, a NASA scientist, have each suffered personal tragedy and carry emotional baggage. They are assigned to tutor the ambassadors in human ways and to guide them on a worldwide goodwill tour. Molly and Paul observe as the extraterrestrials commit faux pas while experiencing human culture. They struggle trying to define a romance and partnership while dealing with burdens of the past.

However, mankind finds implementing actual change difficult. Clashing value systems and conflicts among subgroups of humanity erupt. Inevitably, rather than face difficult choices, fearmongers in the media start to blame the messengers. Then an uncontrolled biological weapon previously created by a rogue country tips the world into chaos. Molly, Paul, and the others must face complex moral decisions about what being human means and the future of mankind.

What is a
more than ordinary life?

Each person's life is unique and special. In that sense, there is no such thing as an ordinary life. However, many people yearn for lives more special: excitement, adventure, romance, purpose, character. Our site is dedicated to the premise that any life can be more than ordinary.

At **MoreThanOrdinaryLives.com** you will find:

- inspiring stories
- ideas and resources
- entertaining novels
- free downloads

https://morethanordinarylives.com/